BEYOND THE MIST

By

Joyce Humphrey Cares

Mainstream Romance

DEDICATION

To my sons, Mark and Eric, who burst with ideas, creative energy, and encouragement.
To Dorothy, my friend and first reader of my novel and Pauline, a friend, who read every word.

BEYOND THE MIST

To help link the past and the present, two sets of footprints are led by a ghost on a romantic journey into a time of treachery and betrayal.

Prologue

New York City, New York
May 14, 1985

When the apparition appeared, it appeared at night—the way bizarre visions usually do.

It was Sunday and one minute after midnight. The second-floor bedroom's French doors, across from where Alexandra Pirrot stood, beckoned to the six-year-old girl. She crept to the other side of the room and stared out the glass panes. An ominous fog coiled as lifelessly as a lethargic snake. She looked up at the halo around the full moon, as it cast an eerie glow into the dimly lit room.

The city was quiet. Alexandra stood on her tiptoes with her nose pressed to the pane of glass near the brass door handle. She stared out over the wrought-iron railing that encircled a small balcony. The lantern of a tall black post lamp at the curb lit the sidewalk and street. Her eyes wide open, she fixed her gaze on a woman in a long black cape. Long streamers hung from the bow tied at her neck. She watched the woman pull her hood tightly around her face with one hand. The other held the cape off the ground as she ran between the tall trees and low bushes of Central Park that stood in silhouette against the buildings that reached to the sky and surrounded the small sanctuary of New York City.

She watched the woman run into the street as a police car cruised slowly down the almost empty avenue. The car sped up as the traffic light on the corner turned yellow. Alexandra's heart began to beat a little faster when she realized the driver didn't seem to see the woman when she darted past his car. Alexandra watched her open the side gate at the edge of the slate patio leading to the library on the first floor. As she slipped into the grounds of the mansion, a gust of wind blew up the hem of her cape. The shimmering silk of her skirt gleamed in the moonlight. Alexandra heard the gate slam shut and stared as the woman drifted toward the French doors and disappeared.

Footsteps approached the bedroom door. She spun around and rushed over the pastel-colored carpet covering the floor where the canopied bed sat. Slithering under the bed, she pulled up a pleat of the bedspread that dusted the floor and rested it on her head. She lay on her stomach, leaned on her elbows with her chin in her hands, and peeked into the room. With half-closed eyelids, she waited. Finally, the hinges of the bedroom door creaked open. She heard a click and the bedside table light switched on. She listened to her mother hum the lullaby she sang every night when she tucked Alexandra into bed.

She gazed at her mother's pale blue gown, encrusted with sparkling jewels, as she stood in front of the closet door. She watched her slip a ring from her index finger, then place it in a box sitting on top of the bedside table. Alexandra scurried from under the bed. "Mama, Mama why are you hiding the ring in the box?"

When Camille Pirrot heard her daughter's voice, she spun around. The box slid out of her hand. As she picked it up, she noticed a chip on the corner of the box that hit the floor. Rubbing her hand over the nick, she stared into Alexandra's eyes. "You must not scare me like that Alexandra—just a minute." Camille pushed on the latch of the wooden box, making sure it was securely fastened. She turned and pulled on the closet door knob. She opened it just enough to reach the top shelf. Her long slender fingers slid along the polished wood of the top shelf, pushing the box to the back of the ledge. She moved quickly to the middle of the door and nudged it shut with her shoulder. She grabbed the velvet pouch hanging from around her neck on a shiny silk cord.

Alexandra tugged on her mother's gown. She jumped up and down trying to snatch the royal purple purse that was being held just out of her reach. "Let me see! Let me see!" Her large green eyes urged her mother to allow her to look into its hiding place.

"*Voila*, there." Camille took a deep breath as she rescued a key from the pouch and faced the door.

Alexandra heard a click as the key twisted in the lock. She watched her mother pull the key from the lock of the closet door, drop it into the pouch, and hold it just above her fingers. She danced from side to side softly squealing. "Please, please open the closet again. I want to see what's in the box." Her eyes sparkled.

"It's nothing, *ma petite fille*, my little girl." She patted Alexandra on the top of her head and smoothed her child's thick auburn curls that bounced up and down.

"When I looked out the French doors, I saw a woman in a long cape standing on the patio below us. Was she with you?" Alexandra asked.

Camille's eyebrows drew together as she walked toward the doors and glanced down at the patio. "Alexandra, you have quite an imagination. No one is out there."

"Where were you, Mama?"

"Don't ask so many questions. It's past midnight. You should be fast asleep."

"Please tell me where you were. Please."

"I was at a magnificent ball." Camille gave Alexandra a tender pat on her derriere. "Now off to bed. I'll come and tuck you in after I put on my dressing gown."

"Mama, tell me about it…tell me about the ball. I beg you."

"Oh, all right." Camille's smile reached her eyes. "Come with me to the library and I'll show you a picture." She took her daughter's hand and gave it a gentle squeeze. "I guess a few more minutes won't hurt."

Camille's gown rustled as she walked down the winding staircase. The leather heels of her satin shoes tapped in staccato time as she walked across the marble floor of the entryway. The patter of Alexandra's bare feet echoed her mother's steps as she ran beside her.

Alexandra climbed into the winged-backed chair in front of the fireplace. She stared at the flames jumping from the logs and waited while her mother fingered through the books in the floor-to-ceiling bookshelf.

"Hurry, Mama, I can't wait. You're taking too long," she cried out as her mother pulled a large hardback book from the middle shelf near the mantle.

Alexandra scrunched herself up into the corner of the chair so that her mother had room to sit down next to her. She leaned her head on Camille's breast when she sat next to her. She could hear her mother's heartbeat. She squirmed with anticipation as she watched Camille flipped through the pages of the book. She stared when her mother stopped turning pages.

"Look at the women with beautiful ball gowns. See the sparkling stones on their dresses and high-heeled shoes. Their hair is piled on top of their heads with curls falling to their shoulders, just like I'm wearing mine tonight. The men are wearing white wigs. Their hair is long and pulled back and tied behind their heads. The trousers of their silk suits are tight around their calves. You can see their white stockings and buckled shoes," Camille whispered.

"Oh, Mama, it's wonderful." She touched the men and women, who seemed as if they were dancing in a large room with mirrored walls. The musicians were sitting in one corner. "I can almost hear the music. What does it say?" She pointed to the caption at the bottom of the page.

"It says Versailles, France, 1786," Camille answered.

"Why did you hide the ring? Tell me about the ring."

"One day my ring will bring you into another time…a time you would never be able to imagine. In this time, you will be caught up in evil and revenge. You must always keep the ring with you. It will protect you."

Alexandra wasn't sure what evil and revenge meant, but she was sure by the serious look on her mother's face the words meant something bad. She knew what "protect" meant. Her mother and the household staff constantly watched her closely. She always felt loved and very safe. Alexandra saw a tear run down her mother's cheek. "What's wrong, Mama?" Her tiny hand reached up and wiped the tear away. "Mama," she whispered.

She waited a few second for her mother to answer. When she didn't hear Camille answer, she grabbed her mother's hand and held it tightly. She watched her lean back and close her eyes, then leaned over the photograph to take a closer look.

Startled by a rustling sound, Alexandra lifted her head—the scent of rosemary, lemon, and jasmine drifted into the room. She turned toward the sound and gazed as if hypnotized at the shadow of a woman in a long dark cape as she passed by the doorway and disappeared into a haze-filled hallway.

Chapter One

New York City, New York
May 14, 2010

After the lawyer finished reading her grandmother's last will and testament, Alexandra ran from his office and hailed a cab. "Central Park West. Hurry, please," she shouted to the driver. She knew it wouldn't take long to get to the family home—now her home. New York City traffic was light.

Her auburn hair was tied back in a ponytail. Tendrils had pulled loose and now framed her flushed face. Her clothes were wrinkled, but it didn't matter. She was on a mission. She couldn't wait until she moved in at the end of the week. She had to find the key to the closet—the closet where her mother hid the box when she returned from her trips to France. After her mother died her grandmother took over the key.

She ran up the front stairs. When she reached the door, she repeatedly hit the doorbell with her thumb. After a few seconds, she pushed on the button without releasing it.

The family butler, breathing heavily, threw open the door. "Oh, Miss Alexandra, it's you." He took a deep breath and smiled. "Are you here to stay?" he asked in a heavy French accent, as he brushed a white speck from the jacket of his formal black suit.

"Not today, Gérard. Sorry if I disturbed you, but I forgot my key. I have to pack up my apartment. I'll be here in a few days. Right now, I'm here to find something. I'm going up to my grandmother's bedroom. It won't take long."

"May I help you?"

"No, thank you, Gérard. If I need any help, I'll call you." She smiled at him.

"I was starting a fire in the library to take the chill off the house. You might want to sit in there for a while and rest."

"Thanks, Gérard. That's sweet of you. If I find what I'm looking for, I may relax there for a while." She threw the words over her shoulder as she slipped past him. Alexandra took the stairs to the second floor of the main staircase, two at a time.

She rushed down the hallway and threw open the door of the master bedroom where she used to hide under the bed waiting for her mother to come home when she was a little child. She pulled on the handle of the drawer in the bedside table and reached to the back.

"Aha, here it is." Alexandra pulled out the royal purple pouch where her mother hid the key to the closet door "That was easy to find." She tugged on the drawstrings. "*Voila.* Here it is." Alexandra dug into the bag and pulled out a key.

Unwillingly, Alexandra held her breath as she twisted the key in the lock of the closet door next to the canopy bed. When she heard the click, she turned the doorknob and threw open the door. She blew out a large breath as she stood on her toes and stretched her arm to reach the back of the shelf. "It's here," Alexandra shouted over the loud pounding of her heart. Her fingers eased the box forward. She looked up when it teetered as it reached the end of the ledge. It slowly began to fall. Alexandra reached up and caught it before it plummeted to the hardwood floor. The same thing had happened the night she hid under the canopy bed to see what her mother did with the box. She remembered she startled her mother when she got excited and made noise as she wiggled so she could see better. Her mother dropped the box and couldn't catch it. It chipped as it hit the floor. She heard her mother's soft reprimand.

Hugging the postcard-sized box to her chest, she dashed down the circular staircase. Her boots pounded on the floor of the entrance hallway as she ran to the library. She pulled off her boots and tossed them. They landed near the bookcase with a thud. Wiggling her toes, she pulled up her legs and sat Yoga style in the winged-back chair—the same chair where she had cuddled up to her mother the night she first found out about the wooden box. It was the chair where she had sat and looked at the picture of the 'Ball at Versailles'. Her face flushed and her heart thumped. Her fingers trembled. She held the box tightly.

The Brahms lullaby that her mother sang to her every night at bedtime ran through her head. "Lullaby, and good night, your mother's delight…" The words calmed her. She sat back in the chair still holding the box—the box she had always been curious about—in her lap. Alexandra stared at the fireplace. She heard the crackle of the logs and watched the flames of the fire jump on the hearth.

Alexandra placed the box on the table next to her. She was almost afraid of what she might find. The chill in the room made her hug herself. She waited. When the room warmed up a little, she moved her chair closer to the table.

She barely heard the click of the button on the lamp as she leaned over and twisted it on. She shivered as she ran her fingers over the highly polished wood of the box that sat in her lap. Her fingers ran over the chipped corner. *I missed my mother very much. I didn't mean to startle her that night. I was just hiding under her bed to try to see what was in the box.*

She gazed around the room. *I have to open it.* Alexandra wrapped her shaky fingers around the top of the box. She pulled off the lid. She stared at a postcard-sized painting of a chateau on the side of a mountain that was wedged into the box. It was faded and frayed at the edges. Alexandra slowly slid her fingers under one of the corners of the painting and eased it out. She flattened the bent edges as she brought the picture nearer to the light. Alexandra examined every inch of it. The chateau overlooked a small town—as if protecting it. It looked majestic and had an energy about it. She had dreamt about a chateau on a mountain that looked just like the one in the picture.

After a while, she turned over the small piece of heavy paper. The faded serif letters of the notation on the back made her lean closer. Alexandra traced the words with her index finger and translated the French. "Maison Familiale, Giverny, France, seventeen hundreds," she whispered. *But whose family? Whose chateau? Is that where my mother went when she disappeared for days? Does it belong to my family?*

Alexandra leaned back. As she moved, the box slid off her lap onto the red and navy Oriental carpet. Something small and round, wrapped in a piece of lavender cloth, rolled toward the hearth. She leapt off the chair and grabbed it before it landed under the grate in the fireplace. She didn't want it to get burnt.

She fell back into the chair and took a deep breath. Her fingers shook. She cautiously pulled back the folds of the silky material. Her brows drew together. *It's the amethyst ring.*

Alexandra remembered what her mother said the evening they sat together in this chair. *You must always keep the ring with you. It will protect you.*

As soon as she slipped the ring onto her index finger, visions of men and women dancing floated through her brain. Candlelight reflected in the prisms of a large chandelier that hung in the middle of an enormous ballroom and bounced off the mirrored walls. She could hear the music as she glimpsed at the group of musicians in the back of the room. She could hear the waltz they were playing. "It's the picture from the book my mother showed me that night, but it's come alive." She thought she saw her mother dancing in the ballroom. She covered her eyes. When she uncovered them, the people in the picture were standing still—like statues—and the music had stopped. It was a tableau. A sudden sense of foreboding engulfed her like a shroud.

She called to Gérard as she stuffed the box and ring into her purse and ran to the front door. "I'll be back in a few days with my things." She let the front door slam behind her.

Alexandra frequently had dreams of eighteenth century France after she moved into the house on Central Park West. She kept the ring close to her bed in the bedside table after she settled in to the bedroom where her mother and grandmother had slept. In her dreams, she saw rebels burning and killing, and watched the aristocracy and clergy being pulled into wagons that took them to the Guillotine. Sometimes the visions were so real she would wake up in a cold sweat. Most of the dreams focused on Paris, France.

One morning she sat at the breakfast table with Josephine, the housekeeper and her old friend. Alexandra remembered how Josephine and Gérard had taken care of her when she was young when her mother or her grandmother would disappear for days at a time. They were more like parents than servants.

She decided to question her housekeeper about her mother's disappearances. "Josephine, did my mother or grandmother ever tell you where they went when they left on their trips? You know, all the trips they took when I was growing up. Did you ever see them wearing ball gowns?" she blurted out.

"No, Mademoiselle." Josephine looked down at the floor. "They just said for us to take very good care of you and they would be back soon." She tucked the strand of white hair that had escaped the knot at the base of her neck.

"Did you ever meet my father?"

"No. Is that all?" Josephine asked as she looked away. Her face drained of color. She rubbed the palms of her hands on her flowered apron that covered her long, gray dress.

Alexandra stared at her. "Did I say something to disturb you?"

"No, Mademoiselle. I'm just a little tired. I had a nightmare and didn't sleep very well last night. I'll rest later."

I have them sometimes, too. It must be this house. Alexandra smiled. "Thank you, Josephine. I'll be home for dinner." Alexandra walked toward the stairs leading to the second floor. She twisted around and looked at Josephine. "Wait! I'm leaving for a vacation. I think I need a holiday. I'll be gone a couple months. I'm going to France to visit an old chateau in Giverny that's an inn now. I saw a picture of it in a box that belonged to my mother. I'm visiting there to do some research on my family history and enjoy the countryside." Alexandra patted Josephine's hand that lay on the table. "I'm going to see if the chateau belongs to my family. You'll be able to catch up on your sleep while I'm gone. You've been working very hard helping me get settled."

"I'll see that Gérard puts your suitcases in your room. When are you leaving?" Josephine pushed on the arms of the wooden chair and eased her large body out of the seat.

"I'm leaving at the end of the week."

"Let me know if I can help you with your packing." Josephine forced a polite smile. She hurried toward the kitchen as soon as Alexandra started upstairs.

Josephine pushed through the swinging door. She held it for a second, looking over her shoulder. She made sure the door closed behind her before she flopped down in a chair at the table where Gérard sat polishing silver. She sighed loudly.

"What's wrong?" He stared at Josephine's face. "You look as if you've seen a ghost. You're as white as this rag." He held up his polishing cloth.

Josephine sighed loudly. "She's asking about her mother and father, and her grandmother." Her brows drew together. "I was afraid to tell her what I know. She told me she's going on vacation to the chateau. Do you think we should tell her about her family before she flies off to France?"

"Don't worry." Gérard slipped his wire-rimmed glasses off his thin nose and set them on the table.

He ran his fingers through his full head of white hair. "She won't find out anything. Her mother and grandmother never did. It will be all right."

"But she's going to the chateau."

"Calm down. Just act normal. We don't want her to start asking more questions."

"Maybe she will be the one, Gérard...the one to...Perhaps Mademoiselle Alexandra will be able to solve the delicate situation in France," Josephine whispered as she wiped the beads of perspiration from her brow with her apron. She shook her head. "Maybe she will be the one."

France Airport Paris
July 12, 2010

Air France 747 hummed toward the airport. Alexandra looked out of the plane window at the panorama of Paris, where all the roads of France seemed to lead either in or out of the city. As they got closer to the runway, the city took shape. People strolled on the sidewalks, ducking in and out of the shops and gardens.

"There's the Arc de Triomphe. It's one of the most famous monuments in Paris," she said to the women next to her. "The cars speeding on the twelve roads that entered and left the circle look like race cars. The Arc was built to honor those people who fought and died for France during the war. Beneath the arch there is an eternal flame for an unknown soldier in WWI. I'll also be in Paris for Bastille Day. The celebration of when the French revolution started. There's sure to be a parade and a ceremony at the Arc."

She began to get excited when she saw the myriad of people on the Champs-Elysées. The city was alive—even early in the morning. Alexandra looked down upon the calm waters of the Seine River that wandered through the city dividing the left and right banks of Paris. The overcast sky did not dull her bright mood. "Finally, good food, French wine, and lots of sightseeing." She rubbed her eyes.

Alexandra had drifted in and out of sleep after she had boarded the plane at Kennedy Airport. She'd had unpleasant dreams of disheveled aristocrats crowded on wooden carts, where one woman screamed, a man in a clerical collar prayed, and a young woman cried. Most of the people sitting on the hard floor of the cart stared straight ahead with looks of desperation on their faces. The images disturbed her on the overnight flight from New York City. *I have no idea why I'm seeing scenes of eighteenth century people.*

She leaned back in her seat and smiled. She had walked away from her marriage and adulterous husband. Now she had a successful career with the FBI and a home overlooking a beautiful park. "I'll have a lot of time to search for long lost relatives, but most of all I can do whatever I want to, and I won't be on a schedule." *And no more men.* She sighed deeply. Her life was exciting now. It had been one year, four months, and three weeks since her divorce, but then she wasn't counting. Alexandra heard the woman sitting in the aisle seat across from her clear her throat.

She glanced out of the corner of her eye and saw the frown on the woman's face. "I always talk to myself," Alexandra said, laughing. She looked out the window as she heard the woman laugh.

Alexandra twisted a strand of her hair around her index finger. It caught on her amethyst ring. A vision of the chateau with a carriage roaring up to its large, oak door floated through her mind as she worked at untangling her hair. The image made her uneasy.

She leaned back and closed her eyes. Alexandra heard her boss's voice. "You're one of our best agents in the New York City office, but you need a vacation." She'd agreed and was finally on her way to the chateau in the picture. She would trace her family history in France instead of sitting at a desk with a cup of coffee sifting through reports, or rushing to some God-forsaken place to catch a criminal.

The ping of the seat belt sign startled her. She pushed back the long sleeve of her T-shirt and squinted to bring her wristwatch into focus. It said seven-twenty. Okay she was off to a good start. Air France was landing right on time. She was now wide awake and ready to start her rest and recreation. She pulled on her boots, buckled her seat belt, popped her seat into an upright position, and waited.

The crunch of the landing gear and the squeal of the wheels made her excitement grow. She felt the bounce of the plane as it hit the tarmac. She caught sight of the airport's bold sign, *Charles de Gaulle,* as they taxied on the runway.

Alexandra reached for her backpack underneath the seat in front of her and foraged through it as the plane continued on the landing strip. When the plane rolled to a stop at the gate, she pulled out her smart phone and flicked it open. She checked her messages. There was only one—a text from her boss telling her to have fun and to get lots of rest and drink some good wine.

"Thanks," Alexandra said.

She gazed out over the full plane and watched the passengers as they reached up and grabbed their carry-on bags from the overhead compartments. She ducked just in time. The man in front of her almost hit her in the head with his bag. The person behind her bumped her seat several times as he pulled out his bag, which seemed to be stuck under his seat. The travelers pushed into the aisles. They were all wide-awake and seemed to be in a hurry.

When it was her turn, she pulled her backpack onto her shoulder and moved out into the aisle. *"Au revoir."* Alexandra smiled at the flight attendant, standing near the door, as she left. She moved slowly, following the passengers who didn't rush past her—to the luggage belt where she would pick up her suitcase.

Alexandra twisted her amethyst ring while she waited, *"N'etait jamais un tel evenement si inevitable pourant tellement complement imprevu,*" she whispered. The French phrase reverberated through her brain as she watched the bags fly through the flaps at the entrance of the carousel being bumped and banged on the belt as they made the journey to their owners. "Never was any such event so inevitable yet so completely unforeseen," she translated the French while she waited for her hot-pink suitcase to soar through the flaps and race toward her. *Why did the quote from Alexis de Tocqueville pop into my mind?* Alexandra shook her head and wrinkled her nose. She had a strange feeling in the pit of her stomach.

At last she saw her bulging suitcase. "Thank goodness it arrived and didn't end up on a tarmac in the deep jungles of Africa." She was distracted for a second. Her gaze caught on a woman in a long, black cape and hood pulled closely around her face. The woman stood at the far side of the carousel. *She looks just like the woman I saw running across the street near my house when I was little. In fact, I remember it was the night I hid under my mother's bed. I lost sight of her after she came through the gate and ran onto the patio. It can't be her.* Suddenly she realized her bag was in front of her. She dropped her backpack and leaned forward just in time to grab it off the conveyor belt before it passed by her. She was too excited to wait for another revolution.

She almost fell, but caught herself on the edge of the carousel. Alexandra glanced up and looked around, but the woman was gone. She straightened up, pulled out the handle of her baggage, and dragged it to customs. *I hope I'm going to be lucky as usual!* She waited and watched.

When the agent saw the FBI emblem on her passport, he brought his hand down and stamped her passport with a huge thud. Then, giving a small bow he swept both of his hands forward with gusto in the direction of the exit.

Her blush was instantaneous. *That's never happened before.* She nodded thank you, grabbed her passport and suitcase, and moved quickly out of the way before one of the passengers questioned her about her first class treatment.

Alexandra followed the arrows to the meeting place—ground transportation. Her boots tapped on the floor of the terminal. She reached the lobby and scanned the crowd. "There he is." Alexandra spied a relatively short, round man who reminded her of a beach ball. He held a sign lettered in large black print—Mlle A. Pirrot—high in the air. A black beret sat jauntily on his head and a red scarf, tied around his neck in a perfect square knot, filled the space between his chin and the top button of his white shirt.

"*C'est moi.* It's me. It's me," she called out as she stood on her toes and waved.

The little man rushed forward. When he reached Alexandra, he stuck out his hand and snatched her suitcase. "My name is Jacques." He tore off his cap and bowed deeply. "Mademoiselle." He eyed her carry-on and smiled, showing the glint of a gold tooth.

"Bonjour, Jacques." Alexandra let her backpack slide off her shoulder. "I'll keep this."

She gripped it tightly as she rested it on the sidewalk. Her shoulder was beginning to ache from the weight of the bag.

He had no trouble dragging her checked luggage to the nearby curb where he had left his auto.

Alexandra heard several shrill whistles. She looked at the policeman approaching the car and then looked up at the No Parking sign that stood next to the taxi's passenger's door.

We got here just in time." Jacques turned and rushed by the policeman and yelled. "Going. Going." He motioned to Alexandra. "Follow me, Mademoiselle Pirrot. *Vite*, hurry."

She saw the scratches and a large dent near the back door handle of his small car when he yanked it open. Alexandra wondered if a ride to the chateau with Jacques might be her first adventure of the trip and perhaps one she might not want to take. *Well, it's too late now. It might be a trip with a detour to a hospital.* She grabbed her backpack, tossed it on the seat behind where Jacques would sit, and jumped in. She landed on the seat beside it just as the door came crashing shut behind her by Jacques' gentlemanly force. Alexandra shuddered.

She looked over her shoulder and watched Jacques waddle to the back of the car. It didn't surprise her when she saw him yank open the trunk door. He seemed to do everything with gusto. She kept an eye on him as he examined her suitcase and then the space in the trunk. She glanced back at the policeman who reached into his breast pocket.

Alexandra heard a grunt and moan. A loud thud made her turn and look over her shoulder. She watched Jacques intently out the back window. Her suitcase, half in and half out, hung over the end of the trunk. She stared as he pushed it into the tight space with his foot. "I hope he doesn't collapse," she mumbled. She looked as his chest heaved up and down. "I don't want to have to give CPR."

She breathed a sigh of relief when she heard a final "Voila." She watched him pull a once white handkerchief out of his pants pocket and wipe his forehead. She turned and looked out the front window. The policeman had a pad and pen in his hand. She decided to lean back and relax.

I won't have to pay the ticket.

She waited for Jacques to reach the driver's side of the car then leaned over and rolled down the window. "Are you all right?"

"*Mais oui*," he yelled flinging open his door. He looked at the policeman. "I'm going. I'm going."

Alexandra kept an eye on the policeman as he moved to the car behind them. She laughed. *Guess he got lucky.*

"Very bad traffic today, Mademoiselle, this is rush hour and it's almost Bastille Day." Jacques sprung into his seat. "In two days, on the fourteenth, all of France will be celebrating." He slammed his door shut.

"What?" Alexandra leaned forward. Jacques sputtered his words so quickly, it was hard for her to understand him over the noise of the traffic and the policeman blowing his whistle.

"It's vacation time. Everyone is leaving Paris." He pumped the gas pedal and revved the motor of the car. His arm muscles bulged as he turned the steering wheel. Without hesitation, he shot into traffic.

Alexandra sucked in her breath. *This is going to be an experience! Hope I get to the chateau in one piece.*

Chapter Two

Road to Giverny, France

Alexandra's back smashed against the back of the seat. She took a deep breath, righted herself and tried to chill out. *I'm not letting anything get me excited. I'm finally in France and on my way to Giverny and the chateau in the painting.* She leaned forward. "How long will the trip take to Chateau Verny?"

"*Trois heures.* It's not too far." Jacques honked his horn and darted by two cars, zipped by a cab, and seconds later almost ran a delivery truck off the road. He merged with the traffic into a third lane of a two-lane highway; he slammed the gas pedal to the floor and tailgated the car ahead of him.

Alexandra held onto the back of Jacques' seat with white knuckles. Her amethyst ring cut into her finger. *One hundred and ninety-eight kilometers. Let's see going through small villages after we leave the city, three hours seems about right. Though he drives like a crazy man. He might decide to levitate the taxi and fly over the traffic.*

She stared at the shops and cafes that zoomed by as the driver snaked through the crazy Paris traffic. *I only hope I'm alive when we get there.* Her hands formed into fists.

"Look out the back window. The Eiffel Tower is on your left." Jacques swerved; he barely missed a man on a bicycle. "We'll be crossing to the other side of the Seine soon and will head northwest."

Alexandra stared at the Eiffel Tower. *Somewhere I read it is 1063 feet high.*

She watched the elevator, crammed with tourists; ascend the south pillar of the tower. "It looks over Paris as if to protect it." *Too high for me to climb.* Her eyes drifted to the Fountains with bubbling water and statues surrounded by beautiful gardens carpeted with low and brightly colored flowers. So *romantic! I'll be walking through them when I come into Paris in a few days.*

Alexandra twisted her ring. She stared out the window ahead of her, past Jacques' hands that gripped the wheel, at the road. "Look, look at the people in ragged eighteenth-century clothes running down the street. They must be starting the celebration early."

"What?" Jacques glanced over his shoulder. He raised an eyebrow.

She stared out of the front window again. "Never mind. They're gone. I just...I just...It was nothing." She twisted her ring. *What's going on? Now I'm seeing things when I'm wide awake.*

"We're crossing to the Rive Gauche." He pointed toward the left bank of the Seine River. "Look at the artists with their easels and paints on the left bank of the river. They are there every day, sitting on small stools and making beautiful pictures on their canvases."

She looked at the patrons that sat in the chairs around café tables on the sidewalk outside the restaurants to seize the morning sun and catch up on the news. "Most of the outside tables of the cafes are filled." She could almost smell the coffee and taste a croissant with sweet butter and jam. "I can't wait to sit at one of those tables and people watch."

"What?" Jacques turned to look at her.

She shuddered. "Please look at the road, *merci.*" Alexandra watched the heavy traffic. *The cars and trucks are very close together. I hope his brakes are good.*

Jacques shrugged and turned back to the traffic on the avenue. In a few minutes, he began to hum the French anthem off key.

"Do you think the sun will come out?" Alexandra looked out on the dismal day.

"Mademoiselle, Paris is supposed to be overcast for a few days. Maybe even rain. But where you are going it will be nice. You'll have lots of sun. I'm sure of it."

He should be a travel agent—never looking at the bad side of a vacation day.

They left the super highway and traveled on two lane roads. The traffic thinned. Alexandra settled into the well-worn leather seat and watched the scenery. Vineyards and farms lined both sides of the roads. Farmers worked the fields with their machines. The land tracts that were fertile and green stretched on forever. They looked as if they led to nowhere. White cows stood in yellow fields where flowering mustard plants bloomed. Small stone houses dotted the hills.

She smiled as she leaned back and relaxed.

"What are the yellow machines in the vineyards?" Alexandra felt safer asking a question since the roads were almost empty—there was no one for Jacques to bump into. She hoped a cow or dog wouldn't wander into the road as he sped along.

"They will help the men in the fields pick the grapes. Soon they will be put to work. Make sure you visit some of the wineries. You'll be able to taste some very good wines. French wines are the best in the world." He put his fingertips together and threw a kiss into the air.

Alexandra smiled. *I don't think I'll mention that California has some pretty good ones too, but I'm tempted.*

She opened her backpack and peeked at her painting. "Jacques, how long has the Chateau been operating as an inn?"

"Since 1959. Some of it was destroyed by fire during the Revolution and then more of it during World War Two. But it's all been rebuilt in the eighteenth-century style. The furnishings are either reproductions or real antiques. You will enjoy staying there. *C'est magnifique.* The owners are very nice. The chef is the best in the area."

The car bounced on the uneven cobbled streets of the first small village Jacques drove through. "Ouch." Alexandra rubbed her left hip. "No springs, I guess. Jacques, please slow down."

He complied and slowed the auto.

She twisted her ring again. "Be careful. Watch out," She shouted. "Don't drive so close to those people. You'll run them over."

"What, Mademoiselle?"

"Don't run down those people."

"What people?"

"Don't you see the wagon and the men and women in ragged clothes walking beside it? Look at their faces. They look sick and hungry and they can hardly walk."

"No. No. Where are they?" He stared. "I don't see anyone." His forehead was wrinkled. He pulled his eyebrows together.

Alexandra glanced out of the back window. She searched the road. "Never mind, they're gone now." She rubbed her eyes. Her ring pressed into her lid. "I'm seeing things, Jacques. Just tired, I guess."

"You'll be okay after a good night's sleep and some good French food." He shook his head side-to-side and frowned. Back on a stretch of two-lane highway, Jacques sped up again.

When they passed through another village, Alexandra took a good look. "Does every village have a clock tower on a church and shops in its square?"

"Oui."

"I love the violet, canary yellow, and scarlet flowers. They make the square look inviting." Alexandra stared at the women scurrying from shop to shop. They carried string bags. Long loaves of bread, packages wrapped with white butcher paper, and fruits and vegetables stuck out of them. "The houses I see on the side streets with geraniums in terra cotta pots sitting on their doorsteps are wonderful." Alexandra sighed as they drove by the bakery. "I'm dying for some French bread—with nice, sweet butter."

She was getting hungry. She had not eaten much on the airplane. When the hostess had raced around passing out meals at dinner and then at breakfast, Alexandra had a glass of wine and bread for her evening meal and a cup of coffee and a sticky bun at breakfast. Airplane food wasn't on her list of something she had to have. She was waiting for French food like Josephine cooked.

When they reached the edge of the village, Alexandra smiled at the two dogs that raced up and down along a fenced-in yard. They barked furiously at the car. A woman in the next yard sat on a stool with a bucket. A cow and its calf stood next to her. She looked up and waved. Alexandra waved back. They passed a medieval church with a clock and bell tower in the village of Giverny. Its chimes rang eleven times.

Jacques' voice startled her. "Look, Miss Pirrot, there it is. Look half way up the mountain. There it is the Chateau Verny. Isn't it *grande?*" He pointed to his left.

She glimpsed down at her wrist. "It's almost three hours to the minute, Jacques, and we made it in one piece." She felt a chill along her spine as she looked out the window and up the mountain. Alexandra caught her breath. The mountain appeared to rise out of the fields. She saw the chateau and several small buildings in ruins that dotted the mountain behind the manor house come into view.

Chateau Verny, built in the beginning of the eighteenth-century and modernized in the mid-twentieth-century, rested stately on the side of the mountain. As in her picture, the land and estate were small by the usual chateau standards, but it looked down on the valley and stood as the protector of the town. The internet brochure she'd downloaded about the chateau mentioned there were twenty-five rooms and the chateau sat in the middle of a chestnut grove that was hundreds of years old. She thought she saw a lake behind the woods that wasn't in her picture. She pulled out her painting and held it on her lap. Alexandra glanced back and forth from the painting to the real thing. She examined each section of the painting and the chateau on the hill.

"Everything is the same. The slate roof, conical spires with turrets, gabled dormer windows, and a Rapunzel-like tower reaching toward the sky are all there." She stared at the rambling estate. "The article I read stated the fence surrounding three sides of the chateau still had most of the original iron. I'm amazed that it still looks in good shape. Is that true, Jacques?"

"*Oui*. Almost all of it is from many hundred years ago."

"There are no urns with cherubs sitting on the pillars in the painting. They look old but must have been added much later. Maybe a hundred years ago?"

'Don't know when but they have been here since I came eighty years ago." Jacques turned left off the main road. The car bounced up the winding road. When he reached the gate, Jacques stopped suddenly. The car rocked back and forth. He gave several quick pushes on his horn.

Alexandra heard a click. She watched the gate of the wrought-iron fence slowly swing open. Then felt the bumps again as Jacques proceeded at warp speed up the stone and dirt road to the front door of the chateau.

"Oh, for a padded seat," she said as she breathed a sigh of relief. *The trip will be over in a few minutes.* Alexandra caught her breath when Jacques slid to a stop at the chateau's front door, gravel spewing from under the car's wheels. She braced herself and hung on to the back of the seat as her body was thrown against her backpack. "I'm supposed to feel calm. I'm on vacation." She took a deep breath.

"What?" Not waiting for her to answer, Jacques flung open his door and jumped out of his seat before she was able to sit upright.

When she sat up, her eyes turned toward the chateau. She watched Jacques run up the stone stairs and bang the large, black iron knocker up and down several times. When her stomach settled down, she pulled on the handle to open her door. Jacques beat her to it. He jerked open the door and offered her a hand. She hadn't seen him return to the car.

"Are you all right?"

"Nothing like a grand entrance. I'm fine...I guess." She felt her cool face with her hand and imagined her freckles stood out on very pale skin. "Don't...Don't worry."

Alexandra tossed her backpack over her shoulder and jumped out of the car. She steadied herself as she walked leisurely toward the front door.

She looked at the perfectly manicured lawn and then over her shoulder at the valley and the small town nestled at the foot of the mountain. Her boots crunched on the pathway. She stared in awe at the red and purple bougainvillea vines in full bloom that climbed the chateau's walls and the well-established gardens filled with flowering shrubs and plants on either side of the steps. *Everything is so beautiful.*

She glanced at a gardener, on his knees, weeding near the front door. She smiled when he looked up. His brows drew together as he stared at her. Alexandra wondered why he cautiously studied her. *Does he know me? I don't know him.* She shook off the strange feeling that he seemed to recognize her.

They must have a slew of gardeners. The grounds are beautiful. Watching her feet, she stood for a second and stared at the massive oak door, then climbed the uneven stone steps. She was surprised when she looked up and gazed into the bright blue eyes of the woman in the doorway. Alexandra smiled. "Hello."

"*Bonjour, je m'appelle* Marie." An older, plump woman smiled warmly as she tucked a piece of long white hair that had escaped the bun at the base of her neck back into its place. There was no evidence of makeup on her plain face. Marie wiped the palm of her large hand on the gray apron covering a long, flowered dress and extended the hand. *Entre, s'il vous plait.*" Alexandra stared at her. *She looks a lot like Josephine.*

"*Bonjour.*" Alexandra felt her firm grip. She glanced around. Jacques had disappeared.

Alexandra stepped into the entryway and stared. "It's elegant." Startled, she twisted her head and turned toward the sound of a slight ding. She saw Marie standing next to a desk in front of a set of French doors. Her hand hit the bell on the table next to her for a second time. This time, Alexandra was not surprised.

"This is beautiful." She stared into a mirror with a gold-leaf frame hanging on the far wall. It was double her size. "My hair is a mess," she said pressing the stray curls of her long, auburn hair behind her ears. She looked around at the dark, wood paneled walls. Hearing a soft tinkling sound, she glanced up at the glass chandelier above her head. A light breeze flowed into the entrance hall from the open French doors. The soft sound came from the prisms of the chandelier as they moved slowly back and forth, hitting each other. Alexandra moved closer to the grand staircase that led to the upper floors of the chateau, to examine the ornate carving of the railing and pillars. She felt as if the eighteenth century had taken over. Alexandra took a deep breath. She immediately felt at home.

"Your credit card, please."

Marie's voice brought her back to the present. She looked at the hand Marie held out. Her palms were dry and lined with thick creases. Her fingers were thick and her fingernails were clipped short. Alexandra fumbled in the pockets of her pack. "Always in the last place I look." She laughed as she pulled it from a small zippered pocket on the front of the bag. She handed it to Marie.

"Your room is on the second floor to the left of the staircase. Right hand side at the end of the hallway. There's an elevator, but the stairs are faster." Marie took her card and slid it through the imprint machine.

"I'll take the stairs. I need the exercise after sitting for so many hours on the airplane."

"Pierre has your bags and will meet you at your room. You'll have a view of the gardens and the mountain. Lunch is at one." She handed Alexandra her credit card.

Marie reached for the pamphlets on the table next to the bell. "You might like these. They describe places of interest you might like to visit while you're here. There's a map of the area in the pile of brochures. Also, if you want to go to Paris, the TGV station is only twenty-eight kilometers away. A taxi can take you there. Paris isn't very far. Only an hour by train."

Alexandra slid her credit card and the area map that Marie had handed to her into her backpack along with the leaflets. "Thank you." She took a second look at the bowl on the table. It reminded her of the one on the hall table in her house in New York City. *It must be Baccarat crystal.* She remembered her grandmother telling her the small village of Baccarat, two hundred and fifty miles east of Paris, was encouraged by the Bishop of Metz to start an artisan business in the seventeen-hundreds. She recalled that the business survived the French Revolution. *It must be an antique.*

Had she not followed Marie's hand when she held out her room key to a tall, pale man in front of her, Alexandra would not have known that he stood near her. He had on a black suit and appeared like a ghost. *Did he come through the wall?* She looked at his feet, wondering if he had on felt slippers. *It looks like they have soft leather soles like moccasins.*

"Merci." Alexandra adjusted her backpack on her shoulder. Her boots tapped on the marble-tiled floor, echoing through the entrance hall until she reached the staircase. The thick carpet muffled her steps. She saw the thinning hair on the back of Pierre's head as he hobbled toward the elevator on her right. She saw him enter the old fashioned lift and pulled the safety door shut. Then she heard the swishing sound of the door as it closed. The lift rattled and clanged as it moved to the second floor. *I guess before Jacques left, he brought the suitcase in. I wonder where else that lift goes?* She glanced at the grandfather clock in the corner next to the elevator. It said eleven-thirty. She had time to get settled in her room before lunch.

Alexandra hesitated when she reached the top step. A life-size portrait of a woman and her dog hung on the wall in front of her. Alexandra stared at the woman in the portrait who had long, auburn hair and green eyes that seemed to look back at her. "She looks as if she wants to ask me a question." A cool breeze passed over Alexandra's shoulders. She shivered. "It's just the way the artist painted her. She's not real." She took a closer look at the painting. In the right hand corner of the portrait, Alexandra noticed a date—1786. It was the same year as the painting in her mother's book—the one her mother had showed her—the ball at Versailles. She looked for the name of the artist. It was there, but illegible. Alexandra turned and looked down the hall. *It's elegant and very European—old world looking.*

Alexandra had no idea a lone figure stared at Alexandra through the hallway walls, as she paced in the hidden passage behind the painting, and that the woman had anticipated her arrival, hoping her problems would finally be solved.

Alexandra passed by floor-to-ceiling paintings and tapestries as she walked slowly down the dim hallway on the pastel-colored Aubusson floor covering. Alexandra stared down at the flowery design of the wide runner. It had a cream-color background with powdery pink, pale sage, chalky blue, and musty violet. It reminded her of the rug in her mother's bedroom.

She peered down the hallway. Pierre stood at the end of the corridor in front of a door. *No more time to enjoy the corridor now.* She walked faster and reached him just as he bent down to unlock the door with an old-fashioned brass key. Alexandra heard the door creak open as he pushed it into the room. She watched him pull the key from the lock. It felt cold as he pushed it into her hand and waited without a word.

Hesitating, Alexandra stood in the doorway. "Thank you." She smiled. She stared at his chiseled block of a face and his large bone structure, square jaw, and bulging eyes that stared right through her. It unnerved her. Flashes of old horror movies flew through her mind. She dug into her pocket and pulled out a few Euros. "*Merci*, Pierre."

Shoving the money into the pocket of his baggy pants, he nodded. The aging servant limped down the hallway. He left as quietly as he had arrived in the reception hall. She shuddered.

Alexandra slipped into her room and looked around. She held her arms tightly around her chest. "I feel as if I'm in the seventeen hundreds." Large pieces of polished, solid wood furniture with beautiful, ornate carvings filled the room. She let her backpack slide off her shoulder, dropping it on the top of the royal blue brocade bedspread that covered the canopied bed and dusted the dark wooden floor.

Alexandra gazed around the room at the small pastel rugs scattered around the floor. Like the hall rug they also reminded her of the Aubusson rugs in her mother's room when she was a little girl. She peered at herself in the full-length mirror occupying part of the wall opposite the bench at the end of her bed. She stood in front of it and ran her hands through her hair. She pushed the loose tendrils behind her ears. She heard a noise. Alexandra pressed her nose against the glass of the mirror. "Is there someone in there?" she said. "I could have sworn someone was looking out at me." Alexandra checked to see if there was a space between the wall and the mirror. She shivered. "Boy do I need sleep."

She stared at her suitcase that sat on a massive, ornately carved bench on the far wall next to the curtains. *I guess Jacques brought it up after he let me off.* She strolled around the bed and drew back the thick, pale-blue velvet drapes hanging from a rod that was attached to a wall a few inches below the high ceiling.

She stood in front of a set of French doors. Alexandra felt the heat from the outside permeate the room. She gazed through the glass into beautiful gardens with bubbling fountains and statues. A row of tall, ornamental hedges separated the formal gardens from a wooded area. She could hardly believe she was at Chateau Verny—the chateau in her picture. Strangely, she felt that she was home.

Alexandra took a deep breath and slowly exhaled. A cool breeze passed through the room. It was over in a second. She felt as though someone had raced by her. She spun around and scanned the room. She hugged herself. An uneasy feeling made her look back over her shoulder. She searched all the walls looking for anything that looked like it might be a door. There was only the door she came through. No one was there. No one watched her. It was quiet. She saw nothing move. Why did she feel edgy?

A faint scent of rosemary, lemon, and jasmine wafted through the room.

Chapter Three

Drawn to the French doors, Alexandra reached in front of her and unfastened the lock. She stood very still, leaned forward, and pressed her face to the windowpane. She fiddled with the drapes. *Is someone out there?* She turned the handles and pulled back the pair of tall walnut and glass doors. The wide-open window offered a view of all the property that had once been part of the chateau's acres. Her eyes scanned the grounds in front of her.

She gazed into the woods on the other side of the hedges. A flicker of movement made her stare into the woods. A lithe, graceful figure of a woman in a flowing, light blue dress, with a matching scarf draped lightly over her auburn hair, caught Alexandra's attention. She watched the woman wander through the ancient chestnut trees.

Alexandra took a step onto the balcony. She reached behind her, closed her hands around the handles, and quietly pulled the doors closed. She tiptoed to the wrought-iron table and chairs that had been placed near the ornate railing, took a deep breath, and kept an eye on the woman.

Alexandra frowned. "I don't feel a breeze," she whispered, noticing that the ends of the woman's sheer scarf moved from side to side. It was as if the ends were picked up by the wind.

Alexandra felt a chill run along her spine. She kept her eyes on the woman.

Her eyes narrowed. *How odd. She doesn't seem to be walking. I don't hear leaves crunching or branches cracking. She seems to glide as she moves in and out of the trees. Who is she? Where did she come from? I need to get a closer look, but I don't want to scare her.*

She bent down and brushed bits of dirt from the seat of the chair. Then glanced back at the woods. "She's gone!" Alexandra leaned over the rail and stared into the gardens.

Where is she? Where did she go? Alexandra peered into the woods. "She disappeared. Her dog is still there."

She edged the chair closer to the rail and sat for several minutes. She heard the echo of the church bell in the village chime—twelve-thirty. "Well, guess she's not coming back." Her chair scraped on the cement floor of the balcony as she pushed away from the table, and she shook her head. Before she opened the door to her room, she gave a quick glance over her shoulder. *Now the dog is gone. Did I imagine them?* "I'll have a logical explanation for my visions, after some food and a good night's sleep. Right now I feel as if I'm losing my mind." *I have to get rid of some of these visions. They're driving me crazy.*

Alexandra paused in front of the full-length mirror. Her ring caught on a strand of her hair as she fluffed it. She leaned forward to untangle it. "What? Is someone there?" She peered closer. *Did I hear a voice? Get a grip, Alexandra. There's no one in the mirror.* She tried to pull it from the wall in order to look behind it. It was firmly attached. "What's wrong with me? My imagination has been playing tricks on me since I arrived in Paris—no, since I got on the plane and fell asleep." She leaned toward the mirror and stared. "If I am honest with myself, the dreams have been happening since I found the ring."

She pulled clothes from her suitcase, tossed them on the bed, dashed into the bathroom, and threw some water on her face. She breathed in the scent of the lavender soap as she washed her hands. "What a soft towel." She patted her face dry and rubbed her hands. She tossed her jeans, T-shirt, and boots on the bottom of the armoire and changed into the clothes on the bed. Alexandra fished her pink lip liner and matching lipstick from her purse. She leaned forward and gazed into the mirror again as she applied them. *No one is there. I just see my reflection.*

She tucked her hot pink silk blouse into her slacks and slipped her feet into brown sandals that she pulled from the bottom of her armoire. She grabbed her room key off the dresser and took several steps to open the door. After she checked to make sure her room door was locked, Alexandra stuffed the key into the pocket of her white slacks. She hurried down the shadowed hallway.

At the top of the staircase, Alexandra stopped and studied the portrait. "It's her. That's the woman I saw in the woods outside of my room." She examined the painting carefully. "She's wearing the same the blue dress and scarf. There's the little dog bouncing playfully beside her—just like he did in the woods." She ran her fingers through her hair. *We look as if we could be twins. Her hair is the same color as mine. Her eyes are green. We're about the same age and height.* A faint floral scent surrounded her. She looked over her shoulder and shivered.

"Maybe she'll reappear in the garden." Alexandra ran down the staircase, turned left—past the grandfather clock in the corner next to the elevator—and rushed into an empty dining room. Winding her way through the tables, she headed immediately for one by the window.

She stood on her toes and stared into the gardens, over the hedges, and into the woods. Her shoulders slumped. "No one is there."

Alexandra heard the chair next to her move. The legs of it scraped on the wooden floor as it moved. She flinched.

"Mademoiselle?"

"Oh, It's you, Jacques. It's nothing, nothing is wrong. I was just startled by the noise."

"Let me help you with the chair."

"*Merci.*" Alexandra smiled as she sat at the dining room table. "Thank you, Jacques, for seeing that my suitcase got to my room."

The buttons of his black jacket strained over his large belly when he bent over and placed a menu in front of her on the table.

I guess he's the waiter now. She wondered how many jobs he had at the chateau.

"It will take me a few minutes to decide, Jacques." She picked up the menu and began to study it.

"I'll be back to take your order. Don't hurry." He smiled.

"Merci." She glanced at the menu. "It's going to be hard to make a choice. Everything looks good."

She looked out into the dining room. There were ten walnut tables with four armchairs at each one. The chairs were made of the same wood as the tables. Each table had a small bouquet with a mixture of purple, blue and white flowers in the middle of the tablecloths. The silver place settings sparkled. The china looked like French porcelain. There were dainty garlands of small flowers on each piece. The table linen was plain and cream colored, and felt soft when Alexandra ran her hand over it. She turned toward the window again and stared into the garden.

"Hello," a deep voice with a French accent said. He pulled his sunglasses to the bridge of his nose and looked at her over the rims. Leaning his hands on the table, he stared at Alexandra.

She turned quickly. After noticing his well-manicured nails, she raised her head and gazed into his face. She looked at his long, classic nose, strong jaw, athletic build, and straight, black hair worn long enough to almost brush the collar of his light blue shirt. A thin scar that ran down his left cheek made him look ruggedly handsome—heart stopping handsome.

She watched him study her for a long moment and then she stared back into amazing eyes that were the most incredible ice blue. They reminded her of Paul Newman's eyes. His smile was warm and genuine. Alexandra couldn't help but think being with him might be very hazardous to her health. Her heart beat a little faster.

"We seem to be the only ones in the dining room. I'm Jean Paul Morneau. May I join you?" He looked directly into her enormous eyes as he spoke.

"Yes, I'm Alexandra Pirrot, Alex for short." She stuck out her hand. His grip was strong and his large hand felt warm as it covered her small one. She heard the scrape of the chair on the floor as he pulled the one across from her away from the table. She watched him ease his large frame into it.

"Alex is no name for an attractive woman. I'll call you Alexandra, if you don't mind?"

"That's fine. My school friends are the only ones who shorten my name. But I thought I would give you the option." She slowly lined up her silverware.

Alexandra glanced up and saw his eyes make a slow trip from her left hand to her face. Her eyes darted to his left hand. She noticed he had no wedding ring, but that didn't mean anything. She remembered her ex-husband James never wore his ring.

Alexandra liked Jean Paul's bearing, athletic build, and edgy good looks. They sparked her imagination. She looked away. *No more men. Not ever again.* A warm feeling crept from her neck to her cheeks.

Jacques appeared. "Monsieur."

Jean Paul nodded.

"May I take your orders?" He turned toward Alexandra.

It puzzled her when Jacques didn't offer her luncheon companion a menu. *He obviously has been staying at the chateau for a while and has the menu memorized or he orders the same thing.*

"I'll have the fish and shellfish stew, some nice crusty bread, and the apple tart for dessert."

"A very good choice. You will enjoy it, Mademoiselle."

Jacques is acting so different from this morning when he picked me up at the airport. Calmer and more formal. He seems to change his behavior when he changes jobs. Being a waiter seems to agree with him.

"*Et vous*, Monsieur Morneau?"

I was right. She smiled. *I wonder why he's staying at the chateau.*

"I'll have the cheese and pâté platter and fruit for dessert." Jean Paul turned to Alexandra. "Do you like white wine?"

Alexandra was about to say it would make her sleepy, but decided she was in France, on vacation and sitting across the table from a very handsome stranger—so wine it was. "Yes, I like it." She didn't care if it made her sleepy. It was the first day of her vacation.

She looked at Jean Paul's perfectly pressed beige suit—expensive threads, she was willing to bet. The only thing she saw that was out of place was the top button of his light blue shirt. It was undone and the knot of his red and navy stripped tie was loosened. *Lunch is going to be very interesting.*

"Jacques, bring us a bottle of Pinot Gris from Alsace and Sauterne with dessert, one from Burgundy, *s'il vous plait.*" Jean Paul looked toward Alexandra. "You will enjoy the Pinot Gris. It has a nutty taste, is not too dry, and will go well with your stew. Sauterne always goes with any dessert. Tell me what you think after you taste them."

"A man who knows his wines." *I must be tired. I usually don't make such dumb statements. He's French; of course he knows his wines.*

Jean Paul looked straight into her eyes again. He smiled. He was obviously enjoying himself. "That will be all, Jacques, *merci.*"

The French accent sent flutters to her stomach. She smiled back at him as he spoke.

"I will be back in a moment with your order," Jacques said. "Would you like me to open the French doors behind you, Monsieur Morneau? There's a nice breeze."

Jean Paul nodded yes without taking his eyes off Alexandra.

Jacques smiled and whistled softly as he walked back to the kitchen.

Alexandra looked over her shoulder and watched the door to the kitchen swing open when Jacques pushed it. It began to close slowly scraping across the slate floor. When it was closed half way, it stopped. Alexandra stared into the kitchen. A heavy oak table sat in the middle of the room. A huge stove sat on the far wall. There were two large ovens above it. Clay pots of herbs were on top of a high windowsill that was over the sink. A large man in a white chef's hat and uniform stood at the table rolling something that looked like pastry dough. *It looks like a wonderful kitchen. No wonder I rarely cook. I need a kitchen like that to get inspired.* She watched Jacques close the door with his foot. *There's the Jacques from this morning.*

"You must be the guest from the United States. Marie told me you were visiting for two or three months," Jean Paul said. He stared at her again.

"Are you on vacation?" Jean Paul asked.

She turned back to Jean Paul. "Yes, I've been working very hard and needed some time off. Some time to have fun." She didn't add that she had not been given a choice by the FBI who had said it was "a leave of absence or no job." They thought she was burned out.

What she said was the truth. She hadn't been happy about being forced to take a leave of absence, but now she was glad she was in France and at the chateau. This was going to be an interesting trip. "I also want to do some research on the French Revolution and hopefully trace my family history."

He raised an eyebrow. "You picked a great place to stay. The Chateau has a lot of history. It's been here for several hundred years. The food is wonderful. Do you think that some of your relatives are from this part of France?" He leaned forward.

They may have been from right here. My mother died when I was ten years old. My grandmother raised me and when she died, she left me the home I was raised in and all its contents. I found a small painting of a chateau in a box hidden in my mother's bedroom. It was a picture of this chateau." Alexandra took a sip of her water.

"When I did a search for hotels in Giverny area on the internet, I found that the chateau had been turned into an inn. I couldn't believe it. I called the reservation number. I didn't want to take time for emails to go back and forth. The owner was pleasant and helpful. I decided this would be the place where I would spend my vacation. I made my reservations at once."

Jean Paul stared out of the window with a perplexed frown. His eyes had taken on a steely quality. He didn't say anything.

Alexandra noticed that he seemed preoccupied. She leaned forward—not knowing how to react to his sudden change in mood. "Are you vacationing?"

"I have a room here and stay a few days during the week. I'm the lawyer representing the owner of the Chateau on murder charges. It hasn't been made public yet, but he is suspected of murdering his business partner in the second floor hallway with a knife. You know things like this have a way of leaking out. That's probably why you and I are the only people staying here. I'm sure the word has gotten around. I doubt that anyone wants to stay in a murderer's inn even if it's a beautiful chateau."

He glanced up. "Jacques."

I didn't hear him come to the table. Do all the people who work here have soft leather soles on their shoes?

Jacques had returned with a bottle of wine in one hand and an ice bucket in the other. He set the silver bucket and stand next to Jean Paul, then pushed the wine bottle into the ice and swirled it around for a few minutes. He pulled out his corkscrew.

Alexandra heard the pop of the cork as Jacques twisted it out of the bottle.

Jean Paul tasted the small sip of wine that Jacques had poured into his glass. "Perfect I'll pour the wine Jacques, merci."

"Your lunch will be ready in a minute." Jacques threw the words over his shoulder as he disappeared quietly.

"This is very good." Alexandra took a thoughtful sip. "I didn't hear anything about a murder. Something like that would never deter me from staying anywhere. What do they say—innocent until proven guilty." He was so easy to talk to. She felt as if it was the most natural thing in the world to be sitting here in a dining room in France with him. She was glad he had approached her and asked to join her.

Alexandra was trying to forget about criminals. She didn't want to talk about work, but she couldn't resist—she felt this was an exception. She was sitting across from the accused man's lawyer, a position she had been in often at trials—when she testified against their clients. This time she could just listen to his story. She didn't have to defend her investigation. Alexandra took another sip of her wine. She felt her body warm. *Oh, what the hell.* "What happened? Did he commit the murder?" *Why did I ask that? No good lawyer would tell me his client is a murderer. They're all innocent.* She stared at her wine glass. The corners of her mouth turned up slightly. She was almost hoping he wouldn't answer her question. She was here for rest and recreation, not to think about murder.

"He's accused of killing his business partner—stabbing him to death as I said. They found him with the knife in his hand," He answered her with one raised eyebrow. "But, let's not talk about murder," he said. His eyes were fixed on her.

She knew he must be surprised to see relief in her eyes.

"Here comes our lunch." Jean Paul placed his napkin in his lap. "Merci, Jacques."

She noticed he looked uneasy and decided to get off the subject of murder. "Is your home near the chateau?" Alexandra pulled her napkin from the table and dropped it on her lap. She felt better seeing him smile when she changed the subject.

"I moved back from London to take over my father's law practice a few months ago. I live in Paris in an apartment when I'm not staying here at the chateau investigating leads for the case. I have a permanent room on the third floor."

"Ah, London, my second favorite city. Did you defend murderers there?"

"I went to high school and college in England. After I graduated from law school in London, I worked for a British firm. We did a little bit of everything. My father wanted to retire and it was time for me to make a change. So…here I am."

He glanced out the window. After a moment, he leaned closer to the pane of glass next to him.

"Do you see something?"

"I thought I did. I thought I saw a woman."

Alexandra leaned toward the window and stared into the garden. Her shoulders slumped. There was no one in the garden. Her lady in the portrait had not reappeared.

He smiled. "Where are you planning to visit, Alexandra?"

As she described her plans, she listened to Jean Paul's suggestions of places she hadn't thought of seeing. When Jacques set another piece of apple tart in front of her, Alexandra was so engrossed in the conversation she took a bite without realizing it was a second piece.

"Would you like some more water, Mademoiselle?" Jacques asked.

She flinched. "No." She looked up. "No, *merci*. The wine is fine." She watched Jacques add wine to her glass. When she picked up her fork, she realized she was on her second piece of tart. "How did you know I could eat seconds? Jacques, it's wonderful. I thought I saw the chef rolling out the dough when you opened the door to the kitchen. It must have been baked while we ate our first course. You're right, it was delicious. Tomorrow I'll have fruit like Mr. Morneau." She smiled at Jean Paul. "I couldn't resist pastry on my first day in France."

She felt a confused sense of familiarity, as she sat at the table with Jean Paul. She didn't understand it. "That's all my family talked about—the pastry in France. They always had French chefs so I grew up eating French food, but it tastes better here in France. Our housekeeper taught me to make special dishes. It all has to do with butter, eggs, and cream."

Moving away from the table, Jacques grinned like a Cheshire cat. "They're really getting along. I detect a romance is brewing at the chateau," he whispered as the kitchen door swung closed behind him.

"Shall we share another bottle of wine?" Jean Paul finished off the last few drops of Sauterne left in the bottom of his glass.

Alexandra glanced at her watch, "Oh, my goodness, thank you, but no." She pushed her plate to the middle of the table. She heard the clock chime. "It's five o'clock—almost midnight for me. We've been talking for four hours. It's not the company. I am barely able to keep my eyes open.

I'm off to a good book and bed. I have to be ready early in the morning for sightseeing." Alexandra twisted her ring as she stood up. "It's been nice meeting you."

She heard the rustling sound of satin material come from the doorway of the dining room. When she turned, the woman in the painting at the top of the stairs stood there staring at her. She was dressed in a high-necked, navy-blue gown. The long, thin fingers of her right hand rested on the button of her collar. Alexandra closed her eyes tightly. As soon as she opened them, the woman was gone.

"Is there something wrong?" Jean Paul asked. "All of a sudden you paled."

"Oh no," she protested. "Just jet lag. Perhaps I'll see you at breakfast?" She wanted to change the subject again, but this time it was so he wouldn't persist. She didn't want him to ask about what she was reacting to—she didn't want to explain what she had seen.

"I hope so," Jean Paul said as he stretched his long legs and pushed his chair away from the table.

Taking a step toward her, he reached for her hand. Jean Paul raised it to his lips. He bushed them lightly over her fingers.

"Your ring is beautiful—an amethyst? The platinum setting is very unusual. Is it an antique?" He studied her ring as he held her hand.

"I'm not sure. It was in the box with the painting left to me by my grandmother. The box I told you about—remember?"

"Oh, yes. You'll have to show me the painting. Until tomorrow, I look forward to seeing you for the Bastille Day celebration." He grasped her hand and laid it against his cheek.

"*Au'voir.*"

"*Au'voir.*" She looked up. *I was right. I bet he's at least a foot taller than me. He must be at least six foot four.* His hand felt warm. She felt her breath catch in her throat. She could feel his eyes swoop from her head to her toes as she walked away from him and wandered into the entrance hall. Alexandra put her hand to her face. She felt warmth creep up her cheek. She was sure she blushed again. "Have a nice evening." She tossed the words out over her shoulder as she left the dining room. *You'd think I was a teenager! The way I blush. Thank goodness I'm not tongue-tied. I'm never at a loss for words.*

* * * *

When Jean Paul had stood up, he realized she was smaller than he had expected. He sat down at the table and waved to Jacques. "A cognac, please," Jean Paul called out. He leaned back in his chair and stared out into the gardens. He watched Jacques set a snifter with gold liquor in front of him. *She's here to trace her family. She may be of help to me.*

He picked up his glass and took a sip as he watched the sun begin to slide behind the mountain. The purple of encroaching night softened the hedges and woods.

He never dreamt when he heard that an American tourist with a French name would be visiting the chateau, she would be such a wholesome beauty. He was happy he had opted for lunch today instead of work. He had sat across from a sexy and beautiful American with long, auburn hair and beautiful, green eyes—he liked the way her smile reached her large eyes.

He had noticed her eyes sparkled with intelligence, as he'd watched her blush under his gaze and smiled. The soft scent of her perfume had tantalized him each time he'd leaned toward her. He could still smell her vanilla and jasmine scent.

A warm breeze blew through the French doors. He sat back and thought about his long lunch with Alexandra.

Chapter Four

Alexandra smiled. "This is going to be an interesting trip," she whispered, climbing the stairs. "My new friend is not only handsome but also charming. Be careful, Alexandra. Good old James was like that too, in the beginning." *No more men. I'm not here for a man or excitement. I'm just in France for a vacation and to find out about my ancestors.*

She moved down the corridor to her room. Halfway down the hall she felt a cool breeze. Alexandra looked back over her shoulder. Shadows filled every corner. Her feet pounded on the carpet as she ran. She unlocked the door of her room and flung it open. *Has someone been in here?*

The bedside light had been switched on and the covers turned down. She opened the armoire. Her suitcase had been stored in the back. Her dresses and blouses had been hung up. She pulled out the drawers of the dresser the rest of her clothes had been folded and piled neatly. *Alexandra get ahold of yourself. You're in an elegant chateau. They take care of your belongings. The help turns down your bed at night and makes up the room in the morning.*

All the wine has made me tired and that bed looks so comfy. "I've got to stop over-reacting." Alexandra slammed the door shut. She threw her clothes on the floor of the armoire, grabbed her XXL Syracuse University T-shirt and pulled it over her head. The bathroom's tile floor felt cold on her bare feet as she brushed her teeth and splashed water on her face. Just as she was about to jump into bed, she noticed a pink rose had been placed on her pillow. "Better than a mint, especially after the meal I've had."

She held the rose up to her chin and breathed in its delicate scent. It reminded her of the past. Pink roses had been in her bridal corsage.

After she filled a glass with water from the bathroom, she stuck the rose into it and set it on the dresser. Tomorrow she'd get a bud vase. Alexandra decided to leave the drapes open so that she could enjoy the full moon. She leapt into bed, wiggled off her ring, and unbuckled her wristwatch. Alexandra placed them within reach on the bedside table. A light breeze brushed over her shoulders. She shivered. It was as if someone walked by her. She pulled her covers up to her chin. She stared at the door. It was closed. Alexandra scanned the room. No one was there.

"I'm losing it." She threw back the duvet and crawled over the comforter to the bench at the end of her bed. She reached for her backpack. "It still feels heavy. I guess they didn't empty this." Alexandra searched in the main compartment for the book she started reading on the plane. After she found the book, she dropped the backpack on the floor and scrambled back to the head of the bed. She was beginning to feel cold. She grabbed the extra pillow, fluffed it up, and shoved it behind her back. She pulled up her covers. "Now I'm cozy."

"Let's see, where did I leave off?" She flipped through several pages. "Oh well, it doesn't matter. This seems close enough." Alexandra started on page two hundred and five.

It was one of those books she called a beach read. Missing a few pages wouldn't hurt the plot. Besides, she had read the last pages and knew how it ended.

It wasn't too long before the words began to blur. She leaned over and read her watch. "It can't be six o'clock. Okay, I'm holding it upside down. It's nine o'clock. That makes it three in the morning for me. I'm not on French time yet. If I have a good night's sleep, I'll be ready for sightseeing. I have to get rid of all these visions." She flicked off the bedside lamp and snuggled down under the duvet.

Alexandra woke up with a start. Her eyes popped open. A flash of light ripped through the French doors. She lay very still for a moment, and then picked up her head from the pillow and looked around the room. It took a few minutes before she realized where she was. She thought she heard a rustle and stared into the room trying to figure out if it was the brightness of the full moon or the light from the huge cracks of lightening coming from the mountain, or if it was something else that jarred her out of sleep. When the lightening stopped, she heard a voice.

"Don't be afraid, don't...be...afraid," the voice uttered.

"What? Who is it?" Alexandra sat straight up in bed. She struggled to focus her eyes and saw a woman stepping out of the mirror.

The light that spilled into her room was bright enough for her to see the silhouette of a nobly dressed, eighteenth-century woman standing just outside the mirror. Jewels covered her neck from her chin to her shoulders. Her dress was also dotted with the same type of stones. Alexandra sat up and leaned toward the side of the bed. Alexandra stared at her.

"Please help me," the woman cried and extended her hands—then stood motionless.

Alexandra grabbed her covers and pulled them to her nose. *Maybe if I don't answer her she'll go away. I must be dreaming or the wine has made me delusional. Alexandra you're an FBI agent, come on.* She threw back the duvet and jumped out of bed. When her feet hit the cold floor she was wide-awake and what she was looking at was not a dream. The figure was real.

"Where did you come from?" She clasped her hands to stop the trembling. "My God! I'm in a chateau in France with a woman coming out of my mirror." She jumped out of bed and planted one foot in front of the other as she began to move toward her visitor. When she felt her legs begin to wobble, she stood still for a second—her body tensed and her throat tightened. As she began to move toward the woman again, her heart pounded. The palms of her hands began to sweat. The small rug at the side of the bed shifted beneath her feet.

"Damn!" Trying to break her fall, she reached out. Her hands flailed. She stumbled—landing on the floor. Alexandra hit her head as she landed on the floor. She was stunned for a second. When she lifted herself to her knees, she saw that the woman's shoes sparkled, too. She felt dizzy. She rubbed her forehead and looked up. The woman was gone. As suddenly as the woman appeared, she disappeared like a vapor into the full-length mirror. Alexandra stood and stared. "Come back, please."

A clock struck eight. Alexandra wasn't sure where its chimes came from. As she listened, Alexandra realized she could hear the sound of the clock's bell echo through the mountains. It sounded as if it came from the church of Giverny. It didn't sound as if it came from the front entryway—near the elevator. She suspected with all the turmoil at the chateau someone forgot to wind it.

She had trouble waking up. Alexandra looked at the foot of her bed. The covers were pulled from the bottom. They were tangled and hanging half on the bed and half off, because she had tossed and turned all night waking frequently. She struggled to untwist from the mess she made. Finally she threw off her covers. "Damn I'm going to be late. Wait, why am I in a hurry? I'm on vacation." Sunlight streamed through the French doors. The rays danced on the walls of the room. *Was there someone in my room last night? Or was it just one of my strange dreams?*

"Maybe I should go back to sleep to see what happens? No enough is enough. This is the start of my vacation. I'm not missing breakfast or my day of sightseeing." *My God, I'm talking to myself and it's getting worse.* She stood up and started toward the bathroom.

Alexandra picked up her makeup bag and tossed it on the shelf over the bathroom sink. She leaned back and glanced over her shoulder and stared. "No one is here. The mirror is just a mirror."

She stepped up to the tub, flung back the white curtain as if she might catch someone standing there waiting for her with a weapon in hand. She turned on the faucets. "I don't believe an eighteenth century woman came out of my mirror. It just isn't possible." She pulled the shower curtain back across the tub so that when she turned on the spray it didn't wet the floor.

After a few minutes, she reached behind the white drape at the head of the bathtub and adjusted the temperature of the water. She switched the water lever from bath water to the shower spray. When a nice, steady stream of warm water came from the showerhead and the bathroom filled with steam, she dragged her T-shirt over her head and pitched it into the bedroom toward the bench at the end of the bed.

"I'd never make it as a Boston Red Sox player." Alexandra glanced back over her shoulder. "But…maybe I could. I'm only off by a few inches." She laughed. The shirt had missed the bench and landed on the floor in front of the mirror.

Alexandra climbed over the side of the old-fashioned claw-foot tub and let the warm spray cover her body. She felt edgy. She kept going over in her mind what had happened last night. She breathed in and out deeply. Then she stood in a trance until the water turned cold. "I must have been dreaming. I don't believe in ghosts." She clasped her arms around her chest to stop her shivering. The temperature in the bathroom had dropped a few degrees as the water cooled.

She reached around the curtain and grabbed her watch off the shelf above the sink. "Oh damn. I have to get going." *I have to learn to slow down. I'm on vacation.* She turned off the water knobs, climbed over the side of the tub, and grabbed the large, fluffy towel from the rack beside her. She wrapped it around her body. Her trembling stopped as she began to warm up. With the palm of her hand she wiped the fogged mirror. She bent forward and stared into the mirror. Alexandra noticed a small bruise and bump on her forehead. *That's it. I hit my head when I fell last night. Maybe I lost consciousness for a few seconds and it's all a hallucination from the fall.*

Alexandra plugged her hair dryer into the adapter in the wall, looked into the mirror at her long, wet, auburn hair and blew it until all the water evaporated. She tucked it up with a clip, applied color to darken her light eyebrows and eyelashes, brushed her face with transparent powder, undid the clip, and raked her hand through her hair. She let it fall where it may.

"I saw a jewel-encrusted woman before I fell. There must be a logical explanation." Alexandra flicked off the bathroom light and dashed out of the dark into the light of the bedroom. The sun that seeped through the French doors made her feel warm. Alexandra sighed. She pulled clothes from the dresser and armoire.

She tossed her towel onto the end of the bench at the foot of her bed and dressed quickly in lacy aqua underwear, a turquoise silk blouse, and tan slacks. "That should do it." When she leaned down to grab the straps of her sandals, something shiny caught her eye. She dug her fingers into the pile of the rug and retrieved a stone. She cupped her hand and held it in her palm. Alexandra watched the sparkle of its facets reflecting in the mirror as she turned it over with her index finger several times.

"A diamond. Where did it come from? I think it's real—fakes don't sparkle like this stone. If there was a woman covered with jewels in this room last night, she lost a stone." She peered into the mirror and shuddered. *What would I do if someone looked back at me?* She bent forward and put her ear close to the glass. "No one is talking to me or to anyone else. There's no one on the other side of this mirror, Well whoever it was that stood at the foot of my bed last night isn't anywhere in this room now or in the mirror," Alexandra whispered as she slipped the stone into her pocket. She applied some lipstick. "Where's my Oscar de la Renta? She rummaged through her makeup bag. Ah, here it is. Just one little spritz."

The door slammed shut behind her when she left her room. She twisted around and turned the key in the lock. When she heard it click, she slipped the key into her pocket and rushed down the shadowed hallway to the main staircase. Alexandra stopped at the portrait. She clutched her arms tightly around her chest as she studied the woman's face. *She seems so sad.* Alexandra felt a sudden chill. "Alexandra, stop obsessing about her."

The aroma of freshly brewed coffee rushed to meet her as she entered the dining room. Alexandra scanned the tables. *Well, I guess I didn't have to hurry. Jean Paul isn't here. Maybe I missed him.* Disappointed, she walked to the buffet against the wall behind her. She filled a small plate with a freshly baked croissant, butter, and a dollop of raspberry jam. She started to leave and turned back. She grabbed a slice of cheese. "I need some protein." She wandered to the outside patio and sat at a table where the hedges were low, so that she could look over them into the woods. She rested her elbows on the table with her chin in her fists and stared. She didn't see anyone, but she was beginning to calm down and enjoy the peace and quiet.

"Coffee, Mademoiselle?"

She flinched. "Oh, bonjour, Jacques. Yes, please. Black." She smiled. "Did I scare you?"

"I was deep in thought."

She watched him tip the spout of a small, silver coffee pot into the creamed colored cup with a row of gold leaves just below the rim. It sat on a matching saucer. Both were sitting in front of her.

"*Merci.*" She took a sip.

"*Bonjour,*" Jean Paul said.

Her stomach reacted to his sexy voice. She looked up and smiled. Jean Paul wore jeans that fit as if they were custom made. She decided they probably bore a designer label and his sweater looked like it was hand-knit in a fine merino yarn.

Alexandra felt the warmth that crept up her face. *Why am I always blushing when I see him?* She had a soft spot for strong, confident men.

"Is that all you're having for breakfast? You'll need more food than that to sustain you on a day of sightseeing. You certainly don't look as if you have to count calories."

Alexandra glanced at his plate. It was filled with three different cheeses, sliced ham, and French bread. "Well, you must be hungry."

"Where are you off to today?" Jean Paul looked into her eyes as he slid his well-toned physique into the seat next to her.

"Coffee, Monsieur?" Jacques appeared at the table before Jean Paul could motion to him.

"*Merci*, Jacques. Black and two sugars," Jean Paul said.

"My first stop is Claude Monet's home," Alexandra said.

"Sometimes I go there to think. Walking through the gardens helps me to sort out the information my clients give me."

He stared at her. There it was again—the subtle sexiness of the scent she wore. It made him want to reach out and touch her. It was her wide smile and full lips that took his breath away. He wanted to get to know her.

"I've read a lot about the home. I'm dying to see it and the gardens."

"I'd go with you, but I have a prospective client to interview today."

"Another murder case?" Alexandra asked.

"No, a land dispute, but if I don't solve it, either my client or the other man mentioned in the suit may commit murder. They are both very high strung. I think they're on the brink of exploding. It's a challenge dealing with them."

"You can come with me on one of my other tours." *What made me say that?* She glanced sideways to see his reaction.

"I will." He smiled. "The gardens here at the chateau are quite spectacular. We should take a walk through them. There are many species of flowers, vegetables, and fruit trees on the five hundred acres. I've been told there is even a small family chapel somewhere on the property," Jean Paul said.

She noticed that he looked and talked to her as if he found her interesting and wanted to get to know her. "They might be fun to explore." Her heart skipped a beat. *Was he interested in her? Alexandra, remember no more men.* "I'd enjoy walking around the property." *So much for my resolution.* She felt her eyes crinkle at the edges. She had smiled more in the last two days than she had in a long time. "I would have thought there would be more land."

"There was, but a lot of the acres were sold off. The owners over the years needed the money to run the chateau and the land. It's expensive to keep the property up so acres have been sold of little by little. The Dumonts must be having trouble making ends meet. Since the murder, there are lots of vacancies. I hope Monsieur Dumont will be found innocent and things will turn around for them. I hope they don't have to sell any land. It's a wonderful place to stay and the food is the best in the area."

"What about the stone houses that are on the mountainside? The ones that have been left in ruins?" Alexandra asked.

"They belonged to the chateau owner in the early seventeen hundreds. A small plot was given to a farmer who worked the land and paid taxes to the king. One of the reasons the revolution started was that the farmers couldn't live on what they earned because the taxes were so high. They went hungry and had to give up their land. After the Revolution, the houses were deserted by the rebels and were left to decay."

"The French revolution was a terrible time in history." Alexandra frowned.

Alexandra looked down at her watch. "Monet's house will be open soon for tourists. Guess I'd better get going."

"May I give you a lift?"

"No, thanks. It's sweet of you to offer. Jacques says it will only take about thirty minutes to walk into town. It's such a beautiful day, I'd like to explore and take some photos of the scenery and the village. Plus I need to walk off the tart or tarts I ate last night." *I don't want to be too easy.*

He looked at her pale face and raised an eyebrow. "You look tired."

"Oh, it's what I call the first night syndrome. I always have trouble adjusting to the time change." *I'm not going to tell him about my visitor—he'll think I'm a grade A nut case.* "Will I see you at dinner?"

"Not tonight. Monsieur Dumont is in prison in Paris. I need to consult with him. Won't be back until tomorrow. We'll celebrate Bastille Day together. Would you like that?"

She tried to hide her disappointment that he would be gone for the rest of the day. She grinned broadly. "I'll be looking forward to spending the holiday with you." It felt good. She could feel his eyes follow her as she left the dining room.

"Until the fourteenth, then."

In the reception hall, Alexandra saw a heavy-set woman sitting in a large ornate chair at a table of polished wood in the same style. She really hadn't looked at the furniture carefully yesterday. They were beautiful antiques and were perfect pieces for the entranceway.

She watched the woman run her hand through her gray hair—hair that Alexandra was sure had once been neatly combed. The hem of her loose fitting, 1950s style navy dress hung almost to her ankles. A pair of square-toed shoes peeked out from under the dresses hem.

"*Bonjour.*" Alexandra walked toward her. The woman didn't look up or respond. "*Bonjour.*" She moved closer and repeated her greeting.

"Oh, I'm…sorry, *Bon…Bonjour.*" The woman dropped her pen. "Since my husband left for prison, I've had to do everything. The books are driving me crazy. *Trés difficile.*" She stood and extended her hand. "I'm Madame Dumont. You must be our American guest. I think I talked to you on the phone. Sorry I wasn't here yesterday to welcome you. I hope my Housekeeper was helpful and made you feel welcome." She sighed.

"Yes, she was very nice, *merci*. I'm sure Mr. Dumont will be all right and will be home before you know it." Alexandra moved next to the table. "Don't worry about me. I understand. I'll manage." She looked into Madame Dumont's eyes. "The chateau is wonderful. I am enjoying myself already. It's everything you said it would be when we spoke."

Madame Dumont exhaled loudly. "You just don't know. They dragged him out of here in handcuffs." She took short breaths. "*C'est tragique.*"

"It will all work out." Alexandra reached forward and patted the top of her hand. "Do you have some suggestions of places near here to see?" She wanted to distract her host. "I already have plans for today, but I would appreciate your suggestions for other days." Alexandra hoped that she might suggest places the usual tourist might not visit.

"I am remiss." Madame Dumont shuffled through papers in the top drawer of the table. She pulled out several brochures and handed them to Alexandra. "Here are some places you might enjoy visiting. They are in towns around here. They are places not often frequented by tourists. You can reach them by car. If you take a taxi, the fare will be minimal. Also, Rouen might interest you. Where is that pamphlet?"

"Don't worry, I'll remember what you tell me."

"Joan d'Arc's statue is there and the town is very interesting. There are many antique shops and a botanical garden. The Rue de la République has many shops and museums. There's a great clock—Gros Horloge—in an overhead arch on the main street. It is very old. It dates back to the fourteenth-century. The history books say its inside works are from 1389. It's at the beginning of a cobblestone street leading into the old part of town. You'll see medieval towers and carvings," Madam Dumont said. She hesitated. She picked up her pen. "I'm sorry. I must get back to work. Have a nice day." She turned back to her books.

"Merci." The poor woman! She is so overwhelmed. "I have to get my things from my room." Alexandra turned and ran up the stairs two at a time. She stopped at the portrait. The painting seemed to give off the same fragrance she had smelled in her room the day she arrived. She bolted down the hall, glancing over her shoulder as she ran; the floral scent followed her down the hallway.

Alexandra unlocked her door, threw it open and stood just far enough inside the room so that she could shut the door. She locked it from the inside. "If anyone is here, go away. Go away," Alexandra yelled. She didn't hear anyone answer. "No one is here. At least no one I can see." She sighed. "Oh God. What am I doing?" She peered around the room, looking in every corner. She opened the armoire, pulled back the hangers that held her clothes, and then stared into the mirror. She sat on the bench at the end of her bed. Her breath came from deep in her stomach.

She picked up her backpack and shuffled through it. "Let's see—wallet, sunglasses, map, camera," she said as she took inventory. Alexandra added the brochures that Madame Dumont had given her to the pile she received the day she arrived. She looked around. "Where's my room key? Slow down, Alexandra, where did you have it last?" She scanned the room again. "Oh, thank God, I left it in the lock. Why did I do that?" She shook her head. *Unlocked or locked—it doesn't seem to matter. Ghosts can get into any place they want to.*

Alexandra ignored the portrait as she dashed down the staircase. "Bye." She waved to Madame Dumont and lifted her backpack higher on her shoulder. She left through the front door and rushed down the gravel road to the front gate.

Chills climbed her spine when she passed through the gate and looked back. She was sure she saw a woman, wrapped in a long cape with a hood pulled up over her head to cover her face, walk across the front lawn heading in the direction of the woods. *Calm down.* Alexandra pulled her camera from the back pocket of her pack and snapped a picture of the woman just as she turned the far corner of the chateau. *Now I have proof there is a third guest at the chateau.* She checked the pictures in her digital camera. She pushed the button and scanned the photos. She looked at the picture she had just taken. The photograph was blurred. She was unable to make out the figure. *Should I go back and look for her? No, I don't want to take the time. I want to get started on my sightseeing. I'll search for her later.*

Chapter Five

Once inside St. Radegonde Church, Alexandra stood for a few seconds, letting her eyes adjust to the dim light. She turned to the plaque and stood close to the wall just within the sanctuary so that she could read about the church. She rested her hand and arm on the thick, gray, stone wall. The coldness of it startled her. She began to read.

It was hard for her to believe that she was standing in a building that dated back to the middle ages—the eleventh century. She studied the simplicity of the semi-circular arches and furnishings as she walked behind the benches and crossed the back of the church. She moved to the far aisle and started toward the altar.

Alexandra examined the statues lining the wall. *They're magnificent.* She was impressed by their Romanesque style.

She bit her lip. She could taste her blood as she held her breath. Alexandra put her hand on her cheek. She knew the color had drained from her face. It felt cold—bone deep cold. Breath, *Alexandra, or you'll faint.* She took a deep breath and exhaled and breathed in deeply and exhaled again.

Not again. She stared at the man who sat on first bench near the plain cross. He wore an eighteenth-century, royal blue, silk suit and a white wig. She slipped into the row behind the man, and then tip-toed toward his seat. She moved slowly and quietly. She didn't want him to suspect she was spying on him.

Alexandra had almost reached him when he stood up and slid to the end of the row. She pretended she was studying the cross, then lit a candle and said a quick prayer, just in case he turned around.

She followed the tap of his leather-buckled, high-heeled shoes on the stone floor as he strolled out the side door. *I have to keep far enough away so he doesn't think I'm a stalker.* Once outside, she stopped and looked behind her for a moment. She clicked a picture of the church. She wanted a photo of St. Radegonde, but she also wanted him to think she was just a tourist if he happened to look back over his shoulder.

Alexandra made sure she kept him in her sights. She watched him hesitate when he arrived at Chemin du Roy. He looked both ways and turned right.

When she reached the intersection, Alexandra stood and kept an eye on him until he disappeared around the next corner. *Okay, enough is enough.* His feet are hitting the ground—no floating. Stop obsessing. I don't believe in ghosts." She turned sharply to the left and reached Monet's house on the River Epte in ten minutes. She enjoyed her walk by the slow-moving river. Willows and poplar trees lined its banks and shifted from side to side in the light breeze.

While she waited in a short line at the ticket office, Alexandra looked out onto the arched Japanese bridge built over a lily pond. A weathered boat sat on the edge of an island in the middle of the water. *It's beautiful. Just like Monet's painting.*

Alexandra paid her entrance fee and picked up a brochure. She watched the young couple in front of her run after their two children who had pulled away from them and were scampering through the gardens, trampling on the flowers. She lagged back so that they would get well ahead of her. Alexandra liked little children, but today she wanted to enjoy the tranquility and peacefulness of nature, and enjoy her vacation.

She started the self-guided tour of the gardens and house. She wandered up the first of eight paths that led to the front of a large cottage painted dusty pink and Christmas tree green. Planted on both sides of each path were hundreds of specimens of trees, bushes, and flowers. They were all in bloom. The colors were spectacular.

She walked up each path, mesmerized by the shades of red, yellow, purple, and pastel. The scent of the flowers overpowered her. Her eyes widened as she read in her pamphlet, "These gardens contain 100,000 plants replaced each year and 100,000 perennials." Butterflies were also enjoying the flowers. She gazed at them as they flitted from flower to flower. The beautiful and serene surroundings calmed her. She was glad she decided to visit France.

She heard a rustle and glanced up. She saw a woman in a long, dark cape disappear behind a mimosa tree. Alexandra wrapped her arms around her chest. She couldn't figure out why she kept seeing the women she first saw when she pressed her nose against the windows of the French doors in her mother's bed room. *Forget it Alexandra enjoy your vacation.* She made her way to Monet's home and began the house tour. The rooms were small and simply furnished. The house was decorated as it had been when Monet was in residence. Alexandra studied the paintings that hung on the walls. Many of them she had seen reproduced in her art history books. Alexandra scanned the pamphlet again. "Monet lived here from 1890 until 1926 with his two children, his lady friend and her six children." *How did they fit into this place?*

The souvenir shop was the last stop. *Where else would a tour end?* "No souvenirs today. I'll be back," she mouthed, waving to the girl behind the counter at the cash register.

A noisy gurgle came from her stomach. She looked at her watch. *It's almost eleven.* Alexandra glanced at her city guide. The closest restaurant was in a hotel that was described as the center of artistic life in the heyday of Giverny. "Artists came from all over the world and stayed at the hotel," Alexandra read out loud from her brochure. "Many of them were from the United States." She skipped to the bottom of the page. "The restaurant serves authentic French food prepared by Jacques Broussard, a graduate of the Cordon Blue." *It's only a block from here.* She decided to try it.

Alexandra walked back past the River Epte and turned left at the Clemin du Roy. Five minutes later she climbed the stairs of the 125-year-old hotel. The wide, weathered boards creaked as she slowly walked up to the door.

Alexandra scanned the menu chalked on a blackboard attached to the wall next to the entrance. Most of the food listed looked rich and heavy. She didn't want a full-course meal and glanced under *lite faire.* It didn't take her long to decide what she wanted to order.

She leaned around the entrance door and peeked into the dining room. There were ten tables. Only three of them were occupied. The dining room wasn't fancy. The tables were plain wood, with paper napkin dispensers, salt and pepper shakers, and sugar bowls. Each table had a small vase with purple and red flowers. The place settings were silver plate. Alexandra translated the sign just inside the entrance, *Seat Yourself.* She chose a table next to the front window.

"Mademoiselle?"

"I'll have the quiche of the day—Quiche Lorraine—and a salad. Oh, also a glass of the house wine—white, *s'il vous plait.* I'm very hungry."

The waiter smiled and pulled a paper and pencil from his apron pocket. He scribbled her order on a piece of paper from a pad half the size of a cocktail napkin and ripped it from the pad.

Alexandra watched him. When he stopped, she smiled. "What do you recommend for dessert?"

"The peaches and strawberries in Pink Champagne. It's a specialty during the Bastille celebrations."

"So much for counting calories, I'll start tomorrow. Whoops, I said that yesterday. Oh well, I'm on vacation."

"Mademoiselle?" The waiter raised his left eyebrow.

I'll have to stop talking to myself. Alexandra laughed. "I'll have the Bastille Day specialty. *Merci.*" She watched him add it to her order sheet.

While she waited, Alexandra looked around the room. She watched two elderly women as they ate the special dessert. Every once in a while they filled their cups from a silver coffee pot that sat in the middle of their table. They seemed to be enjoying it.

Then, she glanced at the older man who sat in the corner. He put his paper down and tucked his napkin into his shirt at the top button when the waiter brought him a large piece of quiche and a glass of white wine. *That looks good. I'm glad I ordered it.*

Alexandra nodded to the young woman next to her who looked up from her book to take a sip of coffee. *She must be a regular and doesn't feel the need to order food, or maybe she's not hungry.*

Alexandra smiled at her then stared out of the window into the square at two men in the throes of building a wooden stage. They talked and laughed as they worked. *Must be for the Bastille celebration.* She stared at the man, who had been in the church, as he walked from behind the hotel and passed by the front door. Alexandra leaned close to the glass and watched him. Her eyes followed him. She felt relief when he stopped and joined a group of men and women in eighteenth century costumes coming from the other direction. She watched them walk toward the platform. She stared at the man as he stood and laughed with the men building the stage. They seemed to be enjoying themselves. Alexandra sighed. *I must be paranoid seeing ghosts everywhere I go.*

"Thank goodness." She breathed a sigh of relief. "He seems to be part of the Bastille Day reenactment. At least I'm not seeing ghosts again. I don't think I am." *This is a real stage and those are, in fact, real people.*

The church bells rang twelve for the noon mass. The group rushed toward St. Radegonde. Alexandra watched them as they hurried through the church's massive wooden door. She smiled.

After lunch, Alexandra stopped at the cemetery at St. Radegonde. She wandered through the headstones of Monet and his family. Fresh flowers had been placed on each grave. *They must be kept up by the Monet Society.*

She glanced at her watch. "It's time I begin to walk back to the chateau." She took out her camera and began to snap pictures along the way. Maybe I'll see the woman in the cape again.

When she entered the hall of the chateau, Alexandra saw Madame Dumont. She was in the same position she had been in when Alexandra left—working on the books. Her hands furiously shuffled through the papers on her desk, but she took a moment to look up and smile when she heard the tap of Alexandra's leather boots on the marble floor.

Alexandra nodded hello and continued up the staircase. Her mouth dropped open when she reached the top step. *The picture is gone.* Her eyes fixed on an empty wall. She looked up and down the hallway to make sure the painting hadn't been moved to another part of the wall before she turned and ran back to Madame Dumont. "Where is the painting that was at the top of the stairs? The painting of the woman with the dog."

"Oh…" Madame Dumont hesitated. "Monsieur Morneau had the servants help him load it into a van. He told me he was taking it to Paris to have it appraised in case my husband's trial doesn't go well and we need to sell it. To have money to live on."

Alexandra took a deep breath. "Who is the woman in the painting?"

"I don't know who she is. I assumed she was someone who lived here at the chateau hundreds of years ago. Mr. Morneau told me who he thought it might be, but that he didn't have any proof. I really didn't pay attention to what he said. These books…you know. They take all my time." She wiped her hands across her brow and pushed a wisp of her hair out of her eyes.

"*Merci.*" Alexandra frowned. She needed to figure out who the woman was and why she was seeing her wandering around the chateau. Alexandra thought that Mrs. Dumont was correct. The woman was someone who had lived in the chateau. She turned to go back to the staircase.

"Wait, I remember," Madam Dumont called. "He said she might be a relative. I don't know what made him think that. I just don't know. When he gets back, maybe you can ask him."

July 14 2010

Strange visions of the past haunted her. Alexandra tossed and turned, finally ending up on her back. She fumbled for her watch on her bedside table and held it toward the moonlight that flowed through the French doors. It was a little after midnight. *Will these dreams ever stop?* She stared around the room at the shadows jumping on the ceiling and walls. She couldn't get comfortable. Alexandra twisted off her amethyst ring. Within seconds of setting her ring on her bedside table a woman's voice filled the room. Alexandra shot straight up in bed and flicked on the bedside lamp.

"You must, you must come with me," she pleaded. Her hands stretched toward Alexandra.

Alexandra stared. She sat very still and took a long look at the figure. She realized her visitor, who stood at the foot of her bed, was the same woman who had stood near the edge of the mirror the night before. But this time her voice was adamant and determined. Her mouth was tightened into a stubborn line. Her fingers trembled as she balled them into fists. The woman's long, black cape moved as if the wind blew behind her. It opened to reveal a tailored, dark dress with a high collar. She looked like a matron in an eighteenth century prison. Her hair was pulled back and knotted at her neck. This time the woman had a dark red scarf tied around her neck—no jewels. She cowered back and looked over her shoulder, waited a few seconds more, then took a step back toward the mirror as if she was going to slip away.

"Wait!" Alexandra took a deep breath then exhaled. "Wait I'm coming with you." She jumped out of bed, ran to the armoire and grabbed clothes she had thrown on the bottom shelf the day she arrived. She turned her back as she pulled them on, but glanced over her shoulder every few seconds to make sure the woman stayed put. "Okay I'm almost ready," she yelled.

"Hurry," the visitor pleaded.

Alexandra tucked her T-shirt into her jeans and pulled her navy blue cotton sweater over her head covering her shirt. Not bothering to put on a belt, she plunked down into the chair, tugged on her socks and pushed her feet into her boots. "I'm coming." She took a quick glance into the mirror. When she saw a reflection of herself, Alexandra ran her fingers through her hair. She fixed her eyes on the woman as she moved toward her. Her heart pounded. *It's the woman in the portrait. What is going on? Who cares? If she needs my help, I'll help her.* Alexandra stared into a face filled with anxiety. She hesitated. She couldn't rid herself of a sense of foreboding. "Were you in my room last night? If you were, I have a diamond that belongs to you." She went over to the armoire and shuffled through her clothes. "I can't find it."

"Don't worry about that now. We have to hurry."

I guess the stone doesn't matter to her. She was covered with them. "Who are you?" Alexandra repeated.

"I am Claudette." She grabbed at Alexandra's arm and pulled her toward the mirror. "Follow me," she shouted. The mirror seemed to open like a sliding door. She dropped Alexandra's arm and entered the pitch-black space behind the mirror.

Alexandra felt a moment of trepidation. Then she frantically waved her hand. "Wait! I'm right behind you." She reached out and caught Claudette's fingers just as she disappeared. She felt their warmth as she held them with a vise-like grip. "Don't let go," Alexandra called out.

Tiny droplets of water, from the mist that closed in around them, collected on her hair and forehead. The droplets began to drip onto her neck. With her free hand, she wiped her face with her sweater. The sensation of floating swept over her as they moved forward through the dark passage. She stretched her free hand out to her side and felt the passageway wall. The cold stone made her jump. *It's a tunnel and it's narrow.* Every nerve in her body vibrated.

She wasn't sure what was happening to her, but her thirst for adventure made her follow her night visitor. Within minutes, Alexandra looked down. She stood on a gravel path. She glanced over her shoulder. The chateau stood in the moonlight behind them. She was on the path leading to the front door of the manor house. The sky was clear with bright stars and a full moon. She looked in front of her. The mist had evaporated. A carriage and four horses waited. She jumped when an owl hooted.

Alexandra eyes fixed on the coachman. She watched him grip his long whip. His mouth was drawn into a grim line as he restrained the horses that seemed to want to take flight.

"What am I mixed up in? I just came here for a vacation and to search for my ancestors." Alexandra tried to pull back into the mist. This time Claudette's long, artistic fingers gripped her arm like a vise. She wouldn't let Alexandra retreat into the haze.

Claudette threw open the door of the carriage. With her free hand, she reached up and snatched at something on the seat. She tossed it to Alexandra. "Put it on—hurry. We can't waste time."

After she caught it, Alexandra examined what Claudette tossed to her. *A black, wool cape with a hood. I don't think this will protect me from whatever is going to happen.* Alexandra threw it over her shoulders. Startled by the horses, she jumped and stepped back when she heard them snort. Their harnesses rattled as they tossed their heads. A torch, stuck in the holder on edge of the driver's seat, burned casting shadows across the lawn. She wrapped the cape tightly around her. She had a feeling of dread.

She stared at the coach and the man sitting on the seat with a whip, and then scanned the property around her. It didn't look like it had when she arrived. There were no beautiful gardens or paved roads.

Claudette leaped into the carriage. "Come on, get in," she shouted as she leaned out of the door and grabbed Alexandra's arm. She reached out and pulled her up onto the leather seat next to her. After Alexandra fell into the seat, Claudette slammed the door and then leaned out of the carriage window. "Go as fast as you can, Charles," she yelled.

Road to Paris
June 14, 1789

Alexandra heard the coachman crack his whip. The horses' harnesses snapped as the carriage jolted forward. She grabbed onto the window frame. Alexandra stuck her head out of the window and watched the clouds of dust rise from the carriage's wheels as it raced down the road. After several minutes, charcoal clouds floated across the moon and stars. The sky was black. Alexandra could see nothing along the roadside except the outlines of fields and small houses that were dark inside. She shivered. Holding the folds of her cape tightly closed, she tried to keep out the cool night air. "This must be what my mother said about the ring. It would take me to a time of evil, but it would protect me. I must be going back in time. Is this what my mother and grandmother did when they came to France?" she whispered to herself.

"What do you want from me?" Alexandra shouted over the pounding of the horse's hooves. She gave Claudette a sidelong glance. Alexandra felt the index finger of her right hand. "My ring!" She checked the pocket of her jeans. "Here it is."

She was no stranger to taking problems head-on, but she didn't know what was ahead of her. She had a sense of foreboding.

I knew when I met Pierre in the reception hall, the day I arrived, he acted very strangely. It was almost as if he knew me. Charles acts if he knows me. I look like the woman in the hallway upstairs that must be why. Alexandra shook her head. "I'll wake up any minute and discover this isn't really happening. It must be one big nightmare."

"What?" Claudette leaned closer to Alexandra.

"Nothing. Nothing at all." She drew in a deep breath and shook her head from side-to-side.

"Keep your cape closed. So no one will see your clothes." She leaned forward toward Alexandra. "You need to help me save my brother-in-law, Henri. He's one of the seven prisoners being held in Paris. I'm afraid something awful will happen to him. I lost my children and my husband. I don't want to lose my brother-in-law. You must help me save Henri."

Claudette stuck her head out of the carriage and yelled. "Go faster, Charles. You have to go faster." Her voice was carried by the wind and echoed through the opened fields.

"What do you mean you lost your children and husband?"

"I can't talk about it. No, that's not what I mean; I don't want to talk about it now." She turned her head and stared at the wall of the carriage. Her body shook. "I need you to help me. No one has been able to. Not even your grandmother or your mother.

The clouds cleared. The moon that had been swallowed by fog now shone into the carriage. Alexandra moved to the seat across from Claudette. The moonlight made it easy for Alexandra to take a good look at the woman. Then she turned and sat sideways on the seat.

"Look at me." She saw a woman with a graceful figure, auburn hair, and sad eyes. She wasn't sure why Claudette always kept her neck covered. Alexandra moved to the seat across from Claudette. She leaned forward and stared at Claudette.

The coach bounced and lurched as they left the chateau grounds. Finally the road became smoother. The coachman slowed down the horses. Alexandra assumed they were on a main road since the bumping had stopped. She leaned out of the carriage and looked down the road. It was packed dirt. She felt the carriage hit a rock. Her head smashed on the doorframe. She rubbed it. *Feels dry. No blood.* She leaned back and tried to think. *Where are we going? What have I gotten myself into?*

Alexandra stared at the woman who dragged her out of her warm bed. "Why me?" she yelled.

"You are the only one who can help. You are your mother's daughter. She almost succeed, but she never came back to the chateau after she showed you the picture of the ballroom at Versailles in the book the night you saw me in your house."

"I wondered if you were the woman I saw that night. My mother died soon after that."

"I thought that's what happened because she wanted to help me, but never came back to the chateau."

"Where are we going?" Alexandra yelled again. She wanted to scream, "Take me back," but she could see returning to her room at the chateau was impossible—Claudette would never order the driver to stop the carriage or turn around. She should have demanded that Claudette tell her where they were going before she got into the carriage and took off. That had been her first mistake. A mistake that might get her killed. A mistake she normally wouldn't have made. She was usually careful—not impulsive. She wondered what was going on, letting herself get caught up in some kind of bizarre joke. "Please, tell me where are we going?" She used a firm voice.

"To Paris. My brother-in-law is in the Bastille. I don't want him to get killed."

The Bastille? It's not there anymore. It hasn't been there for over two hundred years. "The Bastille in Paris?"

"That's what I said."

Alexandra pushed her auburn hair away from her face and shivered. Her heart pounded. She thought about the injuries that might get her a room in a hospital if she jumped from the moving carriage.

"What…What year is it? What is the date?" She stared straight into Claudette's eyes.

"Why? Why are you asking me what year it is?" Claudette looked out of the corner of her eyes. She drew her brows together.

"Just answer my questions." Alexandra leaned forward. Her nose almost touched Claudette's nose.

"It's Tuesday, July 14, 1798." Claudette inched her body back on the seat and huddled up in the corner. Alexandra's harsh tone scared her. She needed her to help save Henri, not to demand answers to asinine questions.

I'm back in the eighteenth century. This is a movie and somehow I've gotten into one of the scenes. I only wish it's a movie. Alexandra started to ask another question, but realized that between the horses' hooves beating on the road and their harnesses rattling, it was too noisy for Claudette to hear her voice.

Alexandra watched Claudette turn to look out the window. *Well I don't think she's willing to answer any more questions right now.*

The road was covered with rocks and deep ruts again. The carriage roared through the night. She heard Charles crack his whip over and over as he urged the horses on.

Well, there is nothing I can do. I'm here until I can get back to the chateau and 2010—if I can get back. Her body began to hurt from being jostled and jarred by the rough and bumpy road. She laid back against the side of the carriage and tried not to worry.

Chapter Six

Alexandra pulled back the curtain that covered the open space in the coach's door and peered out. There was a full moon. It was bright and lit up the road and the land surrounding them. *That's the church—St Radegonde—I was in today.* Her heart raced. Alexandra pulled the folds of her cape snugly around her and leaned back. She tried to think. *I don't know what's going on but I might as well sit back and see what is going to happen. There is certainly nothing I can do now. How bad can things get? Ha! Very bad if it is really July14, 1789.*

Alexandra closed her eyes. *I'm in the eighteenth century and now I'm very far from the chateau. I can't jump out and run.*

The road seemed to flatten out again. She no longer felt her body being bounced and jarred. Alexandra sat up and turned toward Claudette. She decided to ask why she had been chosen to help her. Was it because there was a family connection? Her eyebrows shot up. She couldn't believe what she saw. Claudette seemed to have let the noise of the carriage and the steady pounding of the horses' hooves lull her into a fitful sleep. Alexandra felt her turn frequently and whimper. Once she even cried out and mumbled. Alexandra didn't understand what she was saying. Finally she leaned back, closed her eyes and listened to the noise of horses racing down the road.

After a while, she heard Claudette banging on the ceiling of the carriage with her fist. Her eyes shot open. Alexandra watched her lean out of the window and heard her yell. "Go faster, go faster."

Alexandra pulled back the drape covering her window. Alexandra no longer looked out into darkness. The morning light danced off the walls of the coach. It shimmered through the gap in the drapes. She leaned out. They were still in the countryside—it wasn't like the countryside she has seen on her way from the airport. The fields were unkempt and appeared to be mostly weeds. The people she saw seemed to rise out of the meadows like ghosts—dressed in rags that hung from their bodies and faces that showed hopelessness. The pastures were filled with cattle that were so thin she could see their bones. Many of the homes made from wood and straw looked empty.

She turned toward Claudette and studied her worried expression. "What's wrong?

"I'm worried about Henri. I hope we get to him."

"Why is your brother-in-law in the Bastille?"

"He was imprisoned by a Letter de Cache. The letter that was presented to the court. It said he did terrible things. It said that he was a danger to society, but gave no proof he did anything wrong. I'm sure the king never saw the charges in the letter. The court obviously listened to a disloyal person, who forged the king's name and seal," she said, sarcastically. She wrinkled her nose. "The authorities said the king signed it. The letter was sealed and we were never allowed to see it. We were loyal to the king. He gave my husband and me the chateau when we were married. He was a friend of my brother-in-law, too. He wouldn't have had us arrested. The king was a friend to our family. He wouldn't have let him go to prison"

"Did Henri have a trial?"

"No…No trial and no defense. He thinks that someone at the chateau reported him and had him imprisoned. The letter was countersigned by one of the king's ministers. I think it was the Governor of the Bastille, Marques de Launay."

"Did he know de Launay?"

"No. He doesn't know anyone at the jail and the jailers don't any of the prisoners' names or who they are," her voice broke. "They don't even know what they look like. They have to turn their backs as the prisoners are herded into prison." Claudette used her cape to wipe the tears that ran down her face. "They can't see them when they're in their cells either, because the windows are so small and let in very little light."

"Why does your brother-in-law think this was done to him?"

"Henri had some gambling debts, but was ready to pay them off. So he was certain that it couldn't have been that. He thinks they wanted to dispose of him because he sided with the king. He was loyal to the monarchy. The revolutionaries have vowed to execute anyone loyal to the king. They're against anyone with wealth. They believe it's the wealthy people's fault they are starving and dying because we tax them too much." She sobbed and wiped away her tears again. "Henri can be kept at the Bastille as long as whoever made the claim wants him confined. He may never get out."

Alexandra let the hood of her cape fall to her shoulders. She didn't tell Claudette it was the aristocracy's fault people were starving. She pulled back the curtain and looked out of the carriage window. She could hardly believe what she saw. It was a scene from another dimension. She had seen pictures of the scenery in her history book. "Oh, my God, I really am in the eighteenth century."

"Pull the curtain. It must be closed tightly. No one must see us when we reach the gates of Paris." Claudette glared at her. "We must be very careful—very careful. We'll be there soon."

Alexandra drew the curtain leaving it open a few inches. "Oh no. Oh brother." *If I remembered my college European History, today changed the course of French history.*

"What did you say? Is something wrong?" Claudette leaned toward Alexandra.

"Oh…it looks like rain. The sky is overcast. It's windy and damp. Heavy storm clouds are forming low in the sky in the distance. They look as if they are moving toward us." *No need to worry her. Besides Claudette would never believe me if I told her how today was going to unfold.* She raked her hand through her hair.

Alexandra heard thunder crash in the distance and saw jagged bursts of light rip through the sky. She had read the weather in Paris was cloudy and rainy on July 14, 1789—the day the Bastille fell. But she knew it would be hard to explain how she knew anything about that day to Claudette—even the weather. They drove into the rain.

Claudette pulled her curtain open a small slit. The closer they got to Paris the heavier the rain got. They were in the middle of a storm. "We're almost there. I can see the wall. The coachman is whipping the horses. Any second now we will pass into the city." Claudette raised her voice to be heard above the rumbling of the carriage as they raced down the road toward the walls surrounding Paris.

When they reached the gates, Alexandra leaned across Claudette and peeked out. Groups of men stood guard with guns. They wore drab shirts that were worn and patched. They held back people dressed in rags that stood beside the road and yelled in rough accents at the carriage. The rain was heavy and everyone was soaked. The guards yelled, "Halt, Halt." The rebels began to shoot their guns, when Charles didn't stop.

Alexandra pulled the curtains closed—held them tightly together—and prayed.

Alexandra shuddered at the demonic roaring of the crowds and the pounding of their boots on the cobblestones as they followed the carriage waving pitchforks and scythes. She decided they had probably overpowered the guards and made the carriage their mission—a mission to capture and destroy the occupants. The screams of angry voices echoed down the streets as the mob gained on them. Alexandra felt the carriage rock. She peeked out the window again. The rain had slowed to just a light drizzle.

It was now easy for her to see what was going on. She watched as the crowd nearest them grabbed at the sides of the coach. There seemed to be hundreds of people with dirty, leering faces staring at them. She glanced at Claudette, who cowered in the corner, covering her eyes with her cape. Her hands covered her ears to block out their nasty chanting voices. Alexandra didn't want to die at the hands of rioters. *Obviously Claudette's not going to be very helpful. Not as brave as she was when she dragged me into the coach at the chateau. Well, I have to do something. I'm not getting killed.* Admittedly she made an impulsive decision when she followed Claudette, but now she began to feel compelled to help her.

Alexandra didn't know where they were in Paris or where the Bastille was, but she knew the driver did. She moved to the window ripped open the window drape and leaned out of the carriage. She reached up and pulled hard on his boot. She screamed, over the roar of the crowd, at him. "Get to a side street." *I don't want to be captured by the women citizens. They seem to be the most vicious. Most of them look as if they have escaped from a hospital for the criminally insane.* Her heart pounded in her ears. "Get to a side street," she yelled again. She watched the women raise their fists shaking them at the carriage as they followed it.

Alexandra's body hit the side of the carriage as it turned on two wheels. It slowed down on the road thick with mud. She felt the coach lurch. Her adrenalin pumping, she yelled her next order. "Get to the Bastille." The mud and bodies lying in the streets caused the horses to reduce their speed. Alexandra heard Charles crack his whip over and over. She knew the horses would keep going. They were worked up by the noise of the crowd.

"There's an order out to arrest all carts and carriages entering and leaving Paris." Claudette started to cry. "We have to make sure we find a way to get back to the chateau?"

"You knew about the order and you still dragged me out of my warm bed to go on this trip? How could you?" Alexandra shouted. "I don't believe it. You left out that tiny bit of information."

"I needed to save Henri." Tears ran down Claudette's face. "I'm sorry."

Alexandra took a deep breath and counted to ten. "It's too late now to apologize. Calm down. Please…calm down. We'll figure out how to get back to Giverny later." *Maybe I'll wake up and be sitting in the gardens of the Chateau eating a French roll with strawberry jam while I flirt with Jean Paul. How did I get into such a mess? She knew.* "Curiosity killed the cat. A trait I inherited it from my mother and grandmother. That's how I got into this mess. But finally I found out what my mother and grandmother were doing here."

"What?" Claudette wiped her tears.

Alexandra shrugged her shoulders. She stared at the ragged women who milled around the streets carrying rakes and hoes as weapons. Their bodies were thick with grime; their hair was unkempt and dirty. Some of them wore no shoes; their bare feet sank into the muddy road. They looked as if they had not bathed in months. She could smell the unwashed human flesh as the crowd crushed closer. When she looked into their faces, she could see missing spaces where teeth had been as they cried out oaths. Their eyes looked vacant.

Barking dogs showed their fangs as they ran with the rabble. Both humans and animals looked hungry. They knocked down anyone in their way and ran over the fallen bodies. She could hear their screams. The coachman had difficulty maneuvering the narrow streets lined with the trampled bodies and mud, but he kept going. She covered her ears to shut out the roars of the people.

"Hurry, hurry." Hanging onto the window ledge, she leaned out of the carriage and looked up the street. "There it is. There's the Bastille."

The Bastille

"When we get there, pull as close to the gate as you can," she cried out to Charles.

Alexandra felt a jolt when the carriage stopped. She jerked open the door and jumped out.

She sensed Claudette trying to pull away as she reached up for her arm. Alexandra grabbed Claudette's hand with determination and dragged her out of the carriage. She pulled Claudette along with her as she ran. "Come on. We have to find Henri…remember? You want to save your brother-in-law."

She stared at Claudette's face. Her paleness scared Alexandra. She didn't want one more disaster added to an already horrible situation. Alexandra held onto Claudette tightly. She pulled her close to her side so she wouldn't fall. "Are you all right?" she shouted into Claudette's ear.

"I can't make it," Claudette struggled to sit down.

"Too bad. You begged me to come here with you, now you're coming with me. Remember, I don't know your brother-in-law, Henri." Alexandra seized Claudette's arm. "You have to identify him. Stand up!"

She looked up at Charles. He slumped in his seat—a dagger sticking out of his arm. "What happened? Are you all right?" she shouted.

"One of the guards at the city gate had very bad aim. It's nothing. Just a flesh wound." He pulled the knife out and put it on the seat beside him. "Just in case I need it to use on one of the rebels. Go get him. Get Henri. No time to waste. We can't stay here too long. You need to hurry. You have to find him and then we have to get out of here as fast as we can." He pulled off his cape and wrapped its sleeve around his wound.

"Come through the gate after I open it and follow us as we search each of the towers until we find him. Hopefully, we'll find him immediately and we won't have to search all eight towers." Alexandra pushed up on the latch of the gate. It opened. "Thank God. Luck at last." She hadn't thought about what she would do if the gate had been locked, but that didn't matter now.

Some of the crowd managed to push through the open gate with the carriage. They ran into the Bastille yard falling over each other before she was able to close the gate and lock it. She had to wait for Charles and the carriage to enter. Alexandra looked around—beggars, blind women, and masses of people covered with hideous sores rushed past them and ran wildly around the yard of the prison. As Alexandra waited for the carriage, Matthew 5:45 ran through her brain.

"…He maketh His sun to rise on the evil and the good and sends rain on the just and unjust," Alexandra whispered.

Once Charles drove the carriage onto the grounds of the Bastille, he ran the horses through the mass of people at the entrance trying to block him from moving. He left a small space for Alexandra to reach the gate. She slammed it shut and shoved the bolt across the gate to lock it.

The crowd left on the outside pounded on the iron gate. They screamed oaths. As the crowd who had managed to push into the courtyard scattered, Charles ran the horses to the first tower. Alexandra followed. She grabbed Claudette's arm and yanked her toward the prison. Alexandra's eyebrows drew together as she ran. "We have to move fast." She started to the first tower.

"I'm not letting go of Claudette," she shouted at Charles. "If she decides to escape or we get separated, we'll be in big trouble. Watch us carefully. If you see her without me, grab her." Alexandra's jeans made it easy for her to run—no long skirt and petticoat.

Claudette struggled. She tripped over her long dress and layers of petticoats. "They're going to kill us. Listen to me, Alexandra! These people are going to kill us. Do you hear me…? They are going to kill us."

They don't even notice us. They're only interested in the weapons and ammunitions hidden in the fortress." Alexandra pulled her to the first tower. "Come on. Keep up."

"Go. Go fast," the coachman yelled.

"Look at the dogs. They're going to rip us apart," Claudette screamed.

Alexandra watched the dogs that belonged to the jailers as they showed their teeth and growled. She darted through the crowds. "Don't let them scare you. Pretend they are not there and they will leave you alone. Don't show fear," she pleaded with Claudette. "Keep going. The crowd won't follow you. They don't want to be anywhere near the cells."

"I'll meet you when you come out," Charles shouted. He watched them run to the first tower as he began to move the carriage slowly toward the entrance to the tower. The nervous horses stamped and blew out jets of steam from their noses. Charles had difficulty keeping the carriage upright as the crowd pushed and shoved around him.

Floundering and stumbling, Alexandra darted into the tower as she clutched Claudette's arm.

"Henri, Henri," They screamed. Their words bounced off the walls echoing through the fortress.

Assuming Claudette was now too scared to leave her side, Alexandra finally let go of her arm. It was easier to maneuver the stairs alone without pulling dead weight.

Within a few minutes, Alexandra's eyes adjusted to the darkness of the tower. There was no light. The candles on the walls had burned out. No one was there to re-light them—everyone had left. She felt something dart across her feet. She looked down and froze as she watched a furry creature scurry away. "Oh, my God, a rat." She shivered. *I may be a FBI agent, but I hate rats.*

When there was no answer to their calls, they rushed down the stairs and into the second tower. They ran up and down the hallways. Alexandra and Claudette called and called. Again, no one answered. The smell of unwashed flesh and sweat clung to the walls. It was overpowering. In the third tower, they shouted again over and over for Henri. Just as they reached the top floor, Alexandra heard a thud and Claudette's scream.

"Help me." Claudette grabbed at Alexandra.

Those are the exact words that got me here and in all this trouble. "What's the problem?" She sighed and rested her hands on her hips. Her mouth tightened.

"Wait! I fell. I think I'm bleeding. What am I going to do? My knee feels all wet. I ripped my beautiful dress." She screamed in a panic.

"Sit down on the step." Alexandra felt Claudette's leg. With no light, she couldn't tell if it was bleeding, but it felt wet. Claudette was right. "I'm going to tear off a strip of your dress and wrap your knee—just sit still." She assumed it was blood that covered her fingers, as she felt Claudette's knee. She wiped her fingers on her cape and wrapped it around the wet area.

"It hurts. I can't go any further," Claudette sobbed.

"We have no time to waste." Alexandra tied the strip around Claudette's knee. "Okay, it's wrapped. Get up."

"I'm telling you. I can't move."

"And I said get up. You haven't even tried to stand on it yet." Alexandra reached out, grabbed her arm and dragged Claudette to her feet. "It will be all right. You want to find him don't you?"

"Yes, but…"

They entered the fourth tower and started up the stairs, repeating her brother-in-law's name as they dashed from floor to floor. Alexandra thought she heard "*Ici.*" She waited. "Are you here?" she yelled.

"*Ici*, here," a voice yelled back.

It was so dark they tripped over each other. "Thank God. Come on, Claudette. We found him. Keep yelling, Henri." They followed his voice, as he screamed at them. "I'm at the end of the hallway," he yelled when he heard their shoes pound on the stone floor near him. His voice got louder as they got closer to his cell. "The guards unlocked all the doors and left the prison. The other prisoners left, but I couldn't get up. I'm too weak. I called to them, but they ignored me. I can't walk by myself and they didn't take the time to help me. They were in a hurry to escape."

Alexandra peered into the cell through the small window in the door. She sucked in her breath and held it. The smell of mildew and urine was getting to her. She pulled back a rusted bolt and struggled to open the door of the cell. It scraped on the stone floor as it whined open. Alexandra walked into the cell. Henri sat on a small wooden chair with his elbows on a table of splintered wood. Several matches lay next to his arm. A single candle burned on a black tin plate—its flame dimly lighting the room. A metal cot with one broken leg sat against the wall to her right. It slanted to the floor. The mattress was thin and torn. She thought he heard him mumbling a prayer as he held his head in his hands. His voice was so soft she could barely hear him.

"His eyes are so dull and his cheeks are so hollow. His lips are cracked.

Look at the drops of perspiration on his forehead. He must have a fever." Claudette pushed past Alexandra. "Henri, we're here now. You will be all right." She limped to his side. Alexandra followed. The cell was crowded with the three of them and the hideous furniture.

He looked up when he heard his sister-in-law's voice.

When Claudette reached him, he began to shake. She threw her arms around his body and hugged him. "Is this all you have to keep you warm?" She turned to Alexandra. "Look at this—a rag." She pulled off the torn blanket and bent down to hug him again. They both cried.

Alexandra watched him scrape his black high-heeled shoes back and forth on the stone floor. Their buckles were dull and stained. The leather was scratched and split. She stared at the dirty white wig that lay next to his elbows and his royal blue silk suit that was torn and dirty. When Claudette helped him stand, Alexandra could see that the suit hung loosely on his body. She moved toward him. Alexandra stared at the water trickling down the stone walls of the cell forming puddles on the floor. She stared into the corners of the small room that were filled with shadows.

"We have to leave right now," Alexandra said as she heard cannons begin to fire. She could hear the crash and thunder of the walls surrounding the prison as they fell. "Let's move. Put your arm around him like I'm doing, Claudette." Alexandra pressed her arm under his shoulder fitting it into his armpit. She felt his ribs through the tattered blanket that covered his shoulders and torso when she held him.

"We'll help you walk. Just move as fast as you can. Lean on us." When they reached the staircase, Alexandra nudged her body gently ahead of Claudette and led them down the stairs to the main doorway. She peeked out. The crowd seems to be gone. It's safe to get to the carriage. Just a few stragglers. Henri stumbled as they walked down the staircase. "It's all right. We've got you." She grabbed him tighter. "We'll be at the carriage in just a few minutes."

The thundering sound of the cannon fire got louder and more frequent. When they reached the doorway, she sighed with relief. Charles and the carriage were waiting at the bottom of the stairs. "This is the last step, Henri. Here's Charles."

"Mademoiselle, we're trapped. More people are flooding into the prison; somehow the gate is gone. The cannons shot at it and it fell with the walls it was attached to.

"It will be all right Charles. We'll make it." *I hope.*

"It's going to be a rough ride getting out of here. They're filling the streets. I hope we get out of Paris."

"Charles, I need help getting him into the carriage." She let him take

Henri. Alexandra watched the coachman lift Henri into the carriage, settle him on the seat and cover him with a blanket—that appeared like magic. *He must have had it on his seat.*

"The mobs are looking for the guns and powder. They are not paying attention to us. We'll be fine, Charles. Do whatever you have to do so that we can get to the road. Just go through the gate, turn left and drive north." Alexandra breathed deeply through her nose to rid herself of the odors of the prison. She climbed onto the seat next to Henri, ripped off her cape and threw it over the top of the blanket covering him. She tucked it so it was tight around him.

When Charles whipped the horses, they jumped forward. Alexandra felt the carriage lurch. She caught Henri's body before it slammed into the back of the seat.

"Are you all right?" She felt him shaking and re-tucked her cape.

Charles ran the horses through the space where the gate had been and turned left. The carriage left the Bastille grounds. He maneuvered through the crowds that filled the streets around the prison.

"De Launay has surrendered. Versailles—the City of Kings is next. Vive la France," the mob screamed. No one payed attention to the carriage. The mob was too busy chasing and attacking the governor of the Bastille, Marquis de Launay.

The pounding of falling rocks, roaring cannons and ricocheting bullets could be heard as the three huddled in the carriage.

"Do you have a plan?" Claudette sobbed. She wiped away the tears that ran down her cheeks with the back of her hand.

Alexandra massaged her aching temples with her fingertips. "Not yet, but I'm thinking." She swallowed the lump in her throat. *Oh God, what should I do?*

Chapter Seven

Trip to Abbey Cyr
July 14, 1789

Mobs of people yelled and screamed. Some ran erratically around the outside of the prison as if a pack of wild dogs nipped at their heels. One group tried to surround the carriage. Charles drove through them. He used the carriage like a bulldozer as he moved out of the Bastille area. The coach lurched as its wheels hit the rocks from the fallen walls of the prison. He used his whip on the horses and on the people that clung onto the doors as they tried to climb into the carriage. He turned the horses onto a side street away from the out-of-control mob. Charles struggled to navigate the coach and keep it upright as it shook violently back and forth. He was dauntless. He moved forward ignoring the screams of the crowds.

Alexandra heard a thud and felt the carriage tilt. She leaned out of the window. Cautiously, she hung over the window ledge to see what was going on. "Oh, my God," she stared. "No, no...," she sputtered. Her stomach churned as she watched a man, dressed in strips of rags that hung loosely from his body, slip in the mud and fall.

The back wheels of the carriage ran over his body and crushed him. Blood spurted from his face. Alexandra heard a guttural scream come from deep in his throat. She couldn't believe how fast it happened. Her instant reaction was to knock on the roof of the carriage and yell, "Halt, *Arrete*," but she knew if they stopped they would all be dead within minutes—killed by the angry crowd. She pulled her phone from her pocket. "No bars. It's blank." *Of course it is blank. No towers. It's 1789. Alexandra shape up. You're not thinking clearly.* Her usually calm, green eyes looked anxious.

The horses ran. Their harnesses rattled. The crowd ran. Alexandra could hear their feet pounding behind them. They screamed epitaphs. The mob stopped its pursuit as Charles worked his way out of the Bastille area and north of Paris. He eased up on the horses and the coach began to slow down.

When the carriage slowed, she leaned against the back of her seat and let out a weary sigh. It was quiet. The crowds were far away. The only thing she heard was the pounding of the horse's hooves—no more horrific screams and repulsive oaths. She breathed deeply and thought about what they should do.

They worked their way through the stragglers walking around the outskirts of the prison. The remaining rebels looked for anyone who looked as if they might have some money or food. The noise of the crowd began to sound far away. Soon the noise was barely audible, but Alexandra didn't feel calm; they weren't at the edge of the city yet. She bent over the window ledge again to make sure they were safe. She fixed her eyes on the high pile of rocks and rubble that had replaced the walls of the Bastille. The piles looked almost eight feet like the original walls of the Bastille.

A piercing whine made Alexandra shudder. She stared. "A cannonball just hit the tower you were in, Henri. Thank God we got to the Bastille and got you out when we did."

Henri tried to crane his neck so that he could look out the window, but fell back on the seat. The cape fell off his shoulders.

Alexandra pulled off her sweater. "Here, sit up." She slipped it over his head and slid his arms into the sleeves—then tucked the cape around him again.

Claudette grabbed her brother-in-law's hand. "You're going to be all right."

He turned and stared at his sister-in-law. He shivered when he saw her face turn white. "What is it?"

"The mob is growing. They've stopped parading in front of the prison. They're marching with de Launy's head on a pike toward the main streets of Paris," Alexandra said. She had read about the event in her history books, but seeing it happen made her feel faint. She took a deep breath. *He was a traitor and attacked the people. The revolutionaries got their revenge.* "Don't stop, Charles," she yelled.

She turned to Henri and saw the sweat that spilled in thin streams down his cheek. She felt his royal blue coat. It was soaking wet. His body shook. His face was deathly pale. Alexandra put her hand on his forehead. "You're burning up. Lie still. Don't talk. Just rest." She helped him lay down on the seat and made sure the blanket covered him.

"Who are you?" He peered at her clothing. Henri had never seen the shirt and pants she wore before.

"Don't worry about me. We have to get you help." Alexandra leaned out of the window. She called up to Charles. "Hurry! We have to get Henri to a doctor."

"I know a convent near here. We can stop there. The nuns will help us find a doctor," he shouted back at her. He whipped the horses and raced to the outskirts of Paris and to the Abbey Cyr.

After about twenty-five minutes, Alexandra felt the carriage wheels swerve and slide to an abrupt stop. When she heard loud shrieks, she leaned out of the window and stared.

Abbey Cyr

A flock of nuns ran toward the Abbey. Their crisp wimples fluttered about their heads like large seagulls. Alexandra watched the nuns come to an abrupt stop when they saw the coach, they looked scared. She stared at the looks of horror on their faces when the scared horses reared up. She sighed deeply as she watched them dart past.

The nuns seemed extremely agitated. The leader, whom Alexandra assumed was the Mother Superior, threw open the Iron Gate and dashed toward the Abbey that was surrounded by a high, stone wall and a portcullis. The nuns followed, tripping over each other as they rushed toward the large oak door of the convent.

They disappeared just as the right, back wheel of the carriage hit something large. Alexandra heard a loud thud and felt the carriage roll backward a few feet. It rolled into a deep rut and stopped, tottered for a few seconds and then tilted half in the rut and half out. Alexandra shuddered as she felt her body jerked backward and hit the wall of the carriage.

"What happened?" Alexandra yelled.

Charles looked back and surveyed the damage. "The back wheel fell off. And broke in half. We hit a huge bolder."

"It's only a matter of time before the carriage turns over. We have to get out right away," Claudette helped her brother-in-law sit up.

"It will be all right," Alexandra said. *What else can happen?* "Everybody out! Be very careful. Move slowly. Once we're all out, we'll get Henri." Alexandra patted Claudette on the head as she pulled open the door of the carriage and moved slowly to the ground. She looked up at Charles. "*S'il vous plaît.* Help us with Henri, please." She took Claudette's hand and helped her climb out.

Charles jumped off his perch and hurried to the carriage door on Henri's side of the carriage. He pulled open the door, reached his arms around him and pulled Henri out of the seat as if he were a sack of flour, threw him over his shoulder and set him down and helped him stand up. "This is the Abbey of Cyr. The nuns will get us help. Go into the courtyard," Charles shouted.

They started toward the Abbey when they heard a large crash.

Alexandra looked back. The carriage lay on its side.

"What was that?" Henri called out.

The sky had settled into a soft black. The stars and moon illuminated the path to the entrance of the Abbey. "Don't worry. Let's go. Follow me." Alexandra bolted through the gate and crossed the large courtyard with a deliberate pace. She waved her hand to Claudette and Charles to follow. They walked slowly behind her as they helped Henri. When she reached the heavy, wooden door, Alexandra pulled on the rope in front of her. She heard the echo of a bell ring inside the Abbey. She sighed with relief when she heard the grinding of a key in the lock and the bolt scrape across the door as it was pulled back.

The door opened a crack. The older nun held onto the doorknob and peeked out at them. When she saw they weren't revolutionaries, she stepped back and let the door swing open just wide enough for them to enter. "Enter." Her hand motioned for them to come forward. "Quickly, move quickly." She grabbed Alexandra and pulled her into the entranceway. The others followed and stood closely together behind Alexandra.

They each dipped their fingers in the stone container with holy water that hung just inside the door and crossed themselves. The large hall was cold. The candles in the sconces on the walls gave off just enough light for them to see the person in front of them. Their shadows played on the walls. The heels of their leather shoes echoed on the stone floor.

The walls also made of stone were jagged and wet.

Alexandra looked around. She shivered. *We will be all right, I hope.*

"We need help, Reverend Mother," the coachman pleaded. "Our carriage wheel broke and we have a sick man." Alexandra stared at the Abbess who appeared to be in the seventh decade of her life.

"Come to my office." Her voice was strong and forceful, but she walked slowly, using a cane for help. It tapped on the floor as she moved.

They followed her into the main part of the Abbey. When they passed the chapel, Alexandra heard voices whispering prayers and the rapid clicking of rosary beads echoed in the hallway. She peeked into the small room and saw a group of nuns kneeling toward the altar and whispering in French. They turned their heads and stared at the group. Then went back to their prayers. The Reverend Mother led them to the back of the Abbey. Alexandra was right behind her. *No one can be closer to God than a group of nuns. We'll be safe.* She took a deep breath.

The Reverend Mother walked down the hallway. She reached a large, heavy door and inserted a black, iron key that hung on a chain from her waist into the lock. A cold breeze hit Alexandra as it swung open. She stared at the Abbess. She moved, bent over, leaning on her cane, as she walked slowly to the large chair behind a desk that sat in front of deep red curtains. Her plain, black dress dragged on the floor. She struggled as she pulled out her heavy chair. Alexandra hurried to her side and helped move it. The nun sat down. Alexandra stared at her. Up close, she looked pale and feeble. She leaned over the desk and lit the lone candle that sat in a metal dish in the middle of her massive desk.

The dim light made her look old and wrinkled, but her voice was strong and her face was stern. She leaned back and waited. Alexandra thought there was a grace about her.

Sitting in her chair, she looked very powerful—her arms stretched out on the wooden armrests. She sat up straight against the back of the chair. She stared into each of their faces without smiling. "Please sit down." She motioned for them to bring the chairs closer to her desk with the fingers of her hands. The Reverend Mother frowned as she watched Alexandra help Henri drag his chair close to her desk.

"He is very ill." Alexandra looked directly into Mother Superior's eyes. "Please, we need help for Henri. Do you know a physician? *Aidez-moi*, please help me."

Claudette wiped the tears that ran down her cheeks with her sleeve. "*S'il vous plait*. He's very ill. He's been held at the Bastille." The tears streamed down her neck. "Will you help us?" She wiped away her tears again.

Alexandra leaned forward in her chair. "The wheel of our carriage is broken. We can't travel with a sick man if we have to walk." Alexandra smiled as she grasped the Reverend Mother's hand. "We must get back to our chateau. Can you help us?"

"He can stay here. We can help him, but you three can't stay." She pointed to each one of the group. "One person we can hide, but not four. We will get him a doctor. You may come back for him."

"We can't leave you." Claudette grabbed Henri's hand. "We can't leave him, Alexandra," Claudette cried out.

Alexandra, eyeing him from an angle, saw that his face was ashen and tiny beads of sweat had formed on his forehead. She leaned forward and wiped them with her sleeve.

"You must go on without me. I will be safe until you come back. Please, Claudette. Go on without me. I will be all right," Henri spoke in a hoarse whisper.

The Reverend Mother turned toward Alexandra. She shut her eyes for a few minutes and folded her hands. She took a deep breath. She maintained a stoic expression "The revolutionaries check on us often. So far they just stop by. They don't demand to search the Abbey. However, I'm not sure how long it will be safe here." She sighed. "The revolutionaries are becoming braver. They use to leave the church alone but not anymore. I don't know when they come back and demand to search our Abbey.

"There is talk that they want to confiscate the treasures of the church to fund their revolution. They say we conspired against the new government of France. We are becoming their enemies. They may close the Abbey and make us leave or even take us as prisoners." Her hand gripped the large, silver cross with a lone ruby embedded in the center that hung around her neck.

"What should we do?" Claudette turned toward Alexandra, her face crumpled with disappointment.

"He is in good hands. The nuns will see that he gets help from a physician. We can come back and get him in a few days." She leaned forward in her chair. "Can you get us something to wear so that we blend in with the crowds?" Alexandra leaned forward, her elbows planted on the desk. Her hands were clasped together. She held them in front of her mouth.

"Our coachman has a small injury. It has stopped bleeding, but if you give me some brandy and clean rags, I'll be able to clean it up," she whispered.

"I'll be all right, Mademoiselle," Charles whispered.

"No, Charles. We have to clean it so that the germs don't make it worse. It could get infected. You don't want to suffer more, do you? Or have more pain?"

"Yes, I'll get you everything you need," the Reverend Mother said.

"You'll have to dress as the poor. It's dangerous for the aristocracy."

"How long will it take to get our new clothes?"

The Reverend Mother reached behind her and pulled a black rope that hung from the ceiling behind her chair. Then she reached forward and held Alexandra's arm. "Not long. It will be all right my dear. " She looked straight into Alexandra's eyes and smiled. "It will be all right." She patted Alexandra's hand. "You'll all be fine."

Alexandra smiled. She turned toward Claudette. "He will be fine, Claudette. He's in good hands." Alexandra smiled and gave her a hug.

They watched a small, plump women in black appeared.

"Sister Marie, bring us some clothes from the storeroom, and rags and brandy to clean a flesh wound, please," the Mother Superior said."

They watched the sister disappear, only to see her return as if she were in a revolving door. She held folded clothes stacked from her waist to her chin in one of her arms. The rags and brandy were tucked in the hollow of the other. She scurried to the desk and whispered something to the Reverend Mother.

"Well, one of you Mademoiselles will have to dress as a man. You have to decide. Be quick. I'll return in a few minutes. After you dress, you must leave immediately." The Reverend Mother and Sister Marie helped Henri get up from his chair. "We'll take him to the dormitory and hide him. He will be all right," Mother Superior said in a voice that was like a mother soothing a crying baby.

"All right, I'll be a man." Alexandra let out a deep breath. "Let me clean Charles' wound first." She moved toward him. "Sit down, please." She gripped the material of his shirt and ripped the section around the wound. "It looks pretty good. I don't think the blade went in very deeply." She worked rapidly, rubbing the brandy on the wound, and then wrapping the wound with a clean piece of white material around it. "It will be all right, Charles."

They both dressed quickly, pulling on dark, baggy pants and over-sized, natural, cotton shirts over their own clothes. They slipped on dark green, untailored coats over their clothes and pulled red, felt caps on their heads. The patches of red, white, and blue on the front of their coats were sewn on the left side, over their hearts. Alexandra took the smaller of the square-toed, high boots and pulled them on. She folded the tops down and looked at them. "They are too large, but the heels are low so they shouldn't be too hard to walk in."

Turning toward Claudette, she sighed. "Well, don't you look cute?"

Claudette laughed nervously.

"Do we all have the tricolor insignia, the cockade?" Alexandra checked Claudette's chest to see if it was attached to the coarsely woven, gray, wool shawl with fringed edges to make sure it was displayed. "It will help us to be safe. Take the scarf off."

"I don't want to."

Mother Superior checked their outfits. She hesitated when she adjusted

Claudette's scarf. "Don't worry, the scarf is all right. You all look fine. If anyone stops you, they will think you are part of the revolution."

"What is Claudette hiding?" Alexandra turned to ask Claudette just as she rushed toward the dormitory. Her plain, tan dress was covered with a cream and navy blue striped apron. A shawl covered her shoulders and flew behind her as if a wind drew her toward her destination.

"Where are you going?"

"I'll be right back." Claudette flung the words over her shoulder as she pushed open the door to the dormitory.

"Claudette. Get back here Claudette." Alexandra watched her disappear behind the closed doors. She grabbed her cowboy boots and stuffed them in the deep pocket of her long coat, and started to run after Claudette. Just as Alexandra reached the swinging door, Claudette rushed back through it and bumped into her. "I had to say goodbye to my brother-in-law. I had to give him something."

Alexandra stumbled as she moved toward the door, but righted herself before she fell. *I have to get use to these shoes.* She stopped and folded her arms across her chest. She shook her head. "It's time to go." She led Claudette and Charles to the courtyard. "Tuck your hair up under the mop cap, Claudette."

"*Merci*, thank you very much, Reverend Mother. We'll send a messenger to let you know when we will return for Henri. You don't have to answer if the time is alright." Alexandra smiled.

"The sisters and I, with the help of our handyman, will hide your carriage. We will try to have it fixed." She reached for the small bundle on her desk. "This is in case you get hungry."

Alexandra looked over her shoulder as the three moved toward the gate. "Thank you again. *Au revoir.* You've been a big help. *Merci*, Reverend Mother." She stuffed the bundle into the pocket of her coat.

"It's getting dark, so if you go through the woods, you will be well hidden. Be very careful. The revolutionaries are on the roads. They are everywhere. We will see you soon. God be with you."

"*C'est tout dire*, then we've said all there is to say." Alexandra waved.

After the door slammed shut, she heard the key grind in the lock. *I hope we all get back to the chateau in one piece.* "*Vite, allez.*" Alexandra gave Claudette, who stood in front of the closed door, a gentle shove. "Go, go." She left her hand in the middle of Claudette's back in case she needed to give her another little nudge again. They moved into the darkening night, through the courtyard, until they reached the gate.

She unlatched the gate of the Abbey, swung it open, and pushed it back. They ran through. Alexandra heard it scrape along the dirt path as it swung slowly closed.

"*Vite*, hurry. Get into the woods and hide behind that large bush." Alexandra pointed to her right. "I hear voices." She slid behind a large pine tree near the road and peeked out onto the path in front of the Abbey. She watched as a group of men pushed through the gate of the Abbey. "Listen." She put her index finger to her lips. "They're yelling for the Sisters to open up."

"My brother-in-law." Claudette turned to the Abbey. "I have to go back." She stuck out her chin defiantly as she began to move to the path they had just left.

Alexandra grabbed Claudette's arm roughly just as she tried to move out of her reach. "*Arretez*. Stop. Do you want to get us killed? He'll be fine. The nuns will take good care of him. I'm sure he is well hidden by now. They will protect him," she said through teeth that were clamped together so tightly her jaw hurt.

"You hurt me," Claudette whined as she rubbed her arm.

"Please, I hardly wrestled you to the ground," Alexandra said.

Claudette sniffed. "What?"

Alexandra smiled. She was grateful for the darkness. "Stop whining, Claudette, we're going to have a long trip and we all have to cooperate with each other. Into the woods and pay attention to me."

Their feet crunched on the dried leaves and branches as they ran. "Stay in the trees." Alexandra realized it was going to be harder in the dark, but the light from the moon and stars would help them navigate. They would be able to see enough so that they wouldn't run into trees and bushes. She moved further into the woods as she searched for their hands.

Alexandra reached out. "Hold hands so we don't get separated." Before she laced fingers with Charles, she checked her boots with her free hand to make sure they were well hidden and wouldn't fall out of her coat. She wasn't giving up her favorite pair of cowboy boots.

She forced her feet to go forward as she led them through the trees, keeping the road in sight. She led them north. Alexandra heard the roar of the crowds in the distance. She put her finger to her lips. "Shhh, we must be very, very quiet. The mobs are leaving Paris and coming this way. They're getting closer. Hurry, we have to get further into the woods. Don't let go of my hands."

Claudette began to cry.

"Claudette please...please be quiet and don't be afraid. I told you everything will be fine." Alexandra let a long breath escape from her lip. *This is going to be a long night.*

Chapter Eight

On The Road to Giverny
July 15, 1789

Claudette fell to the ground. She brushed a tear from her cheek and pulled her shawl tightly around her body to shield herself from the cool night air. "It's been hours."

"The sun will be coming up soon and things will get better," Alexandra said.

"I can't go on. Just let me stay here. You can bring help back." Claudette slumped back against a tree and slid to the ground. Her arms were wrapped around her drawn-up knees. She sobbed. "I'm hungry and weak."

Always the drama queen, she never changes. Alexandra quietly sucked in a large breath of air, trying to hide her exasperation. *Count to ten, Alexandra. Hold your temper.* "I'm exhausted, too, but we have to keep moving. We can't give up." She knew from history that the revolutionaries spread into the countryside, killing the clergy and aristocracy and destroying property. She knew no one or nothing was safe. She didn't know how much time they had before an unruly crowd might catch up with them.

"Stop crying and listen for a moment," Alexandra whispered. She put her finger to her lips. "Ssssh! Please be quiet for a minute." When she didn't hear voices, she dragged Claudette to her feet and pulled on Charles' arm. "Come on."

"Brush yourself off, Claudette." Alexandra patted her on the shoulder and led Claudette and Charles deeper into the woods. "The sun is coming up. We have to get into the heavy growth of trees to hide." She reached into her pocket and handed each a chunk of brown bread. "This should help." Alexandra watched both of her companions swallow the bread almost whole.

She felt relieved when Claudette seemed to finally calm down and she followed behind Alexandra without saying a word. They moved quickly. It got darker in the trees and it was harder to see the ground. They tripped over tree roots and rocks. "We can't give up." Alexandra forced them to press on. "We have to keep going. Please…move deeper into the woods. It's almost morning." Rivulets of sweat ran down her neck. *Claudette gives up and cries and Charles follows quietly waiting for me to tell him what to do. He's been a servant too long and she's been part of the aristocracy too long.* Alexandra was beginning to feel the stress of being in charge of two people's lives.

Her feet sank into wet leaves and mud. Soon the trees thinned and the first pale light of day filtered through their branches. She was nervous about what they would find when the woods ended.

Claudette began to cry again. "I'm tired and wet. I don't care if we get caught."

"Stop! Just be quiet." Alexandra glared at her. *The tears and the whole complaining bit is getting old and boring. I'm getting very sick of it.* She shook her head and looked down at her mud encrusted boots and pant cuffs.

Alexandra tried to brush off her trousers. They needed more than a casual wipe. Her cheeks felt damp. She rubbed her hands over them, then held out her hand and looked at her fingers. They were stained with blood. Alexandra didn't remember how many times tree branches had hit her in the face, but she decided there had been enough of them to draw blood. "We'll be out of the woods soon, Claudette, and I can't take anymore crying."

Alexandra shoved back the tree branches in front of her. The sun shone brightly. "Look! A farm house." She pointed into a field that had once been elegant, but was now overgrown and neglected. There were no farm hands working the land. Everything was dead. The fields had once been filled with hearty plants of corn and wheat that were now shriveled or wilted and lying on the ground. The weeds had taken over.

"Maybe we can get help." She let a long breath escape from between her lips. It came out like a very noisy sigh. "You must still do what I say and don't ask any questions. Let me do the talking." She bent down and let go of the tree branch.

"Ouch." Claudette pushed back the branches.

"I'm sorry, Claudette. I thought you were beside me. You're okay. No blood drawn."

Alexandra rushed with her companions into the field. They stumbled over each other toward a small, crudely built home with an attached barn. Rags hung from the windows covering the openings. Her heartbeat echoed in her ears.

"It looks abandoned. I don't see anyone in the field. No signs of life." Alexandra pounded on the door with her fists. "Hello? Is anyone in there?" She waited. Nothing. Her voice was the only sound she heard. It was quiet.

"I'm going in." Claudette elbowed her way past Alexandra and pushed on the door.

Alexandra jumped when she heard a large thud as it hit the wall. She glanced at the wall as they entered and saw a small dent where the latch hit. "Couldn't you have nudged it open? Did you have to fling it open?"

I know she can move fast if she wants to. I'll remember that if we get into trouble and need to hightail it. Alexandra smiled and waved her hand at Charles encouraging him to follow them. "It's okay."

Claudette stopped when she marched over the threshold. She took a step backward. "There's no floor."

Alexandra entered and stood on packed down brown dirt. "Of course there's a floor—it's just not marble or wooden boards with a soft carpet." Alexandra stood on the earthen floor. "It's a floor to them. See how the poor live. Look around—take a good look." Alexandra turned toward Claudette.

The faint sunlight of early morning shone through a small window. On a wooden table, a single candle burned in a metal holder. "Well, someone left in a hurry. They forgot to blow out the candle. They must have seen us coming." Drops of water bounced off the coffee cup on the table. Then Alexandra felt water drip on her face. She brushed the drops away as she looked up. Water trickled through a hole in the straw roof.

"It's nice and warm in here." Claudette ran toward the fireplace—a large fireplace that stood a few inches above Claudette's head. She flopped into a straight, high-backed, wooden chair in front of the large fire and pushed her feet near the glowing coals on the hearth. "What now?" She stared at a cast-iron kettle that hung from a rod attached to the back of the fireplace. "Something smells good." She leaned over and looked into the kettle. "I don't think it's this. The pot is filled with something that looks like water with a small potato, a few carrots, and a small piece of meat."

Alexandra felt the cup on the table. "This is warm." She picked it up, leaned close to it and breathed in. "It smells like coffee."

"It's bread that I smell…bread." Claudette eyed the loaf pan that sat on the hearth and reached for it.

Alexandra swatted at her fingers. "I'm hungry too, but it doesn't belong to us."

Claudette twisted her hands. The corners of her mouth turned down. "Suppose whoever lives here isn't friendly. We…we have to go."

"There was someone here and not too long ago—probably just a few minutes ago. We're going to wait." Alexandra stayed next to her. "They may come back. We'll take our chances if they do. We'll ask for help and hope that they are on our side."

Claudette stared. "What?" She began to stand.

Alexandra moved in front of her. She grasped Claudette's shoulders. With a gentle push, she nudged her back into the chair. Claudette began to struggle to get out of her grasp. Alexandra kept a firm grip on her shoulder. "Pretend, if you are able to, that you are a revolutionary." Alexandra patted her on the top of her head. "You're dressed like one, now get into character. You have to get over having someone waiting on you all the time."

They waited. After several minutes, a door at the back of the kitchen opened just enough for an old woman to lean her head into the room. She pushed open the door a little more and held onto the handle tightly so that she could slam it shut if she was uneasy about who was on the other side. She carried a candle in her free hand. The candlelight reflected in her eyes as she peered into the room and stared at Alexandra. "We have no grain, no bread and we're almost out of food. We paid our taxes. More aren't due yet. They've even taken away some of our land." The words spilled out of her mouth. Clutching her apron with her free hand, she pushed on the door and slowly moved into the room. "Are you here to put us in jail?"

Claudette started to speak, but a sharp look from Alexandra stopped her from interfering.

"We don't want to hurt you. We just want to get to Chateau Nervy." Even in the dim light Alexandra could see the woman's face. Her skin was tanned and lined with deep crevices. It looked rough, like well-worn leather. Her creases were embedded with dirt. When she rubbed her face the dirt streaked her cheeks. She was stooped as if she had worked very hard in the fields her whole life. Alexandra gazed into the woman's lifeless eyes. "Please, will you help us?" She smiled.

"You're really not here to hurt me?" she blurted out as if it was hard for her to believe her visitors wouldn't harm her. The woman's eyes darted around the room.

Alexandra moved closer to the old woman and stood in front of her.

"We won't harm you." Alexandra grasped her rough, dry hands and covered them with her own.

The old woman looked up into Alexandra's eyes and smiled. She seemed relieved. She looked at the two women and the man, who had the look of a peasant. They needed her help. She spoke more slowly. "We have a wagon. You may use it." Her smile showed many missing teeth. "The chateau is not too far away. Just up the road, a few kilometers. But you must be careful…very careful," she said looking at Alexandra. "Come with me. Go first." She gave Alexandra a firm push with the palms of her hands. "We go to the barn. Hurry."

"Obviously she has a kind heart. We don't need to worry." Alexandra motioned to Claudette and Charles. "Come on, she wants to help. Follow me. She wants us to go to the barn."

The woman pulled the door just enough to fit her body in sideways. She slid into the space and pushed on the door with her stomach to open it all the way. She pushed away the beads of sweat that formed on her forehead and pointed to the wagon just inside. "Fill with hay." She pointed to the stall beside her. The woman handed them each a pitchfork. She turned and hurried to the back of the barn.

"Now where's she going?" Charlotte flopped down on a bale of hay.

"She'll come back," Alexandra answered. "Come on, help me. The woman is too old to do this work."

Alexandra looked up and saw the old women returned with a team of horses. She led them slowly out of the barn, holding onto their reins, their manes were matted. Their ribs pushed against thin skin. That looked dried and bruised.

"They've seen better days," Alexandra mumbled. She pulled her coveted boots from her pocket to make it easier to throw the hay into the wagon. She laid them next to Claudette. "Make sure I don't forget these." She knew the boots would be safe because Claudette didn't appear to have any desire to help. Protecting Alexandra's boots would be her excuse.

The old woman motioned to Charles. She stood on her toes and whispered something to him. He nodded his head and began to help her hook up the horses to the wagon. When he finished, he grabbed the pitchfork that Claudette held and started on the hay.

"Ha. The lazy one." The old woman pointed to Claudette.

Alexandra glanced at Claudette who didn't seem to hear the comment. She lowered her head to hide a smile. *Everyone gets her number sooner or later.*

When the wagon was half full of hay, the woman ran between them and grabbed the pitchforks. "Get in. The man drives." She limped to the front of the wagon and started to lead the team out of the barn. She held the team of horses while Charles climbed up onto the wagon seat and grabbed the reins.

"Wait, my boots…" Alexandra snatched her coveted boots and stuffed them back in her coat.

"What's so great about your boots?" Claudette tried to grab them.

"Come on, Claudette, stop. We don't have time to play games." Alexandra jumped into the wagon. She dragged Claudette up into the space beside her. "You wouldn't understand."

"Lay down." The old women paid no attention to Claudette, who coughed and wheezed as she threw hay over her. When the wagon was full enough to hide the women, she slapped the horses. "Go. Go. Be very careful."

The wagon jolted forward. Charles looked straight ahead as he guided the horses out of the barn.

Alexandra sat up and watched her toss her pitchfork into the barn and push the door closed. She waved at the woman as she ran to the house.

"*Merci*," Alexandra yelled. The cart bounced down the road. "*Merci*," she yelled again, trying to make herself heard over the rattle of the horses' harnesses and the pounding of their hooves on the dirt road.

"Stay down. There are beggars on the road ahead of us. It's a large group. We have to be very careful. Don't make a sound," Charles called back over his shoulder.

Alexandra pushed herself under the hay just as she felt the cart slow down. She heard the crack of the whip and Charles yell, "*Bonjour*, Citizens. Going to market to buy flour. We need to make bread to fill our stomachs."

She heard the crowd laugh. "Only if you're lucky," they yelled back. "But things will change. We'll have all the bread we need."

"Liberty, equality, and fraternity," Charles yelled at them. "Just thought I'd shout the revolution motto to make sure they think we are one of them." He looked over his shoulder at the mound of hay and chuckled.

It wasn't too long before Alexandra heard nothing but the wheels of the wagon as they bumped on the ruts and rocks in the road. *My back will never be the same.* She peeked out over the side of the wagon. She saw empty fields and no one on the road. "Okay, Claudette. You can sit up now."

"We're in the town. Not too far to the chateau," Charles called out as he whipped the horses.

Alexandra climbed onto the seat next to Charles and held her coat tightly around her. They rode by the River Epte. They were almost at the church when Alexandra heard the pounding of boots running toward them. "Oh. No! No! Claudette, stay down. Stay down under the hay."

Alexandra stared as a group of men plunged their torches into the base of the box hedges surrounding the cemetery next to the church, St Ragegonde. They paid no attention to the wagon. The bushes began to burn and quickly spread to the grass around the headstones.

"Look straight ahead. You don't need to see what else is happening," Charles said.

Alexandra followed his stare—she saw three men chase a priest into the church. "What are they going to do?" She heard glass breaking and loud thuds.

"It sounds as if they are destroying the inside of the church. Pretend you don't see them and be quiet—both of you." Charles stared down at the horses.

Alexandra heard sobs from the back of the wagon. "Claudette, stop. You've got to stop. We're going to get caught if anybody hears you." Alexandra felt better when Claudette settled down and her sobs stopped.

She sat with her head straight looking at the road, but had to see what was happening and glanced out of the sides of her eyes. Alexandra shuddered when she saw the priest flying through the air as he was thrown from the top of the highest steeple. His screams were blood curdling when his body landed in the flames. She felt the screams deep in her bones. *If they are starting to go after the clergy, I hope Henri is okay.* When she heard the crowd surrounding the church cheer, she retched. The violence was more than her stomach could bear.

"Take deep breaths," Charles whispered.

Alexandra inhaled and exhaled deeply. Finally, after several breaths, the sickness in her stomach disappeared. She touched her neck, making sure all her hair was tucked into her cap. She watched the peasants cheer. *They seemed to be much more interested in destroying the church than chasing a wagon going down the road.* Alexandra only began to feel safe when Charles had placed a great distance between their wagon and the rioters. "Hurry, Charles." She knew situations could change suddenly and the rioters were in a state of frenzy. She prayed no one would notice them.

Chateau Verny
July 15, 2010

Alexandra stared up the mountain. She saw smoke coming from the left section of the chateau. Suddenly the weather changed. It became misty and cool. Alexandra heard the soft patter of rain on the wagon. The drops dampened her face. She could see fog forming ahead of them. The mist got thicker and swirled in front of her as the wagon drove up the mountain. Her cloths began to feel damp. She couldn't see her hands. She knew Charles was still on the seat next to her because she heard his heavy breathing.

It got harder to see the chateau. The mist became a wall of thick fog and circled around them, covering the road. She couldn't see the horses. Alexandra saw nothing ahead. She felt the wagon slow down.

"Why are the horses dawdling?" Alexandra yelled.

"We're going up the mountain and the horses are tired. They don't have much food, just like the people. The chateau is just ahead."

"Tell me what the old lady said to you in the barn," Alexandra said as she leapt from her seat when the wagon came to a complete stop.

"She said things will go well for you because you are a good person."

"*Merci*," Alexandra called over her shoulder as she ran. *I hope she's right. If I run straight ahead, I'll be at the front gate of the chateau in a minute.* The quiet—the eerie quiet made her nervous. She pulled off her cap and let her wet hair hang loose. It clung to her face. She strained her eyes to see the fence that surrounded the Chateau. *It must be here.* It was so foggy she had to use her hands to search. Finally, her fingers ran over the cold bars of the gate. She reached up above her shoulders, found the latch and pulled on it. Slowly, the gate squeaked open a crack. She pulled again. It didn't move. Her fingers were stiff and cold. She looked down at them. They were white. Alexandra nudged the gate further with her body. It moved a few more inches giving her enough room to slip through so she could get on the Chateau's front path.

The gravel path crunched under her feet. She felt the stones through her eighteenth-century boots as she stumbled forward to the door of the chateau. She gazed around and was surprised. She caught her breath, tipped her head back and looked at the sky. It was a perfect day. The sun shone in a blue sky filled with white clouds. The manicured lawn that she had seen on the day she arrived was still there. A group of gardeners worked on their knees, weeding.

Alexandra savored the feel of the sun on her hair and relished the warm summer day. She began to feel warm and threw off her coat and held it over her arm. The rain and cold were gone. She ran up the stairs and flung open the chateau door. Her eighteenth century boots pounded on the marble floor of the entrance hallway as she walked toward the staircase.

When she saw Madam Dumont, sitting at the front table, she slowed down.

"Still working on the books?" Alexandra stopped. She took a deep breath and smiled.

"*Oui.* It never ends." She looked up and smiled.

Alexandra looked behind her. "I'm sorry. I've tracked in some mud. I seemed to have made a mess."

"Don't worry. Pierre will take care of it." She looked up at Alexandra and then back to her books.

Alexandra watched Pierre turn and stare at her as he stood at the staircase. *Thank God I am back in the year 2010.* She thought she heard him say, "You made it back. Bon." She stared at him as he lowered his gaze and looked back at the staircase. He rubbed his dust cloth over the railing, polishing the oak.

Alexandra rushed by him, taking the stairs two at a time. At the top, she stopped. The painting was back. She studied the portrait. The woman's eyes seemed to look right through her.

Now she had a name, Claudette. Alexandra had met her. She glanced at the portrait hanging next to Claudette, and then studied it. It was a portrait of a man in a royal blue suit and white wig. He looked about six feet tall. She felt his dark brown eyes look into hers. He had a handsome face with a classic nose and was physically fit. *He looks very much like the man I saved— the man at the Bastille. That must be a portrait of Claudette's husband. They must be brothers.*

Alexandra moved slowly and stopped at a portrait of two children—a small boy and a girl that looked a few years younger. The boy had brown curls and big blue eyes. The girl had red curls and large green eyes. She had a playful smile. *Why didn't I ever notice these paintings before? I guess I was concentrating on Claudette. They are a handsome family, or they were a handsome family.* Alexandra felt a cool breeze pass across her back.

"Boy, I'm tired. I wonder why? Couldn't be because I was up all night. Think I'll close my eyes for a few minutes."

Trying to put all the pieces of the puzzle together, Alexandra lay in a troubled sleep. The bell on the clock of the village church rang six times. It echoed through the mountains. No chimes from the clock near the elevator. She thought she might wind it herself. If it was like the one at home, the key was probably in one of the side doors. It would be easy to start.

Alexandra sat straight up in bed and tried to erase the crazy dreams of ghosts chasing her through a prison. A dark cape covered her. She tossed it off and it landed at the foot of the bed. She shivered. Looking at herself in the mirror, she saw that she was on top of the bedcovers in her underwear. "I don't remember taking off my clothes and putting a cape over me when I collapsed with exhaustion on top of the covers at nine this morning. The last couple of days have been so stressful I don't want to remember anything." *Does the cape belong to Claudette? Did she cover me up?*

Well, if it belongs to her, she can just reach through the mirror and grab it.

82

Chapter Nine

Evening at Chateau Verny
July 15, 2010

Alexandra jumped off the bed. She glanced at her hands as she flung open the drapes. Her index finger was empty. She took a quick look around the room. The ring wasn't on the floor in front of the mirror. She picked up the cape and ran her hand across the duvet. She looked at the top of her bedside table. It was behind the lamp. She reached for the ring and slipped it on.

She stared out of the French doors. The sun had begun to slide behind the mountain. Alexandra watched the drapes shift back and forth and a cool breeze moved through the room. "Claudette, are you here?" she called out as she glanced around the room. "I know it doesn't matter what room I'm in, Claudette. You will find me wherever I go." She waited. "Claudette!" No one answered.

"Enough of your nonsense. If you're not going to show yourself, I'm taking a shower." On her way to the bathroom, she tripped stumbling over the muddy boots she had worn on her trek through the woods—the boots from her trip back to the French Revolution. *Where are the rest of the clothes I had on?* She looked around the room. Alexandra bent down and looked under the bed. When she stood up, she spied a piece of material sticking out of the closed door of the armoire. She jerked open the door. The clothes were rolled in a ball on the lower shelf.

"Thank you, Claudette," she groaned. "I keep hoping it was a dream, but I was there." She picked up the boots and put them beside the bundle of clothes. *Mrs. Dumont didn't react to my clothes—she must have looked at me, but didn't really see me.* Alexandra shivered. *Why me? Why was I summoned by Claudette?* "Claudette, there has to be a reason you summoned me, but right now I can't figure it out. Tell me," she yelled out into the room, just in case the ghost was hiding in the room. "Claudette, if you're hiding somewhere in my room, show yourself." The room was quiet.

Alexandra was in and out of the shower in a jiff. *I'm human again.* She dressed in light blue, stonewashed jeans and a red, cable-knit, cotton sweater. She sat down on the bench at the foot of her bed and slid on the brown sandals next to her feet. It was too warm for her boots. The weather was not cool and rainy like she had experienced on July fourteenth and fifteenth in 1789. Today it was warm and sunny at the chateau in the year 2010.

Alexandra looked into the mirror. She stared at the scratches on her face. *They're really not too bad, but just to make sure…*She reached for her makeup bag and searched for her liquid makeup and brush. She covered the scratches with a thin layer of makeup, leaned forward and glanced back at her face. *They don't look too bad now. They're pretty well covered. I'm sure no one will notice them unless they look closely. Well, I'm ready for some good, French food.*

She locked her room and dashed down the hallway. Alexandra examined the portraits at top of the staircase. She studied every detail of both portraits. "The man must be Claudette's husband. He looks just like his brother, Henri—the man I rescued," she whispered to herself again. "Henri's clothes were torn, his white wig dirty and he was emaciated, but he had the same eyes, hair and facial features as the man in the portrait. The resemblance is undeniable."

Alexandra stared. An icy breeze passed through the corridor. She ran her fingers lightly over Claudette's hand. "How did I miss it?" She stared back at her index finger. "It's the same ring."

Alexandra touched the ring in the painting. An electric shock moved through her fingers and up her arm. It made her jumped backwards. As she steadied herself, Alexandra sucked in her breath. She glanced back and forth and studied her ring and the ring in the painting. The ring was two loops of platinum that were bound together by very thin, platinum wire. A prong and each side of the ring held a large, round-cut amethyst. A row of small, shaped roses in platinum circled the amethyst. She sat down on the top step of the grand staircase. *What is it about the ring?* Alexandra looked at her finger again.

I haven't seen her wear it. But she has it on in the portrait. Her heart pounded. "Her ring is the one that belonged to my grandmother and mother. It must have been handed down through the generations and now belongs to me! That's it! It's the energy in the ring that takes me back to 1798 and lets Claudette appear in 2010. I haven't seen her wear the ring," she whispered. Gooseflesh rose in her spine.

She felt the air move and glanced out of the corner of her eyes at the portrait. She could have sworn Claudette put her index finger to her pursed lips. As Alexandra rushed to the head of the staircase, she felt two pairs of eyes watch her leave the hallway. "I have to save Henri." Alexandra began to feel a connection to the ghost who sought her out. She peered cautiously over the banister and ran down the stairs. She stared at Pierre, who had inserted a key into the clock's face as he slowly and carefully began to wind the clock. Alexandra waved as she whipped past him into the dining room.

She scanned the room.

"Bonsoir." Jacques smiled as he greeted her.

"Mr. Morneau isn't here?" She gave a small smile.

"No, Mademoiselle. Not yet. He was disturbed when you didn't come to meals yesterday. He asked me to sit you at his table if you came in today."

She followed him to a table by the window. "Merci, Jacques." This time her smile reached her eyes. She fluffed her hair and brushed a piece of lint from her sweater. Jean Paul would join her soon.

"May I get you an aperitif?" Jacques pulled out her chair.

"*Oui, s'il vous plait.* A glass of pinot noir."

"Alexandra, where were you?" Jean Paul roared, as he wove his way among the tables.

There it was—the sexy French accent—but now it had a slightly perturbed edge to it. "I thought we had a date for Bastille Day."

Alexandra ignored his bellow. She felt a flutter in her stomach. *Maybe he's concerned about me.* "*Bonsoir*, Jean Paul."

He pulled out the chair across from her and flopped down with a loud sigh. "*Bonsoir*. I was worried when I didn't see you yesterday. You missed the celebrations. Where were you?" He looked directly into her eyes. "What happened to your face?"

She heard the concern in his voice and saw his frown deepen on his face. Her heart beat a little faster. *I didn't miss Bastille Day. I was there. But he doesn't know that.* "I'm sorry. I worried you." The corners of her mouth turned up. She raised her shoulders in a graceful shrug as she fiddled with her napkin. "I was in Paris on an important errand. I left very early in the morning on Bastille Day. I tried, but I couldn't get back. I'm sorry." She ripped a piece from her roll.

"And your face?" He leaned toward her and ran his index finger down the faint purple bruise on her cheekbone. "What about this bruise?"

She heard his voice soften a little. *I thought I covered it up, but not enough for him to ignore. Boy is he persistent. I can't get anything past him.* "My face? Oh, I was walking through the woods this morning and not paying attention. A branch hit me."

So I told a little white lie. The part about the walk in the woods was the truth, just not when I took it and where. She felt guilty for not being totally honest with him. *How would he react if I told him what really happened? No, I can't tell him. He would think I was losing my mind. I can't tell him.* "It's nice of you to be worried, but as you can see, I'm fine."

Well, as long as you are all right. Did you enjoy the day?" Jean Paul put his hand over hers. "There must have been a reenactment of the storming of the Bastille in Paris. Did you see it?"

"There was…it was very exciting and so…so interesting." *If only he knew.* Alexandra pulled one of her hands away from his grasp and touched it to her cheek. She could feel heat move from her neck to her face. She was sure she blushed. This time it was because she told the white lie, not because of her reaction to his attention. *I'm a terrible liar. But he hasn't seemed to notice my blush and seems to believe me.*

"Have you ordered?"

"No, I'm starved, but I'm not sure what I want." She hadn't eaten in over twenty-four hours. "The chef here makes everything to perfection."

"May I order for you?" He raised his free hand and motioned to Jacques.

"Please. I would like that. Yesterday was hectic. I'm tired. I don't have the energy to make a decision about food."

When James had ordered, she thought he was trying to be in control. Somehow when Jean Paul suggested what she might like for dinner, she wasn't bothered. *Maybe because he asked.* She fiddled with her place setting. *He's an interesting man.*

He took her hands gently in his again. "Let's see, you're drinking red wine." He turned to Jacques, who stood quietly at his side. "We'll both have Beef Bourgogne and a salad. We'll decide later about dessert."

"So what else did you do in Paris?" Jean Paul asked.

Alexandra felt the warmth of his large hands. She enjoyed it. The feeling went right to her heart. "What have you done since I saw you last?" She wanted to get the conversation away from her so she didn't have to concoct more lies. She was having trouble thinking about how to tell him what happened in Paris without mentioning she had experienced the falling of the Bastille. in 1789.

"Well, let's see. I went to Paris to see my client. I got back late in the morning. When Jacques told me you weren't here, I decided to go to the celebration in town. I ate lunch at the hotel and had the Bastille dessert, which I always enjoy."

"Maybe they're still serving it here. I had it the day. I went to Monet's house at the hotel. It was very good."

"We must have been in Paris at the same time for some of the day. I guess we were in different parts of the city."

By a few hundred years. "I guess we were." She smiled. "Madam Dumont said you took the painting at the top of the staircase with you to Paris to have it examined by an art historian."

"Yes. I wanted to get it authenticated. I was sure that the woman was a relative. With the help of the historian, I was able to find the records of the artist and when he painted the portrait."

"What were the results?"

"It was as I thought. She was related to our family way, way back in the eighteenth century. She lived here in this very chateau." He smiled. "I have to be honest. I had an ulterior motive when I took this case. I not only wanted to prove Monsieur Dumont innocent, but wanted to prove the chateau belonged to my family during the seventeen hundreds and was taken illegally by the revolutionaries."

Alexandra stared. "Is the portrait next to her a relative also?"

"Perhaps," Jean Paul laughed. "When I was a small boy, I heard many stories from my grandfather about the chateau and how it was taken during the revolution by the rebels. He said there were papers proving it belonged to our family. It seems that these stories were passed down through the generations—that his great grandmother's mother lived in the chateau at the time of the revolution and there have been sightings of her on the anniversary of Bastille Day. There was never anything in the stories about a brother or husband or any man who might have lived there at the time of the French Revolution.

My grandfather said that when the mobs attacked, she hid any documents that pertained to her and her family somewhere in the grounds of the chateau before she disappeared. But no one has been able to find them." Jean Paul stared at her. He watched the color drain from her face. She looked ashen. "What's wrong? What did I say?"

"Nothing."

He stared at her. His eyebrows drew together. His eyes were wide open.

"It's not what you said about the chateau belonging to your family. It's what you said about a ghost."

He shook his head in disbelief. Hid face took on a look of

astonishment. "It's just a story. I don't believe it."

She smiled. *He doesn't know that there is a ghost. Wait till he finds out about Claudette. She's bound to show herself to him soon.* "On the back of the painting I told you about, the one my mother left me, it says—La Maison de Familiale. The family name is blurred." Her heart began to pound. Her brain moved as fast as a bullet train. "Maybe I'm related to you. I'll help you hunt. I want to find my family roots, too."

"I would love for you to help me and if we are related, it's hundreds of years ago."

"The next time Madam Dumont goes to visit her husband; we can try to find the papers. Two searchers are better than one. We'll be able to cover more ground in a shorter time." Alexandra felt excited. Her heart pounded. Her palms felt damp. She wanted to say 'let's start right away'. She took a deep breath.

Alexandra wasn't sure she wanted to share with him what was going on and what had happened to her since she arrived a few days ago. She was afraid he might think she was crazy; however, she felt she needed to make Claudette reappear and for Jean Paul to see her.

Alexandra knew if she wanted answers about what happened in 1789 she would need his help. When she went back to 1789, Jean Paul would have to go with her. After all, they were both part of the family that lived in the chateau during the French Revolution. *If I tell him how I really spent Bastille Day, will he believe me? Should I dare tell him there is a ghost?* She had to trust her gut. Alexandra rested her elbows on the table, folded her hands together and leaned forward on them.

"What is it Alexandra? You look so intense."

"Jean Paul, do you believe in time travel?" She looked him straight in the eye.

Jean Paul's mouth dropped open with astonishment. His eyes widened. He stared at Alexandra. "What do you mean do I believe in time travel?" He reached out and clasped her hands. "There's no such thing, except in the movies." His brows drew together.

"I guess you don't," Alexandra said.

"Are you kidding with me? Are you sure this is your first glass of wine?" he laughed.

"Of course it is," her voice remained steady. "I'm not joking. Just listen to me. First let me say, every time I walk in the hallway upstairs, I feel the eyes of the woman in the portrait at the top of the stairs follow me." She pulled her hands out of his grasp and grabbed her wine glass. Alexandra took a long sip. She needed to think for a moment. *How much should I tell him?*

"The hall has very dim light. I'm sure it's the shadows that are playing tricks on you." Jean Paul gently pulled the wine glass from her white knuckled grasp. Finally, he was successful in extricating it. He set it down in front of him and stared at her. *She must be imaging it.*

"No. I'm sure her eyes follow me. I can also smell a strange perfume. In fact, I smelled it in my room the day I arrived."

"Go on." He looked intently at her. "I'm listening." His eyebrows drew together again. "My client told me something strange about a portrait in the same hallway. I didn't believe him so I never pursued it. But finish with your story and then I'll tell you what he said."

She returned his intent look. *Well, he's not laughing. He seems to be listening now, so I guess I can go on. He did say finish your story.* She chewed on her lower lip.

"The first night I was here a woman came out of the mirror at the foot of my bed. The woman only stayed a few minutes." She waited. *He's still not laughing.* "The second night she reappeared. It was very early in the morning of July fourteenth."

"You look a lot like the woman in the painting upstairs," Jean Paul said.

"When I took the painting of her to Paris, the dealer confirmed the woman was Claudette Pirrot, the mother of my great-great-grandmother," Jean Paul said.

"Claudette, that's what she called herself. She has never told me her last name."

"My relative appeared in your bedroom?" Jean Paul leaned forward. He raked his hand through his hair.

"She dragged me through the mirror to a coach parked at the front of the chateau."

"*Mon Dieu*, Alexandra. You let her kidnap you. Are you…Are you sure it wasn't a dream?"

"Yes, I'm sure it was not a dream. We drove to Paris in an eighteenth century carriage. I witnessed the storming of the Bastille. I was in Paris on July 14, 1789."

"Don't stop. How do you Americans put it, I'm all ears? She dragged you, really?"

"Well, to tell you the truth, I didn't resist. I went along willingly. Do you know the coachman looked just like Pierre?" She laughed nervously. "She wanted me to save her bother-in-law, Henri, who looked much like the man in the portrait next to Claudette's."

"Where was he—the man, Henri? Where did you find him?"

"He was in a cell at the Bastille and was very ill. He was the only prisoner left in his cell when we arrived. The guards had opened the cells and had run away along with the other six inmates. They left Henri. In all fairness, there was so much confusion they probably didn't realize he was there. They didn't know he hadn't left. He was too weak to leave on his own. We got away from the Bastille by the skin of our teeth. The crowds were wild and pursued us until we outran them. Our carriage broke down. It was impossible for Henri go on foot so we left him at the Abbey Cyr, outside of Paris, promising to come back for him."

"The Abbey Cyr? I don't believe it is there anymore."

"Well, it was there in July of 1789. I visited it."

"You escaped the storming of the Bastille and left him at an Abbey?" Jean Paul frowned and shook his head and sighed loudly.

"You don't believe me?" Alexandra licked her dry lips.

"Actually, I'm beginning to, or should I say I do! You could have gotten killed. It was not a safe thing to do. You are so foolhardy. It was imprudent and rash." He gripped her hands. "You were lucky to get back. How did you do it?"

"It's a long story. Are you sure you want to hear it? " She stared at his unsmiling face. "You think I'm crazy, don't you?"

"No. No, I'm just worried. If you go back again, or should I say *when* you go back," he laughed, "I don't want you to be reckless. I am going with you. No argument." His gazed lingered on her face. His voice was husky. His grip tightened around her hands.

"We have to figure out a way to get Claudette to reappear. I have to get back to 1789 to make sure her brother-in-law is safe. I believe, no, I'm sure that my amethyst ring triggers visits from Claudette and brings me back to 1789. If you look at her portrait she has a ring on just like mine." She held out her hand. "You commented on it the first time I met you. This ring was in the box with the picture of the chateau. I told you about the picture, remember? When I'm with her, I don't believe I have ever seen her wearing it. The ring somehow it ended up in my family. We must be related."

Jean Paul stared out of the window, then at her.

"What are you thinking?" Alexandra asked.

"Let me tell you what my client told me when I took his case. First, he swore he didn't kill his business partner and that a woman flew out of a portrait that hung in the second floor hallway. It was that woman who stabbed and killed his business partner. He said her hair flew wildly around her face, had a crazed look in her eyes and seemed to be in a frenzy driven by rage. I didn't believe him. I thought he was delusional. I even thought of pleading him insane.

"I've searched the chateau and never found a knife and neither have the police. I hunted through his suite and offices." Jean Paul shook his head. "He had no reason to kill the partner. His wife said they had no money problems. I checked his bank accounts—business and personal. It didn't look as if there were problems there. According to everyone, he and his partner got along with each other extremely well. The chateau business was doing well. The rooms were filled almost every month. I'm sure now that he must be telling the truth. I…we have to find out what's going on."

"The woman he's talking about must be Claudette. The other women are not dressed in eighteenth century clothing. The clothes are more like nineteenth century. The other paintings in the hallway are of animals, scenery, or men or children. He said a woman?" Alexandra asked.

"Yes, Claudette must be the person he is talking about. But why would her ghost kill the business partner?"

"I have no idea why she would commit murder. What's her connection to his business partner?" Alexandra looked directly at him. "Perhaps when she reappears we can get her to tell us."

"I'm not sure that Claudette is the one he is talking about, but it certainly looks that way. At least now I believe he may not be making up the story and is as sane as you and me," said Jean Paul.

"Maybe he was confused about the sex of the murderer or which painting he or she jumped out of. When you witness something like a murder, especially one as violent as this one, your perspective can be distorted. We have to find out. Perhaps you can ask him on your next visit," Alexandra said. "Possibly it was someone who worked in the household."

"I will talk to him again about what he saw. It was probably her, but we have to find out why she murdered him."

"Tell my again. Why Alexandra…why did you go with her?" He shook his head and stared straight into her eyes. His eyebrows drew together again. "I worry about you."

"I…" Alexandra hesitated. "It's nice to have you worry about me." Her heart beat a little faster. "My curiosity got the better of me. It happens often in my line of work, but I rarely get into trouble that I can't get out of."

"And what kind of work do you do?"

What the heck. It's bad to keep secrets. I might as well tell him the truth about what I do for a living. What can happen? He can just get up, walk away and never talk with me again, but he wouldn't do that. She licked her lips. "You probably won't believe me." The corners of her mouth turned up.

"What else? What else can you say?" He waited a few seconds. "I don't think anything can surprise me as much as what you just told me." He waited. "Okay, let me have it."

She stared at him. "I'm not just a little affluent woman from New York City. I'm an FBI agent."

"What…That I don't believe. You're right." He was almost shouting.

I guess I'll have to show him. She reached into the back pocket of her jeans and pulled out her I.D. "Believe it." She pushed it into his hand.

He held the card up to the window and studied it. "It doesn't look like a fake. The picture looks like you. That's a surprise—usually this kind of photo isn't very flattering, but yours looks just like you. All right, I believe you."

"Of course it's not a fake." She was happy she finally saw him smile.

He laughed uneasily, as he handed it back. "Any more secrets?"

"No, I promise," she said. The corners of her mouth turned up again. "Are you sure?"

"Yes, I'm sure." Alexandra laughed softly. "When I was with Claudette at the Bastille, she told me that Henri, her brother-in-law, lived with her here at the chateau before he was imprisoned. She also mentioned her children and a husband that died. Things got so hectic we never got back to talking about them," Alexandra said. "We have to find out who lived at this chateau in 1789 and what happened to her husband and children and what happened to her."

Jean Paul stared. "When my grandfather told me the stories about the chateau, and he said there were papers hidden somewhere on this property, I believe him now. If we can find them, it may help us find out what happened to the people who lived here during the Revolution and after."

"Maybe there's a secret room somewhere. When I came to dinner, I think I saw Madame Dumont walking toward her suite with an arm full of ledgers. They looked like the account books I saw her working on the other day. She seems to be overwhelmed. Running the business of the chateau by herself seems to be a burden for her. I'm sure she'll be busy in her suites for hours." Alexandra stood up. "Do you want to start now? We could begin in the hallway on the second floor."

"She's probably in her suite for the night. Her rooms are right next to mine, so there's no reason for her to be on the second floor." Jean Paul pushed back his chair.

"Come on, let's start in the hallway upstairs at the top of the main staircase. We should begin at Claudette's portrait. Maybe there is a hidden panel or room behind one of the paintings or tapestries." She grabbed his hand and dragged him out of his chair. Alexandra gave him a sidelong glance as he followed her. She pulled him to the entrance hall. "Let's hurry." She dropped his hand and took the stairs two at a time. He ran right next to her.

"We should go right. The left wing was burned during the revolution. The papers would have been ashes and long gone if they were there."

Jean Paul shook his head. "How do you know that?"

"I saw a fire this morning on that side of the house. When I returned to the chateau. It was still 1789 and the rebels had attacked the chateau. When I entered through the gate, I was back in 2010. Everything was fine."

"I want to hear about the whole trip, but first let's start to search." Jean Paul was fired up. He didn't hide his eagerness to find the long-lost deed.

"You take the right wall. I'll check the left." Alexandra glanced over her shoulder. She pulled the first painting, a still life, away from the wall and ran her fingers over the paneling. Then she worked her way down the hall running her fingers over every inch of the walls. What she wasn't able to reach she searched with her eyes.

At the end of the corridor, she stumbled when she hit a solid body. Alexandra felt an arm slide around her waist and catch her before she fell. She glanced up. "I was so into the search I didn't see you. Thanks for catching me. I wasn't paying attention to what I was doing."

"There's nothing here. I'm disappointed. There is nothing—not even a clue. There are no slips of paper hidden on the backs of the paintings— nothing—not a hint of a hidden room behind these walls." Jean Paul didn't move his arm.

"No. We have to search the library. In all the murder mysteries, the library is usually the key to the investigation." She giggled as she looked up at Jean Paul.

"Is that how the FBI reasons?"

Alexandra leaned into him and laughed.

"Madam Dumont is going to Paris tomorrow morning to see her husband. I don't have to be at the prison. She'll leave early in the morning. Probably around seven. She visits with him for an hour—from eleven a.m. to twelve noon. She spends more time traveling than she has for a visit. Let's meet early for breakfast. We'll start to search the library after she leaves. We'll have until mid-afternoon. We'll be done long before she gets home. Can you wait until tomorrow morning?" He chuckled.

"Maybe." She looked out of the sides of her eyes and smiled like a Cheshire cat.

Chapter Ten

Chateau Verny
July 16, 2010

Alexandra opened one eye and glanced at her watch and ring on the top of the bedside table. It was six-fifteen in the morning and nearly dawn. She leaned toward the table and switched on the bedside lamp. She looked out the French doors.

The eerie feeling that she had frequently experienced since arriving in France was there again. She jumped out of bed and peered into every corner of the room but she didn't see anyone. No one was there. There weren't even shadows on the walls. The "creepy crawlers" walked slowly up her spine. She didn't know why she was encountering this sensation.

Alexandra rubbed her eyes as she pulled out some clothes. Again her dreams had made her toss and turn all night. Again she was tired. She glanced out of the windows of the French doors. "Thank God no one is there. Okay, bathtubs aren't Claudette's milieu. She picks more dramatic settings." She rushed into the bathroom and jumped into the shower. She let the warm water run until it cooled.

When she walked into the bedroom the lamp light was out. "Is that Claudette playing tricks? My ghost is making this trip very interesting. Now she's shutting lights off. I'm sure she doesn't care about the electric bill." Alexandra checked the lamp and laughed. The bulb had burned out. She was wrong. It wasn't Claudette.

After she dressed, Alexandra checked the mirror. She pulled her hair back, fastened it with a rubber band, touched up her eyebrows and lashes with color and brushed translucent powder on her face. "Well, Vanity Fair would never ask me for my opinion on style unless they decided they needed an interview from a bag lady or someone who escaped from a mental institution. The brown sweatshirt doesn't exactly go with the gray sweatpants and yellow socks. But who cares?" She reached for her sneakers on the bottom shelf of the armoire. After she slipped them on, she double knotted the laces. *That's all I need to do—trip over them and tumble down the stairs.*

Alexandra picked up her key, locked her door and hurried down the main staircase. She bounced through the hallway, wrapping her arms around herself. When she reached the library, just off the entrance hall near the elevator, she opened the door slowly. "Damn." Hearing it squeak loudly, Alexandra stood for a moment in the doorway. Then she closed the door quickly and scurried inside. Her eyes scanned the room as she walked down the four hardwood stairs to a room that brought back memories of her family home.

The walls were paneled with dark wood. A large fireplace with a marble mantle flanked by bookcases lined the far wall. A mixture of reproductions of elegant eighteenth century furniture and real antiques were scattered around the room. They looked exactly like the pieces her grandmother and mother had collected at Sotheby auctions over the years. She sank into one of the soft leather, over-sized winged-back chairs that faced the fireplace and sighed. Slipping off her sneakers, she leaned back and pulled her legs up. She wrapped her arms around her knees. She began to think about her mother and how she sat in a chair similar to this and saw the lady in the black cape and hood walk through the hallway outside the library.

Alexandra stared at the ornately carved mantel of the fireplace. She pushed out of her eyes a strand of hair that had escaped her hair band and sat up straight in the chair with her feet on the floor. She concentrated on the fireplace as she dug her toes into the oriental carpet. The chateau was silent. She had time to think. Her eyes drifted to the bookcases. Alexandra glanced at the antique clock in the bookcase—it was six forty-five.

"Something is very strange about the fireplace and bookcases." She stared. "The fireplace is unusually far from the wall."

The sound of the elevator door sliding open and Madam Dumont's voice distracted her thoughts. Alexandra leap from her chair and ran to the bookcase. She pretended to look for a book. She held her breath and waited. Within a few minutes, she heard the owner shout what sounded like instructions to her housekeeper as her heels tapped across the entrance hall's marble tiles.

Alexandra let out a sigh of relief when she heard the squeak of the hinges of the chateau's front door as it slammed shut. She listened a few more seconds to make sure Madam Dumont didn't return. She heard the loud ticking of a clock that stood in the corner of the entrance hall.

Alexandra looked to the left of the hearth at the bookcase. She pulled the books from the middle shelf and set them on the floor. She ran her hand along the wood and knocked on the panels working her way across the wall. "There's a difference in the sound the closer I get to the mantel. It sounds hollower." She thought she heard an echo. "There must be a hidden room. There's an empty space behind the paneling and marble, just like in the old horror movies. If only I can locate a lever to open the bookcase. There must be a room behind the wall."

Alexandra began to pull books off the rest of the shelves. She put them haphazardly on the floor. French history books translated into English, Jane Austin, C.S. Lewis, Hemingway, Mary Roberts Reinhart and other authors that would appeal to foreign visitors, especially English speaking ones, filled the floor around her feet.

Her obsession with finding a secret room and the noise of the books hitting the floor distracted her. She was so absorbed that she was oblivious of the footsteps that entered the room.

"I knew it. I knew I'd find you here. What are you doing?" Jean Paul stopped instantly as if hit by a barricade.

Alexandra jumped. "You startled me." Her blush was instantaneous. The piles of books circled her like a fort. Her foot caught on one of the piles. She stumbled and swore as the pile scattered.

"I figured you would get up before sunrise," Jean Paul said ignoring her language.

"I couldn't sleep. I never can when I have a lot on my mind. I came down here to study the room."

"Why are you making such a mess?" His voice was soft and his eyebrows were raised slightly. He stared at the pile of books surrounding her.

Alexandra was surprised when she looked down and saw the mess. She understood what he meant—after all she was a guest. "There must be a secret room behind the wall. I'm sure of it. I can hear a hollow sound behind the shelves near the mantel when I knock." She demonstrated for him. "Hear it." She ran her fingers along the inside of the bookcase. "I need to find a latch. Where are you? Where are you, latch?" she whispered. She felt the recess in the wood. "*Voila*. Here it is." Her fingers touched a wooden latch.

"Here's what?"

"The latch, the latch." She pulled on it.

The bookcase groaned as it open a crack. Alexandra moved out of the way and grabbed the edge and tugged on the door. "Help me, please." She turned to Jean Paul. "Never mind, it's moving." The bookcase slowly creaked open into the library.

"First, let me just fix the pile I just scattered." She picked up one of the larger books and stared. "My mother had a book like this." She flipped through its pages. "See here's a picture of a ball at Versailles. She showed it to me one night when I was about five."

The Secret Room

Alexandra leaned forward and peered into the darkness. She pulled on Jean Paul's arm. "Look! Not a room—a winding staircase! We need a flashlight." Alexandra turned toward Jean Paul.

"I just happen to have one." He grinned as he held the flashlight in the air, and then glanced at the pile of books on the floor with a critical eye. "You owe me. First, let's pile up all the books that got scattered. Madam Dumont wouldn't be too happy to see what you've done."

"I'm sorry. I was so excited." She tried to look grumpy, but smiled inside as she lowered her head and let out a small sigh. She raised her shoulders and looked at him out of the corner of her eyes. "Okay, I owe you." She bent down to straighten the books, piling them into neat stacks near the bookcase. "Come on, please help me." She watched his face soften. "She isn't here anyway. I heard her leave," Alexandra said. "But we should be neat."

Jean Paul handed her the last of the books to lay on top of pile next to her. His hand brushed her arm. Self-preservation made her jerk back. Her face felt hot.

She held up the last book and read the title out loud. "*The French Revolution*. That's intriguing." Alexandra stared into space. Memories of the night when she was five and sat by her mother in the big chair floated in front of her eyes.

"Where did you go?" Jean Paul asked.

"Oh, I was just remembering something from my childhood." She set the book on the mantel. "My mother also had a book just like this one. She told me a lot about the French Revolution."

"Okay, done. What now?" Jean Paul asked.

Alexandra eased herself into the open space and found herself on the first step before Jean Paul could say anything. "It's a spiral staircase." She looked up. "Please shine the light up. "The stairs are winding and narrow.

It's pitch black ahead. It must go to one of the turrets. We have to see what's up there. Come on."

"Put your shoes on."

"I'll be all right." Alexandra started to climb, but quickly backed down. Her hands thrashed in front of her face to get rid of the dangling cobwebs. "The passageway is filled with cobwebs and dirt." She stumbled on well-worn risers. "Ugh. Something is crawling on me." She trembled as she stared at the large spider that fell onto the stair in front of her when she brushed the creepy crawler from her forehead. "I never have liked to get under old buildings while investigating a case."

"Be careful! What do you expect? It's a hidden staircase in the walls of a chateau that is several hundred years old and hasn't been used for many, many years. It's not the grand, circular one in the entryway," Jean Paul said with a laugh.

"I know, but you never know what you will find crawling and slithering around a body or closed in space and stop laughing."

The air became heavier as they climbed the spiral staircase. She began to feel claustrophobic. "Ouch." Her toe hit the riser in front of her. She clutched her arms together around her chest. She bent down and checked the step to make sure it was splinter free, and then started up the staircase again.

"Are you all right, Alexandra?"

She looked down at her feet. "My feet are cold. Shoot, no wonder, I forgot my shoes." Alexandra laughed. "I'm fine. Come on." She grabbed his hand and started to climb again.

"You're too slow." The stairs creaked under her weight as she climbed.

"Yeah, but I'm cautious. I'm not the one getting bumped and bruised." Jean Paul shined the flashlight on the staircase. It lit the way as they moved upward. Their shadows played on the wall. "Slow down, Alexandra, you'll have an accident," Jean Paul called to her.

"Damn!"

"What happened, Alexandra?"

"I stubbed my toe again on a loose board."

The steps are getting narrow. Wait for me. Do you have enough light?"

"Yes, it's fine. There's enough light. I'm just going too fast. My hands are cold."

"What am I going to do with you?" He laughed as he patted her arm and held one of her hands. "Stick the other in your pocket to warm it up. Didn't I tell you to put on your shoes? Look, there's a ledge leading off to the right. Where do you think that goes?" Jean Paul shined his flashlight down the ledge.

"Let's check it out on the way back." She glanced over her shoulder and watched Jean Paul turn sideways as he moved up the stairs. *I never realized how broad his shoulders are.*

The air cooled as they climbed higher. The steps groaned against their weight.

"I'm sure we've walked up at least six floors. We must be in one of the towers."

Her body hit the wall in front of her. "We're at the end. Shine the flashlight up and down the wall, please. There must be a door."

Jean Paul slowly shined the flashlight up and down on the wall.

"Wait! Stop! I see a doorknob. It's very low. The top of door is only waist high—my waist." She pointed at the wall. "I don't think I want to touch anything—who knows what kind of spiders are hidden in the cracks." Alexandra sighed. "But I think I'll be brave." She reached out and wiggled the knob that was next to her knees. "It seems to be locked. There doesn't seem to be anything but dirt here." She gingerly felt along the top edge of the door and the floor with the tips of her fingers. "No hidden key." She grasped the padlock and shook it vehemently.

"Here, let me help." Jean Paul reached around her. "Hold this." He gave her the flashlight. She shined the light below the knob while he pulled up and down on the padlock with both hands. "It's rusty, but I'm sure we can get it open if we keep moving it."

Alexandra heard a sharp click as the lock snapped open. "May I do it?"

"Of course." Jean Paul smiled.

She pushed on the door. Its hinges squeaked as it swung open. Alexandra bent down and crawled into the room. It was cold and airless. When she stood up, the ceiling was about a foot above her head.

Jean Paul followed. She noticed that he had to bend his head a little after he stood up. He flashed his light around the room. A candle sat on a rusted metal plate in the middle of the table that was pushed against the far wall. The candle sat in a small pool of hardened wax. There was a cot against the wall to their right and a small iron crib against the wall on the left. Two trunks sat in the middle of the room. The space was so small Alexandra had difficulty maneuvering around the furniture. She stood mesmerized. She noticed the room was a perfect square and it was windowless. The walls were bare except for a small painting of a sleeping child above the crib. She and Jean Paul cast long shadows. The flashlight spread a ghostly luminescence throughout the room.

"Someone slept here. Look at the iron bed and the thin mattress. Looks like someone just tossed a blanket over what must have been a linen sheet." He held up a piece of torn cloth. "They must have been in too much of a hurry to make it properly," Jean Paul said. "The crib has a blanket. It's folded neatly at the foot of the crib."

"What a mess." She sneezed. "The room smells of mold and dust. It hasn't been opened for hundreds of years." Alexandra flopped down on the bed. She jumped up with a start. "How could anyone sleep on this? I can feel the springs." This time she sat down slowly. She shifted her weight until she found a comfortable position.

"Let's see what's in the trunks." Jean Paul sat down next to her on the cot and opened the one nearest him. "There was a little girl and boy here." He pulled out a small dress and pants and shirt that looked about a size larger. "Here's a doll." He picked up a stuffed doll with a china face. Its hair was a mass of blond curls. He leaned over. "Look, an old fashioned, wooden toy. It looks like a top." Jean Paul flipped up the latch on the second trunk. He held his flashlight and shined it into the trunk. He rummaged through its contents. "This one has a few women's dresses and a wool shawl. No man's clothing."

"Something horrible went on in this chateau." Her hair stood up on the back of her neck. "I can feel that at one time this wasn't a happy place."

"Come on. Let's get out of here. I want to see where that ledge goes." John Paul scanned the room with his flashlight and then reached for Alexandra's hand.

"Wait a minute. "What's this?" She looked into the crib. "Let me have the flashlight. I think I see something sticking out from under the blanket." Alexandra brushed cobwebs from a baby blanket as she pulled out the folded piece of paper. "It's a piece of paper." She stopped to inspect the blanket. "This is beautiful. Look at the embroidered material. It's done on silk. The stitches are so fine." She picked up the corner of a piece of paper. "Looks like a letter." She opened the flap of the envelope and withdrew a piece of paper and unfolded it—carefully so that she wouldn't damage the almost tissue-like paper.

Jean Paul handed her the flashlight. "Here, you'll need this."

"The address on top says, Claudette Pache Pirrot, Chateau Verny, Giverny, France." Alexandra brought the note closer to her face.

"Well, well. What does it say?" Jean Paul reached for the letter.

When his hand moved close to her, she held the letter tightly to her chest. She felt his fingers on her arm. Her heart raced and her face got warm. "Just a minute." Her voice caught.

"What...?" He swallowed a chuckle. His face softened. "Okay, read it."

My dearest Daughter Marie and Son Louis,

I'm writing to tell you about your father and me. You father was an officer in the King's army. He was on his way to fight with France in the American Revolution when the ship he was on went down in the ocean and was lost. I was a Lady-in-Waiting to the Queen. We were both loyal to King Louis XVI and the Queen, Marie Antoinette.

Your father and I met on a beautiful spring day and fell madly in love. When we got married, the King gave us this property, Chateau Verny, as a wedding gift.

"She must have written this while she hid here." Alexandra leaned toward the light.

"Go on," Jean Paul said.

If you are reading this, I am gone and Monique, your nanny, has gotten you away from the chateau and will take care of you both.

When the bad times are over, the chateau will belong to both of you. I am being held in my room. I hope I am able to smuggle this letter out to you before they transport me to Paris.

"Somehow she was able to leave her letter here before she disappeared, Alexandra said." She continued to read.

You both are the best of your father and me. I know you will do well in life. Remember that I love you both very much and I hope your lives will be filled with love, happiness, and adventure.

Your loving Mother

"The children must have left the chateau without getting this letter, if they were able to escape." She read the letter again to herself.

"How did they get out without beginning seen? Maybe that ledge leads to a way out." Jean Paul glanced around the room. "This is a good hiding place. No one would be able to find it."

Alexandra twisted her ring. She felt a cool breeze and shivered. She picked up the small blanket at the end of the crib and held it to her chest. When she looked up, she was sure she saw Claudette standing just inside the door near the top of the crib. Alexandra reached out. The vision disappeared. She felt a swish of air and the rustle of satin material.

A tear ran down her cheek. She wiped it away with her sleeve. "Come on. Let's go back and see where the ledge goes." Alexandra folded the letter and stuffed it into the back pocket of her jeans. "What happened to Claudette? Where did her children go?" Her voice softened.

"We'll find out what happened to them," Jean Paul said as he extended his hand. "Will you be all right with no shoes?" He held out his hand.

"I'll get them." She jumped up ignoring his help. "Where was she taken? Why didn't she tell the children—unless she didn't want to scare them?"

"Wait, let me give you some light. Slow down." He tried to grab hold of her arm, but she was gone. Jean Paul stomped down the stairs after her. "You'll trip if you're not careful," he shouted.

Alexandra stood on the last step of the staircase. She peeked around the open door before she stepped into the library. "My sneakers are still here." She ran and plopped down in the winged-back chair. She took several deep breaths before she stuffed her feet into her shoes.

"Let's go." She jumped up and scurried toward the stairs.

"Well, tie your laces first," he chuckled. "Calm down. The staircase has been there for a few centuries. It's not going anywhere."

She bent down and quickly tied her shoes. "I'm very excited. You're right." She stopped and counted to three, then ran up the stairs.

Jean Paul followed. He grabbed hold of her arm. "Let me go ahead, please." Not giving her a chance to respond, he squeezed passed her. "We don't know what we'll find in this branch of the tunnel."

"Wait." Alexandra pulled on Jean Paul's arm.

"What now?" He shook his head and laughed.

"We didn't close the door to the staircase."

"Don't worry, we'll be back before Marie goes into the library to clean. We'll even have time to put everything back where it belongs. She'll never know we were in there."

Jean Paul brushed cobwebs from his face. "The path is getting narrow. Give me your hand." He saw a spider scamper down the wall next to him.

"This tunnel is awful. It's so dusty and the spiders have been hard at work. I'm beginning to think Claudette and her children were the last people in here. No, I'm sure of it."

"Be careful. Don't move." Jean Paul stopped. He looked down.

Alexandra came to an abrupt stop. She felt the muscles of his back stiffen as she bumped into him. "Why? What's the problem?"

"Look!" His flashlight lit up the wooden ledge. He moved a little to the side so that she could see. "Part of the wood has rotted away. See that huge hole? I can't tell how far up we are, so I don't know how far down the hole might go."

"Can we jump over it?" Alexandra looked ahead to see where the other side of the hole was.

"I have long legs and can make it." He leapt over the opening without difficulty before he finished his statement.

"Give me your hands. Don't worry. I won't let you fall. I'll make sure you're all right." His fingers closed like manacles around her wrists.

Alexandra looked down into the blackness in front of her feet.

"You can make it." Jean Paul leaned toward her. "On three, jump— one, two, three."

When her feet hit the floor, he let go of her.

She landed against him. Feeling unsteady and without thinking she wrapped her hands around his chest.

He enjoyed the softness of her body against his. Her perfume still tantalized him. He would never get used to the scent. He drew his fingertip along the side of her jaw and looked straight into her eyes. "Are you all right?" Jean Paul asked after several seconds.

"I'm fine, I'm fine." She pulled away. *Hopefully, he didn't feel the pounding of my heart. What is it about him that makes tingles run up and down my spine?* "It's freezing in here." She hugged herself, trying change the mood. "Just go," she blurted out. She took a deep breath. "Sorry, I mean let's keep going, please."

Jean Paul shined the light so that they could see ahead. "Aren't you glad you went back for your shoes?"

Alexandra laughed. "Yes. Yes. You were right—as always." She moved forward. "If this corridor gets any narrower, a stick figure would have trouble getting through."

"Well, you don't have to worry about that. We're at the end." Jean Paul knocked on the wall. "Hear that hollow sound? There must be a room on the other side." He shined his flashlight up and down the wall. "I hope. There'd better be. I don't relish going back the way we came."

"There's the latch." She reached around him and pointed to it. "Push on it. Pull on it. Open it. Do something," Alexandra cried out. "I can't wait to see what's on the other side."

"Calm down. My, my, such impatience." Jean Paul flipped the latch and pushed.

When the door opened, Jean Paul stared. "We're in a room."

Alexandra edged around him and peered at the floor. "We're in *my* room. This is the armoire that backs up against the wall near the mirror. These are my clothes" She tripped over the small rug on the floor as she stepped down into the room.

"Be careful." Jean Paul reached out for her arm and caught her just as she began to fall.

"Thanks I'm okay." Alexandra stood still. "I never thought of a passageway behind my room. It must be the way Claudette and her children left. Somewhere there's a passageway to the outside of the Chateau. I bet this place is filled with many tunnels and probably more than one goes to the outside. They're like the webs the spiders had spun in the walls."

Jean Paul looked up. "Who is that?" He turned toward Alexandra and scowled.

Chapter Eleven

"Where were you?" Claudette stood with her hands on her hips. Her feet were planted as if glued to the floor. She stared at Jean Paul and leaned forward. She was just close enough so that her index finger could make contact with his chest. She poked at him. "And who is this person?"

"And who are you?" Jean Paul glared as he slowly took a step backward so that he was out of her reach. He didn't want to rattle her. She seemed extremely annoyed. He just didn't like being poked—especially by a very rude woman.

Thank goodness he sees her too. "Jean Paul, this is Claudette. It was her brother-in-law we saved on Bastille Day." Alexandra reached for Claudette's hand and held it. "He's a friend. Please don't worry."

"We have to go back to the Abbey to get my brother-in-law. We must go right now." Claudette turned toward the mirror. She raised her hand and motioned to Alexandra to follow her.

"Just a minute, Alexandra. Where is she going?" Jean Paul asked. "You can't just follow her." He grabbed Alexandra's hands. "Please stay here. Let's talk about this—let's make a plan."

"Hurry. The peasants are storming the chateau. The hedges near the kitchen are on fire." Claudette grabbed one of Alexandra's arms and pulled. She tried to get her away from Jean Paul. Alexandra's arm began to feel as if it was being tugged from her shoulder. She felt herself being dragged toward the mirror. Jean Paul was still holding on tightly to Alexandra's other arm. "Charles is waiting with the carriage. We have to go—right now. I don't want Charles to get caught, or we won't have a way to get to the Abbey."

Alexandra tossed Jean Paul a determined look as she twisted from his grip.

"I'm coming with you." His look was just as determined. He kept his eyes on Alexandra as he followed her into the mirror.

Jean Paul saw nothing but blackness. He had the sensation of floating and felt a wet mist surround him. When it cleared, he glanced over his shoulder. He peered at the silhouette of the chateau. A cloud floated across the moon. The chateau disappeared into the darkness. The air was still.

"Get into the coach." Claudette gave Alexandra a push to the steps of the carriage and shoved her up to the door. She nudged her through it. Claudette flopped down next to Alexandra who sat down and leaned back into the seat.

"Wait for me." Jean Paul rushed up the steps of the coach. "I'm coming with you—so live with it." He didn't like Claudette's angry stare as he slammed the door behind him. Alexandra pushed him gently into the seat by the carriage window.

"We need him. We need his help," Alexandra pleaded.

"Oh, all right. If you really think we need him." Claudette snapped from her seat beside Alexandra. "Lie down and cover up with the blanket next to you. You can make believe you're sick if we get stopped." She sighed loudly.

Jean Paul sat very still. He stared at the two women. "Where are we going?"

"Lie down," Claudette shouted.

Jean Paul put his feet up on the seat and scrunched up as he yanked the blanket over him.

Alexandra leaned forward and reached for the cloak lying on the seat next to him. "Lift up your feet so I can get my cape." She threw it over her shoulders and wrapped it tightly around her. She watched Jean Paul's eyes shift back and forth between her and Claudette. Alexandra collapsed into her seat and smiled. "Lie down. I'll explain," she mouthed to Jean Paul.

Claudette leaned out of the window "Go, go," she yelled to Charles. "Use the path through the woods. The revolutionaries are in the side gardens now. They are making so much noise they won't hear us leave. If they do, I hope we'll be able to outrun them with the horses and get far enough away so they won't be able to catch up."

Jean Paul heard the crack of the coachman's whip and the hooves of the horses pounding as the horses ran to the road leading out of the chateau's iron gates. He frowned. "Where are we going?" he roared. No one answered him.

Road to the Abbey Cyr
August 16, 1789

Alexandra was aware of the quick jerk of the carriage as it turned on two wheels. Her body slammed against the back of her seat. "Is there a problem?" She felt a prickling at the base of her neck. They were still in 1789, but time had advanced faster than 2010 time. "What month is it Claudette?"

"It's August. My brother-in-law should be able to travel now," Claudette yelled over the pounding of the horses' hooves. "It's been several weeks since our last trip to the Abbey. We have to get there quickly."

"What's going on?" Alexandra watched Claudette as she stared out of the carriage window.

"Nothing is going on. Everything is fine," Claudette shouted.

Alexandra had a feeling that if Claudette said everything was fine, it probably wasn't. "Claudette, if you want me to help, you have to be truthful with me," she said.

"Oh, all right. We've veered off the main road. There are mobs gathering. They're stopping carriages. We have to travel on sparsely populated roads. It will not be a smooth ride and it will take us longer to get to Paris and the Abbey Cyr, but it will be safer," Claudette said." The revolutionaries are all over now. Things are getting worse. More people are being killed."

"Claudette, tell me about your brother-in-law. Why was he sent to prison? Where was he living when he was sent to prison?" Jean Paul sat up and leaned forward. He looked her in the eyes.

"I already told Alexandra." She sighed. "He lived with me after my husband died."

"What's wrong?" Jean Paul watched the blood drain from her face.

"You…you look just like the man—the judge—who prosecuted and condemned me to death."

"What?" Jean Paul stared back. He looked mystified. "What do you mean?"

"Quick, lie down and cover up," Alexandra interrupted. She leaned out of the window.

"Halt!" A man dressed in dirty clothes waved a gun at them.

She had never seen a gun like it and wondered what this person was going to do as he plodded toward the carriage. She stared at his unkempt hair that stuck out in all directions from under his red cap. He waved a bottle in his empty hand.

"I said halt," he yelled. He held a long neck bottle in his hand. He took a long swig from it.

They're drunk. It's hard to reason with a drunkard. I hope they cooperate and don't block us from getting to Paris. Alexandra stared at them.

"What's the matter, Citizen? Let us go by. We have a very sick man here. He's contagious," Alexandra shouted.

"Where are your cockades?" he yelled.

"*Ici*, here," Claudette yelled as she leaned in front of Alexandra. "They're right here." She pulled her cape open and pointed to her heart. "Show him." She nudged Alexandra as she watched the man as he moved closer to the carriage.

"*Ici.*" Alexandra pointed to her left chest. She watched him strain his eyes. "We're taking our passenger into Paris. I told you he's contagious, so don't get too close."

The dirt stood out on his face as he paled. He took several steps backward. "*Allez, allez,*" he said and waved them on with his filthy hand. "Get out of here. I don't want to get sick."

Charles whipped the horses. He bore down on them. They plunged ahead like a gust of wind propelled them on. When the men were well out of sight, he slowed them down. Their hooves rhythmically pounded on the road.

Alexandra heard church bells ring. She bent over the window. Looking out, she saw that they had just passed St. Radegonde—the church in Giverney. She looked back. The men who stopped them walked toward the chateau. She fixed her eyes on them. Then she saw flames shooting out of the back section of the chateau. "Oh, my God, my things." She flopped back in her seat. "Jean Paul," she whispered. "The chateau is on fire."

"What is going on?" He sat up.

"Don't you remember your history? The revolutionaries destroyed a lot of the country. They burned homes and killed people. The chateau is on fire."

"Yes, I remember my history. Don't worry about your things. They are in 2010. You're tired. I'll watch for the rebels. You try to rest." He stroked her cheek. "I'll let you know if I see anybody about to approach our carriage. I promise I will lie back and play sick if I think we're going to be stopped again." He kept his eyes on the road and on the once beautiful and plush fields that had turned to weeds and dirt. He stared at the wooden huts and the small stone houses on the hillsides, looking for stray rebels. *What have I gotten into? What have I let Alexandra get herself into?*

"I'm sorry. I didn't mean to get you into this mess," Alexandra said.

"It's all right. I sure as hell wouldn't want you to do this on your own. I couldn't have let you go with Claudette. She's a loose cannon. And who knows what kind of problems or evil people we'll run into."

Alexandra turned to Claudette, but her even breathing made Alexandra realize Claudette was in a deep sleep. *How can she sleep? That's right she's a ghost and has relived this scene over and over.*

"Claudette is asleep. I don't believe it, but it's good for us. She is a bit of a drama queen. She could only get us into more trouble if she's awake—more trouble than we're already in."

Alexandra closed her eyes, but she didn't sleep. *We'll be at the Abbey in a few hours.* She relaxed and thought about what they might find at the Abbey. Had the revolutionaries taken over…Were the nuns all right? Was Henri still there and in better health than when they left him? She wasn't sure what she would do if he had gotten sicker or died. How would she handle Claudette?

When she felt the coach slow down, Alexandra leaned out the window. She reached up and pulled on Charles' foot. "How much longer?"

"Soon. Soon. We have to circle Paris and approach the Abbey from the side where the woods are," Charles yelled. "We'll follow the road that borders the woods we walked through the other day."

Alexandra leaned back against the seat and stared out of the carriage. *At least we won't have to ride through the gates of Paris.* Foreboding clung to her. She bumped her shoulder on the edge of the window when the carriage stopped abruptly. "Ouch."

"Are you all right?" Jean Paul reached for her shoulder and rubbed it.

"I'm fine." She stared out of the carriage as she rubbed her arm. "Look! There's the Abbey. The gates are open. Stay here, Charles." Alexandra threw open the door.

Jean Paul looked out of the door. "Wait." He grabbed Alexandra's arm just as she began to leap from the carriage. "Be careful. There are ditches on the side of the road. They are filled with water." He bolted out of his seat and climbed over the trench nearest him. Jean Paul leaned over and picked Alexandra up in his arms before her feet reached the side of the road and the wet ditch. He set her down on the side of the road.

"What about me?" Claudette screamed. "I thought we brought you along to help. You're not helping me."

"All right, Charles, pick her up and get her over the water," Jean Paul shouted over his shoulder. He walked beside Alexandra.

"It looks empty," Alexandra whispered so that Claudette, who followed in silence, couldn't hear. She raised the heavy iron knocker against the door and let it fall several times. "They're not answering."

"Let's see if it's open." Jean Paul pushed on the door. Its hinges creaked as it swung into the hall.

They left the door open as they entered the pitch-black entryway of the Abbey. The sounds of their leather soles on the stone floor echoed loudly. It took a while for their eyes to adjust to the darkness. There was no candlelight, just the bright glow from the moon and stars. As they passed the chapel, Alexandra peered in and stared.

She looked around and stepped into the chapel. "It's empty. The altar is empty. All the treasures are gone. The furniture is gone, even the benches."

"Where are the nuns? Where is my brother?" Claudette pushed past Alexandra and fell in front of the altar. "It's already August and we didn't tell them we were coming. Maybe they're in hiding some place on the grounds. Let's look around."

"Shush. I hear footsteps." Alexandra turned and looked. She peered into the darkness.

An old man with shoulders curved toward the floor shuffled through the doorway at the back of the chapel. He carried a torch. When he reached the altar, he stopped and waved it around and carefully looked at their faces as he walked toward them. "I remember. Some of you were here with the sick man."

He reached them and stopped. "If you're looking for the nuns, they left several days ago. It was getting dangerous—too dangerous for them to stay here." His baggy pants, untailored coat and red cap were in rags, but his cockade was in plain sight and in good condition. The red, white, and blue ribbon was undamaged. "The rebels started to make demands on the nuns. They wanted them to give up their treasures to fund the revolution. So the Reverend Mother and the nuns packed everything they could carry in their bags. I got them some horses. The Reverend Mother drove the carriage you left here. They disappeared in the middle of the night." He began to shake. "The Monsignor closed the Abbey, but not in time. The Revolutionaries confiscated the building and all the church property that was left."

"Where did the nuns go?" Alexandra took hold of his arm. "Please sit down." She helped him sit on the bench in front of her. She looked into his face. His eyes bulged from their sockets with puffy bags of skin beneath them. His skin was dirty. His clothes smelled of sweat. "Did they take the man left here several days ago with them?"

"Yes. They went south." His eyes kept shifting to the doorway. He looked scared.

"How was he—the sick man?" Claudette tugged on his sleeve.

"He seemed a little better than when he arrived."

Alexandra turned toward Jean Paul. "We have to find Henri. I made a promise to her," she whispered. "I have to make sure he's okay."

"Monsieur, *s'il vous plait*, where did they go?" Jean Paul grabbed the man's arm.

"They went to Bordeaux. The man said something about going to sea—something about the New World. Please let me go. I have to leave. The rebels stop by often. I don't want to get caught talking to you. You don't want to get caught. If they capture you, you may be killed—you'd better leave."

"Henri is safe." Claudette wiped her eyes with her sleeve. She rushed over to Alexandra and hugged her.

"Wait. We have to make sure the nuns are safe and Henri got passage to America. We'll go to Bordeaux and search the records." She took hold of Claudette's arm. "You wait for us at the chateau," Alexandra said as she stroked Claudette's hair.

Alexandra turned. She stared in the direction of the altar where the man had stood. He was gone—disappeared. "Hurry. He may report us to the rebels," she yelled as she ran toward the front door of the Abbey. "Get into the carriage." They fell over each other as they ran to the carriage. "Get going, Charles, before we get caught."

No one paid attention to the water in the trenches.

"My shoes are wet," Claudette whined.

"Don't worry about it. You didn't stand in the water long enough for the water to seep through the leather," Alexandra said, shaking her head.

Charles whipped the horses and the carriage was on its way and they settled in their seats.

Jean Paul looked Claudette straight in the eye and demanded, "What did you mean when you said I looked like the man who condemned you? What happened to you?"

"I was wrong. Never mind." Claudette turned to Alexandra and shook her head.

Jean Paul had an uneasy feeling. The hairs on the back of his neck stood up.

"This is as far as we go." Claudette leaned out of the window of the carriage. She tugged on Charles' boot. "Stop the horses," she shouted.

Alexandra gazed up the mountain at the chateau. She jumped from the carriage. Jean Paul followed right behind her.

The chateau was surrounded by clouds that looked dark and ominous. She felt Jean Paul grab her arm. "Let's go before we get soaked. It's going to pour," Jean Paul yelled over the thunder as it began to rain. They ran.

"I'll be in touch when we get back from Bordeaux," Alexandra yelled over her shoulder and waved to Claudette. Alexandra heard the pounding of the horses' hooves as the carriage pulled away. Claudette waved as the carriage disappeared into the mist.

Chateau Verny
July 17, 2010

Alexandra glanced at Jean Paul when they reached the gate of the chateau. She pushed it open. "Did you enjoy your trip back to 1789?" She looked up at the sun.

"Perhaps it was all a dream and when I wake up, I'll be sitting in the dining room with Jacques serving me a paté and fruit." His eyes twinkled as he put his arm over her shoulder and gave her a hug.

"Be serious. If it is a dream, we're both having the same one. Beside our clothes are dirty and wet, and now there's not a dark cloud in the sky."

"At least I know I'm not crazy. I thought I was the only one who could see Claudette and the cast of 1789."

"Yes, I saw them, too." He shook his head. "I hate to admit it, but now I believe in ghosts."

She pulled up her sleeve and glanced at her wrist. "My watch says July, 2010." She looked around the grounds. "And the chateau looks just as it did the day I arrived." Before the gate slammed shut, Alexandra looked over her shoulder and saw the paved road behind her. "We're back." She smiled. "Do you think we'll find what we need in Bordeaux?"

"I don't know, but I'm just going with the flow, as you Americans say, and see what happens." He took large strides as he walked toward the front door of the chateau.

Alexandra walked fast to keep up with him—taking two steps to his one.

"Do you want to go to Bordeaux now or wait until morning?" Jean Paul asked.

"Now. It's only 4 p.m. It should only take a few hours."

"How did I know you would say that?" He laughed. "Pack for a few days. I'll meet you here in thirty minutes." Jean Paul took the stairs two at a time and held open the chateau door for her. He grabbed her hand and pulled her to the main staircase in the entrance hall. "My car is in the parking lot at the side of the chateau. I'll wait for you out front. "You're right. It will take about three hours. You'll enjoy the scenery." He held her in his arms and gave her a bear hug.

Alexandra, laughing, slipped from his embrace and dashed up the stairs. She felt Jean Paul following close behind her. When they reached the second floor, she turned and ran down the hall. "I'll be ready in a few minutes," she shouted and waved to him as he continued to the third floor. She reached her room and threw open the door. Alexandra glanced around. The room was quiet. *Thank God no one is here.*

Assuming they wouldn't be gone more than three days, she packed a pair of tan slacks, a couple silk blouses, underwear, an over-sized T-shirt to sleep in, makeup, and a little black dress, just in case they found a nice restaurant. Alexandra checked the clock on her bedside table. With ten minutes to spare, she changed into stonewashed jeans, a pale blue silk blouse, and her boots, and refreshed her makeup.

She stuffed a pair of dressy black three-inch heels on top of the bag before she zipped it closed. Alexandra opened her jewelry bag and found the pearls her grandmother had given her on her eighteenth birthday. She wrapped them in a handkerchief and slid them into an outside pocket of her suitcase.

She checked her ring while she waited with her case and leather jacket outside the front door for Jean Paul. *Just in case we need it.* It had been almost a week since she arrived. She couldn't believe how much had happened. *What will we find in Bordeaux? Did Henri get to America?* Alexandra sat down on the top step. She didn't wait long. Within a few minutes she heard the roar of his car's motor and the car's wheels crunched on the gravel path. She looked up and saw a black Porsche, with the convertible top down, pull up next to her.

Jean Paul threw the gear into park, jumped out of the car, and grabbed her suitcase. He tossed it into the trunk next to his duffle bag. He walked to the passenger side and opened the door. "Your carriage awaits Mademoiselle."

His blue eyes radiated with something more than friendliness—she wasn't sure what it was—or maybe she didn't want to know what the look in his eyes meant. She felt them becoming more than friends.

John Paul had dressed casually—continental chic—in faded Levis, no tie, an opened neck shirt, a red cable knit sweater, and loafers. "We'll stop in St. Emilion for the night and get an early start to Bordeaux tomorrow. I called an inn before I came down. I think you'll like Hostellerie De Plaisance. It was a monastery hundreds of years ago. It sits in the middle of a vineyard." He watched her stare at him. "Don't worry. I booked two rooms."

She looked over at Jean Paul. "Actually, I was thinking about how wonderful you are and how you think of everything." Her face felt more than warm; she knew it must be bright red.

Chapter Twelve

St. Emilion
July 17, 2010

Jean Paul fastened his seatbelt, revved the motor, and started toward the gate. It swung open as they approached. Alexandra heard the clicking of the turn signal. She watched Jean Paul veer his Porsche to the right after they drove through the gate and push his foot down on the accelerator.

Alexandra looked behind his steering wheel. She heard the snap of her seatbelt as she pushed it into the buckle. She translated the kilometer speed into miles. They were going over a hundred miles an hour before she could blink. She held on to her seat.

They drove in silence for a while. Finally, she relaxed. The road was empty and the ride was very smooth. Alexandra looked at him out of the corner of her eyes. *He is all man—a handsome man. Stop! This is a fact-finding trip. Not a romantic rendezvous.*

They drove on in silence for a while. She tried not to talk over the roar of the engine and the noise of the wind. They made it impossible to carry on a conversation.

She stared out the front window and enjoyed the scenery. They drove by several wineries, the Rothchild Estate, three churches, and wide-open fields. Jean Paul flicked on his headlights as it got darker. Alexandra's eyelids grew heavy. Jean Paul glanced over at Alexandra and smiled. When she had rested her head on his shoulder, he enjoyed it. He turned on his radio; soft music from the forties filled the air.

The next thing she heard was, "Wake up." Her eyes flew open. She saw a sign that said St. Emilion. Jean Paul entered through one of the seven gates that surrounded the town and drove through a large square. He maneuvered down narrow streets and finally turned left on Place Du Clocher. He pushed the gas pedal to the floor as he drove up the steep hill to the hotel.

Alexandra looked up. The hotel looked more like a chateau than a monastery. It looked as if most of the rooms had balconies. A fountain in the front was surrounded by floodlights. The spray of water bounced off the beams making the rivulet glow.

"We're here." Jean Paul pulled into a space near the front door. "They have a gourmet restaurant with a superb wine cellar. Shall I make reservations after we check in?"

"Sounds good. I always enjoy good food and wine." She looked out over the vineyard. The pink, purple, and red of the setting sun made the hotel glow. It was a wonderful tableau. The sun began to sink behind the mountain. She looked at the vineyard and the sand-colored houses of the town. "This is a spectacular view."

Jean Paul pulled the key from the ignition and hit the button that opened the trunk. He met Alexandra at the back of the Porsche. He was surprised when she reached for her suitcase. *Well she's an independent little woman.*

"Here, I'll take that." He grabbed her case before she could pick it up. Together they strolled to the front of the inn.

Alexandra smiled at the doorman as he tipped his hat and held open the door. The heels of her boots clicked on the black and gray marble floor, echoing through the lobby. She walked to the wide, winding staircase where large urns with deep green ferns flanked the ends of the brass railings, and waited for Jean Paul.

"Hello, Claude. I made a reservation with your wife this afternoon."

"It's nice to see you, Jean Paul. Two rooms, *oui?*" He glanced at Alexandra with eyebrows raised.

"*Oui.*" Jean Paul shrugged his shoulders.

Alexandra smiled. She pretended not to hear the exchange as she looked around. The walnut reception desk was massive. The French doors at the rear of the lobby were open. She glanced at the dining tables with candles and flowers. She leaned forward and saw a patio with intimate tables and chairs behind another set of French doors.

Claude hit a bell next to him. A small man in a black suit picked up their bags and disappeared.

"Sign the register, *s'il vous plait.*" He handed Jean Paul two keys.

"Rooms 323 and 324. Take the elevator to the third floor and turn right. Your rooms are at the end of the hall."

"*Merci.*"

Jean Paul waved to Alexandra. "Okay, we're set. Follow me. The elevator is just around the corner in back of the staircase." He smiled as he pushed the 'up' button.

After a moment the elevator door dinged open. The ride seemed to take forever. She felt the closeness of Jean Paul. He made her heart beat a little more rapidly. She walked beside him to their rooms in silence.

Jean Paul handed her the key to her room. "I made our dinner reservations for nine. Is that okay?"

"That's fine."

He glanced at his watch. "It's seven-thirty. I'll knock on your door at about eight forty-five. That should give you enough time to get ready." He smiled as he turned toward his room.

When she entered her room, her bag sat on a bench at the foot of her bed. She opened it and hung up her dress. She wanted to look her best tonight—no wrinkles in her little black dress.

Alexandra stepped from her bath. She shivered instantly. She had forgotten to turn up the heat in the bathroom before she dribbled a packet of crystals for her bubble bath and slipped into the tub.

She grabbed the white terry cloth robe left on the shelf over the garden tub and wrapped herself in it. *The hotel management thinks of everything.* She walked barefoot to the French doors leading to the balcony. When her feet hit the cold stone, she jumped, but kept walking. After she reached the railing, Alexandra gazed down onto the town of St. Emilion.

The lights in the houses and streetlights lit up the cobbled stone streets and the window boxes filled with geraniums. The streets were almost empty. A few people walked their dogs, a young couple walked hand-in-hand slowly down the sidewalk, and a delivery truck approached the hotel.

Alexandra leaned over the balcony and watched it drive down the well-lit alley next to the building and stop at the rear door. Three men leapt out and unloaded several wooden boxes. *Maybe some of that is food for dinner tonight, or maybe it's French wine.* She stood and looked out over the courtyard. A full moon and stars filled the clear sky. It was a beautiful night. The hotel was quiet and elegant. Everything was perfect.

Alexandra wiggled into her black lace underwear and sheer, black panty hose. She slipped her little black dress over her head. After she reached over her shoulder and pulled up her zipper, she slid her feet into her black, silk heels and fastened her pearls—the ones her grandmother had given her on her eighteenth birthday—around her neck. Just as she finished making sure her makeup highlighted the right features of her face, she heard a knock on her door.

"Just a moment." She took a deep breath, slipped on her amethyst ring, and spritzed on some Oscar de La Renta, her favorite perfume. She walked leisurely to the door in her high heels, counted to ten and slowly pulled the door open.

"Ready?" Jean Paul stood with one hand behind him.

Alexandra watched him look her up and down, then draw his hand out from behind his back.

"For a lovely lady." He smiled and handed her a single, red rose. The scent of her perfume swept over him—it was the same one he had smelled the first time he met her—the one she always wore. It mesmerized him. He looked into her eyes. He had the impulse to wrap his arms around her and cover her tantalizing mouth with his. He bent down and kissed her on the forehead.

Her heartbeat thundered in her ears. Alexandra put the rose up to her face and enjoyed the fragrance of his gift. She was aware her cheeks grew warm as she felt his eyes on her. Alexandra rose on tiptoes and kissed him lightly on the cheek. She liked men who were sweet and thoughtful. Alexandra felt his masculine hands engulf her as he took her gently into his arms and pressed her cheek to his chest. She could hear his heart beat in her ear. It was strong and steady.

Alexandra looked up at his face as she stepped back. *He has a surprisingly endearing grin on his very male face.* "You look very preppy in your navy blazer and gray slacks. The light blue shirt and striped tie are perfect," she said.

"Well, I've spent a lot of time in an English prep school. It was the daily uniform. I like being more casual, but this is a special evening."

Alexandra smiled. "The beginning of an adventure."

They walked to the dining room in silence. His arm hung over her shoulder. Alexandra liked the feel of walking close to him. His arm moved to her waist. She liked the feel of his arm around her waist. His familiarity made her happy.

The maître d' led them to a table in the back corner and handed them menus. Alexandra looked around the room. It was small and intimate. There were only ten tables. She stared at the grand piano that stood in the opposite corner. A man in a tuxedo played slow, romantic music. The table linens were unusual and elegant; they were made of a soft, embroidered material. The silverware and china sparkled in the candlelight.

"Thank you, Pierre."

"*Bon appetit*, Monsieur Morneau, and you *aussi*, Mademoiselle."

"You look exquisite," Jean Paul said after they sat down. He was amazed how the soft glow of the candlelight made her green eyes sparkle and her auburn hair shine as it tumbled over her shoulders. He reached forward and held her face in his hands. Her elegant cheekbones were tinged with pink. He pulled her close and kissed her lightly on the lips. Her face flushed. The glow extended to her throat and disappeared under the neckline of the soft material of her dress. She swallowed and moistened her lips with the tip of her tongue.

Alexandra placed the rose on the table beside her wine glass and smiled. Unconsciously she twisted her ring. *Oops,* she thought and stopped twisting it immediately. She didn't want Claudette to appear. She would ruin the mood. Alexandra glanced around the room. *Perhaps it doesn't work all the time.* She saw no one that looked like her ghost. *Maybe she's being good tonight and letting me have a nice evening.*

She glanced at her rose. Alexandra was conscious of that old tingling sensation she felt when there was a man to share things with. She leaned back in her chair. It was something that she hadn't felt in a long time. Maybe it wouldn't be so bad to have a very close male friend in her life. Then she reminded herself she didn't want a committed relationship. She stiffened.

The change in her expression mystified Jean Paul. He let go of her hand and picked up the wine menu. "Shall we start with champagne?"

Alexandra smiled and nodded. She picked up her rose and took a deep breath. She felt wonderful.

When the waiter appeared at their table, Jean Paul ordered, "Krug NV Grande Cuvee Brut, please."

"Where did you go a few seconds ago?" Jean Paul asked, as the waiter disappeared through the swinging doors of the kitchen.

"What do you mean?"

"You looked as if something was upsetting you." He covered her hands with his large ones. He squeezed her long artistic fingers. "Are you all right?"

"Yes." Something *was* happening to her. He was charming, urbane, and much too sexy. She swallowed and pulled her hands free. "I don't know what you mean. I'm fine." She smiled. "There's nothing wrong."

He drew his brows together. He wasn't satisfied with her answer, but decided not to push it and ruin the moment.

The waiter interrupted. "May I pour the champagne, Sir?"

Jean Paul nodded and tasted it. "It's fine." He waited for the waiter to fill their glasses with the chilled champagne. "Merci." He nodded.

"I think you'll enjoy it. It's fermented exclusively in small oak casks. That's what gives it the unique taste. Are you ready to order?" The waiter placed the champagne in the bucket filled with ice and laid a white napkin over it.

"Give us a few minutes, please."

"Yes, Sir."

They raised their glasses after the waiter left. "Bonne chance, may we be successful tomorrow," Jean Paul said.

Alexandra smiled. "Bonne chance."

"We'll leave early in the morning. It's only about thirty-five km. to Bordeaux, but we have a lot of records to search through. Hopefully, if we're lucky, it won't take us more than a day or two to find what we're looking for. Then we can drive back to the chateau and search there."

"Here comes the waiter again. We'd better decide what we want." Alexandra quickly glanced down at the menu.

While they waited for their food, they listened to the clatter of dishes from the other tables and the soft notes of 1940s music coming from the grand piano. They were comfortable with each other even when they didn't talk.

"I know we will find what we need." Alexandra smiled. "I feel lucky."

"If we don't, we can always go back in time and hope the nuns and Henri show up," Jean Paul laughed.

"Actually that's a good idea," Alexandra said. "I think you're enjoying seeing 1789 first hand."

The waiter returned with their food. After he set their meals in front of them, he filled their glasses with champagne again. "*Bon appetit.*" He left quietly.

Jean Paul waited until she took a few bites of her dinner. "How's everything?" Jean Paul asked.

"It's wonderful. This is best bouillabaisse I've ever eaten. The truffle salad is very unusual and quite good. And your fish?"

Jean Paul stuck his fork in his seared sturgeon. "Great." He smiled.

They slid easily into conversation—laughing and talking. They never seemed to run out of things to say.

"Do you come here often? You seem to know everyone."

"I've stayed here a few times. My parents know the owner and his wife. Their son Charles and I were in boarding school together. We weren't really friends, but we see each other at reunions." He grinned at her. "So tell me what drew you to the FBI?"

"My mother died when I was ten and my grandmother raised me. She died this year. Anyway, to get back to what you asked, when I was growing up, I hung out at my best friend's house all the time. She had a normal family. Not a mother and grandmother who disappeared for periods of time with no explanation."

"What do you mean?"

"It's the ring. Now I know their trips had something to do with the ring. They would be gone for days sometimes, leaving me with the household staff, a French couple. When I was little, I would hide in the master bedroom under the bed on the day they were to arrive home. I saw them hide the ring in a box and put it in the closet. Sometimes they were dressed in eighteenth century clothing—beautiful ball gowns."

"What do you think they got involved with?" Jean Paul asked.

"They never talked to me about it. Maybe they tried to help Claudette and weren't successful. I don't know. Anyway, my friend's perfect family included a son whom I married. The marriage didn't last very long—less than a year. It just didn't work out, but that's a story for another time. At any rate his father was an agent, so after I graduated from law school..." She laughed when she saw his mouth drop open. "Yes, I went to law school and took the Bar Exam, but never practiced law.

"After graduation both my friend and I went into the FBI. She's stationed in Spain now. Maybe I'll visit her before I go home." She took a deep breath. "Anyway, I came home to New York City after graduating from Quantico in Virginia. I worked in the New York City office. I didn't live with my grandmother, but she made sure I got good, home cooked meals. I visited her often. She enjoyed hearing about my cases. I miss her a lot. What about your life?"

"I have a brother and a sister. I had the usual life growing up. I went to schools in England—nothing unusual. It was really quite boring."

Alexandra looked around the restaurant. "It's like being in a different world. It's so elegant with all its European charm."

The waiter appeared with a small menu. "Dessert?"

"Of course. I haven't gotten my fill of French desserts yet. I probably never will."

When the music stopped, Jean Paul and Alexandra looked up. They realized they were the last patrons in the restaurant as they finished sharing an apple and almond pastry.

"Would you like a cognac? We can sit out on the patio and look down on the town. I would suggest a walk around St. Emilion, but your heels wouldn't do well on the cobblestone streets."

"Thank you, but I'm just about ready to fall asleep. It's not the company. It's been a busy day and tomorrow will be even busier."

They walked through the lobby to the elevator. Jean Paul draped his arm around her shoulder as they waited. She again felt a tingling in her spine. The doors opened and they stepped out of the way of a young couple that left the lift. Alexandra eye's followed them as they walked arm-in-arm out of the front door. *In love in France.* She smiled.

Jean Paul caught the door before it closed. As they entered, he leaned across her and pushed the button for the third floor.

At her room, Jean Paul pulled her against him, looked down at her, and traced her lips with his index finger. Alexandra felt the rise and fall of his deep breathing. She tensed at first, but after a few minutes she leaned her head against his chest. This time she heard his heart. It thudded strongly and quickly against her ear. He lifted her chin with his hand. A tinge of excitement swept over her as he leaned down. He was going to kiss her, she was sure of it. She felt him gently nibble at her bottom lip, then he cover her mouth with his lips, tenderly at first and then his kiss deepened. She loved the feeling of his lips and responded.

When she leaned back, she ran her finger down the side of his face tracing the scar. "How did this happen?"

"It was nothing mysterious or exciting. I got it in a skiing accident. I slid into a tree. I'm lucky I only have a scar."

"You are." *We would have never met if anything worse happened to you.* "It's late," Alexandra said as she slowly pulled away. Her emotions were becoming involved and her feelings were getting complicated. She smiled up at him. "And I am really tired. I had a wonderful evening—a perfect evening."

"Until tomorrow." Jean Paul turned toward his room.

"Good night," she called to him as she watched him turn the key in the lock of his door. Alexandra stabbed her key at the lock. On the third try, she was successful and turned it. When she heard the click, she twisted the knob and opened the door. She walked slowly into the room. She kicked off her shoes, threw her clothes on the chair near the window and wrapped the hotel robe around her.

Alexandra strolled out on the balcony and stood barefooted, looking out over the town. Her heart hammered. She began to pace restlessly. She was sure that she would never be able to sleep. Her brain was working overtime. As it ticked away, she began making a mental list.

"Jean Paul is intelligent and charming. He's interested in me. Even a glance from him makes my heart pound. It's been a long time since I've felt this way. Lastly, it's good to be in a man's arms again." She felt confused. "What's wrong with me? Am I falling in love with him?" She felt warm inside and speculated on what kind of lover he would be as she sauntered into the bathroom to brush her teeth.

Road to Bordeaux, France

July 18, 2010

She began to feel excited. "I can hear the screeches of the seagulls and smell the salt air." Alexandra strained her eyes. She looked out over the countryside to see if she could see boats on the water.

"We're traveling southwest on A10—near the water. You'll like Bordeaux. It's a seaport on the Garonne River. The river empties into the Atlantic Ocean. Ships have been sailing from the docks here for hundreds of years." Jean Paul reached over and squeezed her hand. He smiled when he felt her squeeze back.

"Do we have a reservation?"

"I made one at a small inn. They only serve breakfast. We'll eat our dinners at one of the many restaurants in town."

"I'm going to gain weight while I'm on vacation. Especially, since I'm eating so many French desserts, though I seem to be doing a lot of walking—so maybe it won't be too bad."

Jean Paul chuckled as he turned and looked her up and down. "A few pounds won't hurt you."

He drove along the river road for a short time and then turned left onto St. Pierre Street. "You'll like the inn. It is furnished with period pieces from the nineteenth century. When the owner bought it five years ago, he restored it to the 1860s, with modern plumbing, of course. There are only ten rooms for guests." He pulled into the parking lot on his right.

Chapter Thirteen

Bordeaux, France
July 18, 2010

"It looks magnificent," Alexandra stared up at a four-story, stone building with three sets of French doors on each floor. The rooms on the front of the inn opened onto balconies with iron railings, except for the first floor. Those doors opened onto a long porch with rocking chairs that looked out onto the street, a manicured lawn and flowering shrubs. French flags, hung from poles on either end of the second floor, fluttered in the gentle breeze. Gaslights stood every few feet in front of the inn near the street. They gave the inn an old-world look—like Victorian times.

Alexandra watched Jean Paul maneuver his Porsche into a slot to the left of the front door. When she heard the key turn the motor off, she watched Jean Paul push the button for the trunk to open and jumped out of her seat. She ran toward the inn.

"I've got the bags," he shouted. "Finally, she is relaxing and letting me do something for her," he mumbled.

"Thanks." Alexandra was already at the top of the ten steps that ended on the porch. She walked to the front door and let the screen slam shut behind her as she burst into the inn. She stood in the entrance hall. She felt as if she was in the country estate of an aristocratic family. A flower arrangement of red and white roses, and blue flowers she didn't recognize, sat in a brass urn on the large, round table in the middle of the entrance. Padded benches covered with off-white embroidered material were placed around the walls.

"*Bonjour.*" A man with dark hair and white sideburns walked out from behind a large, walnut desk and stood in front of her. "Welcome to Hotel Burdigala. *Je m'appelle*, Leo. We gave the inn that name because when the Celts established a small village here in 300 B.C., they called it Burdigala. Today it is called Bordeaux and is a large coastal city with a port."

"*Bonjour*, Leo. I think Burdigala sounds more colorful and poetic." Alexandra stood in front of him. Her eyes were level with his. "I am Alexandra Pirrot." She extended her hand. "It's nice to meet you, Leo." She looked into the eyes of a small man dressed in light gray slacks and a light blue shirt opened at the collar.

"And you must be Messieur Morneau? Leo Leche." He looked over Alexandra's shoulder. He extended his arm and reached for the bell on top of the reception desk. He slid it close to him and tapped it lightly with his fingers. The sound echoed through the hall.

A stooped old man dressed in black pants, a white jacket, and shirt with a black bowtie appeared at the end of the counter. He dragged his feet to their overnight bags and waited.

"I have put you in two rooms on the second floor. You'll be in the front overlooking the park and the Garonne River."

"*Merci*," they said in unison.

"My first passion is this inn. My next passion is wine. We're having a tasting tonight in the dining room. Would you like to join us? All my guests will be there. We will be sampling wines from all over Bordeaux—Mouton Rothschild, Medoc, St. Emilion and many more. It starts at six."

Jean Paul looked at Alexandra and smiled when she nodded. "We're here to do some research about Bordeaux in the eighteenth century, but we will join you. *Merci*," Jean Paul said.

Jean Paul took Alexandra's hand. "A wine tasting will be fun."

"Anton will show you to your rooms. Until six." He waved.

Anton's gnarled old hands didn't stop shaking until he picked up the bags.

They followed him to an elegant, gray, marble staircase with a thick-piled, red carpet. Brass rods held the rug down on each riser. The elevator stood across from the winding staircase that led to the second floor.

Alexandra looked up at the crystal chandelier above their heads. The prisms moved gently in a breeze from a large, open window at the top of the stairs, making a light, musical sound.

She jumped at the clank of the elevator's chains when it reached the ground floor.

"The lift has arrived." Anton pushed back the brass grill. He waited for the main door to slide open and held it so Alexandra and Jean Paul could enter.

Alexandra moved to the back and leaned against the mirrored wall. She read the sign on the wall next to her. "No more than six persons." She laughed. "Three of us and two overnight cases can barely fit in here." She waited for Anton to push the button labeled 'two'.

The lift shook and shimmied as it moved slowly to their floor. When the elevator ground to a stop, chains clanking, the door slid open. Anton pushed open the safety door. They followed him down the hall to their rooms.

He twisted the key in the lock of 214, entered the room, bent over and dropped Alexandra's bag on the luggage rack. He straightened up as he walked to the door. It took him a few minutes to get back into a semi-upright position.

Jean Paul gave her a hug as she started into her room. "I'll meet you in the lobby in twenty minutes. All right?" He smiled.

"Okay. I can't wait. We're finally going to find out what happened to Henri and the nuns. Hopefully we won't end up in the middle of a revolution."

Jean Paul winked at her and nodded. He followed Anton to room 215.

Alexandra threw open the French doors to the balcony off her room and walked to the rail. She leaned over the wrought-iron fence and stared out over the river. It startled her when she heard someone clear his throat. She turned in the direction of the noise. Surprised, she watched Jean Paul leaning over the railing of his balcony. He was staring out into gardens. He glanced over at her and smiled.

"I'll be ready in five minutes. See you downstairs." She turned and waved as she backed into her room drawing her French doors closed. Alexandra opened her case, dashed into the bathroom, and touched up her makeup that was tastefully under-applied. She grabbed her key. Letting her door slam behind her, she ran down the hall to the elevator. When the door opened to the lobby, she stepped out and bumped into Jean Paul. "You beat me."

"Took the stairs."

"That's what I should have done."

"We still have a few hours until lunch. Where do you want to start?" Jean Paul grabbed her hand.

Alexandra felt tingles run down her spine. "We're near the ocean where the boats landed and left for other countries. Point us in the direction of any church that you think was here in the eighteenth century and is near the docks. I'm thinking perhaps there might be a record of the nuns and maybe Henri in one of the church's archives—if we're lucky. They probably stayed in this area since it's near the water. So, let's start checking the churches around here."

"We're not too far away from the Cathedral. It fits the bill. It was here before the revolution. It's the largest church in the area." He pointed up to his left. "See, the twin spires of Cathédrale de Saint-André. Shall we walk? Hopefully it will be the one we're looking for."

"Sure." She gazed at the spires. "Let's go."

They walked hand-in-hand to the Cathedral. Alexandra didn't even notice her surroundings. She was too excited. When they got near to the entrance of the church, she noticed a woman with dark hair and a light tan complexion. She was dressed in a long dress with a scarf draped around her head and several strings of silver beads around her neck. She held a small basket in her hand.

Jean Paul leaned close to her. "Be careful, she's a gypsy. Just shake your head and move quickly into the church. The gypsies are always begging. They can be very difficult," he whispered.

Alexandra looked straight ahead and ignored the woman who stood very close to the church door. She almost blocked the entrance.

"Be very careful. You are in danger." The woman whispered to Alexandra as she tried to stand closer her.

Alexandra held her arms tightly around her chest as she squeezed by her. She stuck her hand out to where the doorknob should have been and found a donut-shaped hoop ring. She pushed on the door.

"It's an angelus." He reached around her and lifted the ring. He pulled it toward him. The high recessed wooden door with brass hinges yawned open.

Alexandra moved into the vestibule and waited for her eyes to adjust to the darkness. She enjoyed the quietness of the church. It seemed to calm her.

"Let's look for the church offices," Jean Paul whispered into her ear as he led her down the aisle toward the front of the Cathedral. Alexandra glanced at the antique statues, tapestries and frescos. Candles in sconces lighted the walls.

"Look how the light from the candles make the statues cast shadows on the walls. It's eerie." She ran her hand over one of the tapestries. "I wish I had more time to examine these. They're elegant. I just can't imagine someone spending the hours needed to create a piece of art like these. Whoever created these must have had tiny hands to be able to weave these intricate designs."

She stared up the aisle at the gilded altar made of a polished wood. "It's beautiful. Who wouldn't want to take communion here?"

"There's a brass plate on the door in the hallway behind the altar," Jean Paul said. "See? It's on the right." He led Alexandra to the door.

The gothic door, with a nameplate labeled *Church Office*, was ajar. Alexandra knocked softly on it as she slowly pushed it open. She stared at an elderly priest dressed in a black cassock. He sat in a dark red, leather, winged-back chair behind an ornately carved desk. His reading glasses sat on the bridge of his nose as he concentrated on the words in the leather-bound book in his hands. He was taking notes on a yellow, lined pad of paper with his free hand. He looked up when he felt the cool breeze that flowed into the room.

"*Bonjour.*" Jean Paul stood in the doorway.

"*Bonjour.* I'm working on my sermon. Enter, *s'il vous plait.* May I help you?" He closed the book and put down his pen and slid the yellow pad to his right.

Alexandra glanced around the office. Tapestries and paintings lined the walls to her left and right. She moved slowly and stood beside Jean Paul, who had reached the desk in a few large strides.

Behind the desk, red velvet draperies framed the windows. The leaded glass of the windows cut off some of the daylight, but still allowed the room to fill with natural light. She stared at the dark, wooden built-in shelves that flanked the drapes and were crammed with religious and contemplative books—each leather-bound.

The priest straightened his hunched shoulders, took off his glasses and laid them on the desk. "I'm Father Bernard." The priest rubbed his eyes, and then extended his hand.

"Jean Paul Morneau and this is Alexandra Pirrot." Jean Paul grasped the priest's hand and returned his firm grip. "We would like to look through your eighteenth century records. Do you have such records in your archives? *Pouvez-vous m'aider?*" Jean Paul asked.

"We're looking for relatives who disappeared during the Revolution." Alexandra added. "We hope you can help us."

"You're in luck. We do have records from that time. Not a great many, but several notations. It was bad times then, as you know. We have rooms below the church. The revolutionaries never found our hiding place so the records and artifacts from that time were saved." He smiled as he replaced his glasses on the bridge of his nose. "We also were able to rescue some of the clergy and nobles. They usually hid in one of the rooms in the spire of the church that doesn't hold the bellworks. There's a secret staircase in the spire that takes you to the rooms, though sometimes they stayed under the church. There are secret rooms there also. Now we mainly keep church records there.

"When the Reign of Terror reached its peak, the churches were looted and the beheadings of the clergy began. The church tried to help. We hid people until we could get them on a ship or smuggle them into another country."

"We're interested in the summer of 1789—July and August. In particular were looking for records of nuns that traveled here from the Abbey Cyr in Paris and a man's name that may have been traveling with them," Alexandra said.

"If the nuns stayed here, they most likely lived in the spire. The underground is too damp and cold to stay for any length of time. There are small rooms halfway up the tower. If you find their names in the records in the archives, we'll look into the rooms," Father Bernard said. "The man may have gotten on a ship—many escaped that way. He would have been hard to hide for a long period of time. The revolutionaries would soon find out he wasn't a priest, so he probably left soon after they arrived. The nuns would have been considered part of the clergy and would have blended in with the priests. The Revolution went on for ten years, you know. People came and went. However, if they came here, there will be records, even if it's a few sentences."

"We think that's what happened," Alexandra said. "The man got on a ship. We hoped the nuns were saved." She smiled. "Where should we look first?"

"Come with me, we will go to our storage rooms." Father Bernard smoothed his black cassock after he stood. "There was a staircase behind the altar leading to the small rooms under the chapel during that time. There used to be a trap door under the altar. In earlier days, the altar moved. You had to descend one hundred steps under the church to a hallway that led to the cells or as you might say—small rooms. Now we have an elevator at the end of the courtyard behind my office." Father Bernard picked up his glasses, held them up to the light and wiped them with the handkerchief he pulled from his pocket. He motioned for them to follow him.

They walked through an opened-roof courtyard. At the end of the path, the priest pulled on a heavy iron door in the wall. "This is our elevator." After they entered, Brother Bernard leaned close to the panel with numbers and pressed a button that was labeled *Archives*.

As they slowly descended beneath the main floor of the cathedral, Alexandra held her arms around her chest. She felt it getting colder the closer the elevator got to the archives. The lift bounced up and down a few times when it hit the bottom floor. The door creaked open.

The priest handed them candles from a tin box just outside the elevator door and lit them with a twenty-first century lighter. He turned right and proceeded down a hallway that was damp and cold. Water dripped off the thick, stone walls. Sconces with candles lined the walls every few feet. He lit them as they walked down the corridor. They followed Father Bernard through a series of halls that were like the tunnels of a labyrinth. Alexandra felt a cool breeze. Their candles flickered. Alexandra held her hand around the flame so that it didn't blow out. Father Bernard finally stopped at a room with a sign on the door that was labeled 1700.

"Bishop Remy was in charge during the Revolution. They say that he was very organized. So if the records you are looking for do exist, you'll have a good chance finding them. He pulled open the thick wooden door with brass hinges. He lit the oil lamps that sat on the floor just inside the door and pointed to the steel filing cabinets. "The records are in the cabinets." Father Bernard turned. "There's a table and chairs for you to sit at while you do your research." He looked back over his shoulder. "Don't worry about the candles. Leave them burning. I'll take care of them after you leave. Will you be able to find your way back to my office?"

"Yes. We just follow the dates on the doors. The twentieth century documents are closer to the elevator, right?" Alexandra smiled.

"You were paying attention." He turned toward Alexandra. "I won't worry, then." He chuckled. "1930 is next to the elevator. Just push the button labeled chapel to get back up to the courtyard. If you don't come back by two p.m., I'll come down and find you. I wish you luck. Father Bernard left the door open as he turned and started to walk back to the elevator.

"Okay. Thank you. We'll come and get you if we need help." Alexandra's eyes followed him as he left.

"I guess we start by looking for a cabinet labeled 1780."

She picked it up the lantern and held it above her shoulder.

Jean Paul moved toward the cabinets against the wall on his left. "Let's see 1700." He read down the drawers of the file cabinet. "1710, 1720, 1730… We're in luck." He opened the drawer part way.

"There has to be dim light. Parchment fades in the light." Alexandra reached her arm around him to finger through the manila envelopes. The drawer moved open all the way.

"Careful." Jean Paul backed into her. "We have lots of time."

"I'm sorry," she said. "I didn't mean to hit you in the stomach."

"I'm fine," he laughed. Jean Paul thumbed through the envelopes. "*Voila*, here's the one that says 1789. You take August and I'll take July." He separated the piles and handed her the August papers. He leafed through the papers of July and pulled out the tattered papyrus with handwritten text and placed them on the table. "These pages are going to be hard to decipher."

Jean Paul turned toward Alexandra. "Let's sit down. It may take us a while."

They sat down, putting the lamp between them in the middle of the table, and studied the papers.

Jean Paul leaned toward Alexandra." Do you remember their names—the nuns' names?"

"No. The only name I heard was Reverend Mother…Wait! There was a Sister Marie." Alexandra gently turned the parchment pages. "Here they are." She let him see the record on page fifteen, and pointed to a paragraph in the middle of the page. "They came here. I knew it!" She turned the page. "I have to translate. It will take a few minutes. It says the nuns arrived in the middle of the night and asked for asylum. Whoever wrote this said they begged for help. It's dated August eighteenth. It must be them."

"Do the records mention Henri?" Jean Paul asked.

"Not by name, but it says there were five nuns and one young man. My French is not that good, but it says that the young man that was with them was ill." She turned the pages. "There's nothing else. The notations end."

"Here, look." He took some of the pages from her. "It says one of the priests helped the nuns take the man to a ship headed for the New World. It's called the United States today, as you know. The ship he left on was called *The Scipion.* Notations in the margin say the nuns hid in the spire and were guests at the cathedral for several months until they escaped to Austria." Jean Paul pointed to the record.

"You're the Frenchman. I should have let you do the translating." She laughed.

"Come on, let's go see the rooms." Alexandra returned the records to the cabinet and blew out the lamp. She ran out of the room and down the hallway. She reached the door labeled 1950. "Oh damn." She turned and saw Jean Paul laughing as he waited for her at the elevator.

"Don't worry I closed the door," Jean Paul called to her.

When they reached the courtyard, the elevator ground to a stop. Jean Paul pushed the door open. Alexandra grabbed his arm and pulled him to Father Bernard's office. She knocked on the closed door.

"*Entré.*" The priest looked up. "Did you find what you were looking for?"

"Yes, they were here in August of 1789. Can we see the room in the spire now?" Alexandra turned toward the door.

"Yes, of course. You have to walk up a winding staircase. No elevator."

"That's fine," she answered. "It's okay with you, right?" She stared at Jean Paul.

"Yes. I work out every day."

"Which one?" Alexandra stepped back so that the priest could lead the way. They reached two spires.

"This is the one that leads to the rooms." He pointed straight ahead. "The other one holds all the bell works. No one would have hid there. The bells are so loud anyone would have been driven crazy."

He felt along the wall and found a ridge. He pushed on a button hidden behind a metal hinge that looked as if it only held the door to the wall. The door creaked open. Father Bernard flipped a switch and the staircase lit up. "There was no electricity when the nuns stayed here. They had to maneuver the stairs by candlelight. It must have been very hard for them. They weren't young."

Alexandra started to run up the staircase, but slowed down when she heard the heavy breathing of the priest. "I'm sorry. I get excited." She waited for him to catch up and let him squeeze by her so he could lead the way. Alexandra stood quietly when they reached the door to the first room. While she waited for Father Bernard to open it, her heart pounded.

He stood for a moment and caught his breath.

She watched him pull a large, brass key from his pocket and turn it in the lock. It took a few minutes for him to push the door open.

She glanced around the small room. Daylight came into the room from a small window that was close to the ceiling. Her eyes adjusted slowly to the dimness. Alexandra sneezed. Dust covered the floor, and a lone, wooden chair. "They must have been crowded…one bed. A large cot with a lumpy mattress sat against the wall. Do you think they all stayed here?"

Alexandra asked. She ran her hand over the mattress. Her fingers were covered with dust.

"They probably stayed here because I'm sure some of the nuns were old. They would have found it difficult to walk too far up the spire," Father Bernard said. "There were probably more cots and blankets in here. More than one person stayed in the room, I'm sure."

"I don't see anything to prove they were here," Jean Paul answered. "Where is there a place to hide something? I don't see any loose floor boards or a small hole anywhere in the floor." His eyes closely scanned the room. "The walls are made of cement."

"I'm not going to give up. Wait! Let's see." Alexandra moved her hand under the thin mattress and slid it around. "Wait, I feel a lump." Her fingers pushed into a small hole. She wiggled her fingers around in the hole. "Look." Alexandra yanked out a silver cross with a large ruby where the two pieces of silver met. "There was one just like this always hanging from around the Mother Superior's neck. I'm surprised it is still in good shape. Rubies are very soft and damage easily."

"Well, I guess we have proof, unless every nun wears a cross exactly like this one." Jean Paul smiled. "I doubt there is another one like this; it looks like one of a kind."

Alexandra handed the cross to Father Bernard. "This is for you to add to your church treasures."

"*Merci*, I can't believe that no one found it before now, but then we never looked in the mattress and no one has slept on it for hundreds of years." He held the cross close to his chest. "I'll lay it on the altar when we get back to the sanctuary."

"Nobody but the nuns knew it was in the mattress and they've been gone over two hundred years."

"When I found the loose threads and the lump, I knew the nuns must have sewn something into the mattress. I didn't know it was a cross. Others who slept on the cot probably thought it was just a bumpy mattress. No one would have found it unless they knew about the cross and searched carefully. But I'm sure wherever the Reverend Mother is, she is happy it is in a place where it may be appreciated by many and in the Cathedral where it belongs."

"You surprise me. How did you know about the cross?" Father Bernard asked.

"It's a long story. There are family records."

"I thank you for your donation."

"*Bonjour* and thank you for your help." Alexandra waved to Father Bernard when her foot hit the last step of the spire.

"May the peace of the Lord be with you." The priest waved goodbye.

"And also with you," she called over her shoulder.

"Well we found the information we needed to help in the search for long lost relatives."

"Telling a priest a lie, aren't you ashamed?" Jean Paul laughed. He put his arm around her and pulled her close to him and kissed her on the top of her head. "You are such a good person. I'm glad you came to the chateau for a vacation."

Alexandra leaned over and kissed his cheek. "He wouldn't have understood if I told him I saw her wearing it. I don't think I'll have a long stay in Purgatory for a little white lie." She turned to Jean Paul when she heard the church bells chime six times. "Well, that was easy," Alexandra said. "Tomorrow the shipyard, to see what happened to Henri."

He leaned down and brushed dust from her hair. "It's wine tasting time." Jean Paul smiled. He wanted to kiss her, but settled on squeezing her hand as they left the Cathedral.

Chapter Fourteen

Bordeaux
July 19, 2010

"What?" Jean Paul felt a tap on his shoulder. He turned around and looked up.

"Going my way?" Alexandra sat down next to him on the top step of the hotel's front porch. "What are you doing up so early?" She could see the lights in the houses near the inn flick off as the sun began to rise. Alexandra offered him one of the two paper coffee cups.

He looked at her and laughed. "I wanted to see the sun rise. Black with two sugars, right?"

Alexandra nodded. "Of course. It's going to be a beautiful day."

"Thank you." He took a long drink. "Just right."

"By the way, thank you for getting me to my room last night. A wine tasting without eating all day was not very smart on my part, even if they did have fancy hors d'oeuvres. I didn't want it to look like they were my dinner. So I didn't eat too many. Did I make a fool of myself?"

"No problem. Your behavior was beyond reproach last night. You sure are perky this morning."

"I've been up for a couple of hours; I took a long walk and scoped out the warehouses where the records are stored for French ships that have left the docks of Bordeaux and returned to the port over hundreds of years. There are several buildings."

"Well, well, you've been busy. Why are you up so early? It's only six-thirty."

"I am an early riser, especially when I am about to solve a mystery."

He stood up and grabbed her hand. "Come on, let's go."

"Wait. Let me finish my coffee." She took a long swallow, crumpled up her cup and tossed it into the wastebasket on the porch next to the front door. "Look at that! I got it in on one try."

"I'm taking mine with me."

They strolled down the front path of the inn to the main street, turned left on St. Pierre Street and walked toward the Pont de Pierre—the stone bridge that led to the old Bordeaux near the sea. "It's not too warm and a mile walk will be good exercise." Alexandra heard the clock of the Cathedral chime seven. She enjoyed the tree-lined road that led to the port warehouses and docks. Foot traffic began to get heavy. Men and women carrying briefcases hurried past them to tall buildings in front of the docks. They dashed through the streets, jaywalking and running past red lights. *Just like the United States.*

Jean Paul and Alexandra were very close to the docks. The warehouses were just ahead of them.

"It's a good thing that we got an early start. There will be a lot of records to go through," Jean Paul said.

"Well, we know Henri probably sailed on the *Scipion*, a ship built by the French Navy. If the records of the church are correct, we have a place to start. What are you staring at?"

"You know you look exactly like Claudette." He took a large swallow of his coffee, crumpled his cup and tossed it into the trash can at the head of the path leading to the gate house.

"You really think so?"

"You have auburn hair. It's long and curly, like hers.

"I'm from the Pirrot side of the family. Remember?" Alexandra said.

"I still think you look like her."

"Well, people who study and believe in reincarnation would tell you we change over the generations and we are born to a new body. You could be born as a male if you were a female, or as someone's brother if you were a son." Alexandra laughed. "Maybe I'm a reincarnation of Claudette this time around."

"What time do you think the offices at the docks open?" Alexandra asked as they crossed the bridge over the Garonne River.

"The warehouses store cargo taken off ships and cargo to be loaded on the ships. We just have to find the building with all the old records. The offices at the docks open early—by six a.m. and close late—eight p.m. We have all day." He grabbed her hand and pulled her to the booth ahead of them.

Jean Paul knocked on the glass window of the small building labeled Logis-Porté—Gatehouse—fortified with brick walls and bulletproof glass.

"What was that?" Alexandra heard a large thud. She strained her eyes as she peered through the glass that started halfway up the gate." She smiled. "You must have scared him. He was leaning back in his chair and fell off."

Jean Paul laughed. "He must be on the night shift and was probably sleeping." He looked through the glass; the man was sitting on the floor. When the guard righted himself, "Buildings records?" Jean Paul yelled through the glass. "Where can we find the old records from the eighteenth century?"

The guard rubbed his eyes. He struggled to stand. When he was upright, he slid back the glass partition and leaned out over the ledge. "Down two warehouses, turn right. It will be the first building on your left," he mumbled.

They walked to the entrance of the historical wing of building three. Jean Paul knocked on the door. When they heard a continuous buzzing, Jean Paul grabbed the handle and pulled it open. The clerk sat behind a large, metal desk. He looked up from his computer when they entered.

"*Bonjour.* May I help you?"

"*Bonjour.* I'm Jean Paul Morneau. This is Alexandra Pirrot." He smiled. "We are doing some genealogy research. May we look through your records for a ship called the *Scipion* and the dates it sailed during the seventeen hundreds? We're looking for a sailing date in the summer of 1789 going from here in Bordeaux to the United States. We're interested in the names of the crew and any passengers that sailed on the ship."

"That was during the Revolution. The records are skimpy, but you can look at them. They're in warehouse number three. Go out this door, turn right and walk down the wharf past about five buildings. The historical building will be on your right. Here's a slip." He placed it in Alexandra's hand and watched her stuff it into the pocket of her slacks. "Hand it to the guard. He will direct you to the right stack of boxes. Be careful, Miss. He won't be able to read it if it gets too wrinkled. "Keep it flat. Don't fold it."

"*Merci,*" Alexandra said. "It must be a slow day. Did you see? He was playing spider solitaire," Alexandra commented as they left.

She grabbed Jean Paul's hand and pulled him toward the repository. After they reached the door, she knocked. When the door slid open, she saw a tall man standing in front of them. "May I help you?"

"Yes, please." She dug into her pocket, smoothed out the pass before she handed the uniformed man the slip.

He studied the paper. "*Entré.*" He walked to his desk and booted up his computer. After a few minutes, he looked up. "The records for the ships that sailed in the 1780s will be on the left hand side on the top shelf at the back of the building. They are at the end of row ten. There's a ladder." The guard stood and walked in front of them. "Follow me." He grabbed a roll of plastic tape from the top of his desk and handed it to them. He pointed to the end of a large row, then pointed to the section they needed. "It's down there." Please seal the boxes when you finish," he said as he walked back to his desk.

When they reached row ten, Jean Paul looked at the top shelf. The boxes were labeled in large, dark letters. "It's a maze. There must be hundreds of years of records here," Alexandra said as they hurried to aisle ten. She stared at the thousands of brown cartons taped with clear sealing tape.

When they reached the back of the passageway, Jean Paul dragged the ladder from the corner to the last row. He climbed up, ran his fingers over the labels. He searched through the dated boxes for ships and year. "Here it is—1780s. There are three boxes."

"It looks like a lot of ships went in and out of Bordeaux even though there was a revolution going on," Alexandra said, looking at the stack of boxes.

He scanned the labels. "The *Scipion*—years 1785 to 1789" was the third box from the top. He pulled out the boxes one at a time and handed them down to Alexandra. "Just lay them on the floor. We'll put them back up when we finish."

"Be careful." Alexandra watched him back down the steps of the ladder with the box that held the information they were looking for. "Need help?"

"No thanks. Got it."

"Guess we'll have to sit on the floor." Alexandra plopped down with her back to the boxes on the first shelf.

"We could always go back to the office. There were chairs there."

"I can't wait that long," Alexandra smiled.

Jean Paul pulled back the tape and flipped through the manila envelopes. "Here's the one for 1789. Looks like the whole year is here." He flipped through the manila folders. "January, February, March…Here they are—July and August." Jean Paul pulled out half of the papers and handed them to Alexandra.

"Thanks." She began to sift through her records. After an hour, Alexandra put down her part of the stack. She leaned back and stretched her shoulders. "I'm hungry."

"There's a café just outside the shipyard. When we finish, we'll stop there."

Alexandra resumed her search. After a few minutes, she shouted. "I found it! I found the date it sailed!" Alexandra held the page up. "Look! Here it is. The *Scipion* loaded its cargo August 20, 1789 and sailed August 21, 1789 to the New World. It says their mission was to help the Americans after the War of Independence," she read on.

"It sailed early in the morning. The captain was Nicolas Henri de Grimouard. His first port of call for the ship was the West Indies to restock. They reloaded supplies and sailed to Virginia. Let's hope they made it and didn't get lost in a hurricane. August is the month for bad weather in that part of the world."

Jean Paul shuffled through his stack of papers. After a few minutes he smiled. "Found more papers for that sailing." Jean Paul began to read the manifest.

"The *Scipion*—a 74-gun ship of the French navy. Name—*Commerce de Scipion*, Builder—Rochefort. In service 1786. Displacement—2966 gross tons, 5260 tons fully loaded. Length—55.87 meters, Armament—cast iron of various weights. Is docked at slot 240. Provisions—meat, vegetables, fruit, flour, spices, water, and wine," Jean Paul read.

"Of course there was wine. Bet they had lots of wine or they wouldn't be real Frenchmen." Alexandra laughed. "Come on, let's find out where they sailed."

"Don't be impatient. Docked in Bordeau, France—Latitude 44* 50'N. Longitude O* 34' W. Sailing to Port-au-Prince Haiti—Latitude 18*32" N. Longitude 72* 20" W. Final destination Virginia—Latitude 45* 35" N. Longitude 94* 11'W. Trip 3976 nautical miles."

Alexandra peered over his shoulder as Jean Paul read. "Here's a log of the crew's names."

She pulled the paper from his hand and studied it. "The first mate was Pierre Cardone. There were one hundred fifty-five crew, forty officers and twenty passengers." She scanned the list—no Henri Pirrot. "Maybe he was a last minute passenger." Alexandra showed him the sheet. "We have to get back to the summer of 1789 and see if he was on the ship. Since we're at the dock, I hope the ring will bring us back to August 21, 1789."

"All right. Do whatever you do with the ring to get us back there."

"First we have to find a costume shop. We'll dress as the rebels of 1789 and then go back to the docks and see what happens. I hope there's one close by."

Jean Paul stuffed the papers carefully back in the folder and the folder back into the box. He sealed up the box with the tape and climbed the ladder. "Everything's back where we found it. Okay, Alexandra, we're off to a costume shop," Jean Paul said as he pushed the ladder back to the end of the aisle.

They ran back to the entrance of the building and the guard.

"Do you know where we can find a costume shop?" Alexandra asked the guard.

"There's one not too far away. After the guard shack, go straight ahead one block, turn left, second shop on the right."

"Hurry. It's noon. If we're right, they're already loading the cargo. The passengers will be the next to get on."

She rushed toward the shop and pushed open the door. "Do you have costumes depicting the 1780s?" Alexandra said quickly. "We need them right away." She took a deep breath.

"*Mais oui.* How long a rental?"

"Just today—a few hours," Alexandra said.

"Fifteen Euro each."

Alexandra looked at Jean Paul. She watched him nod his head. "Fine." He dug into his pants' pocket.

The shopkeeper disappeared into the backroom. When he returned, he held a plain, gray dress, apron, and dust cap for Alexandra and baggy pants, shirt, and red cap for Jean Paul in his arms. Both costumes had a tricolored cockade on the left chest—right over the heart. "I think these will fit. I have a dressing room in the back." He pointed behind him. They followed his gesture and dressed quickly pulling the clothes over their own. They looked just like rebels from the French Revolution.

Jean Paul and Alexandra rushed back to the docks. When they reached the docks they ran to slot 240 where the ship would have been in 1789. "I hope this works." Alexandra twisted her amethyst ring.

Bordeaux, France
August 21, 1789

Fog spread over the coast, hanging like a gray shroud. It covered the harbor making it hard to see the ships sitting at the dock. A fine mist collected on Alexandra's hair, as she and Jean Paul stood leaning on the rail of the dock close to the *Scipion*. They watched the activity of the sailors on the dock as they load boxes into the cargo hole of the *Scipion*. The wind blew. They could hear the groans and creaks of the ship as it rolled back and forth in its birth.

Jean Paul kissed the top of her head. "You did it."

"Let's get closer to the gangplank. Look, there's a young man in rebel clothes. His cockade is visible. His long, light brown hair is tied in a ponytail. He looks like Henri. He must have hurt his leg. He's dragging his left foot as though it were attached to an anchor," Alexandra said. "I thought he would see a doctor. I guess his problem with his walking was worse than I thought."

"He seems to be all right, except for the limp." Jean Paul stared at the man. "He has a stick to help him walk up the gangplank."

"The deck is wet. I hope he doesn't fall." A tear ran down Alexandra's cheek "He's so despondent. Look at his slumped shoulders and ragged clothes."

"The nuns dressed him well in the ragged clothes. No one will question him," Jean Paul said.

"He has a dog that's walking right beside him who looks fierce," Alexandra said. "I've never seen that breed before. What kind is it?" she asked as she strained her eyes to see it.

"Heavy, broad shoulders, massive head, and muscular legs…thick, loose skin that covers its bulky neck. Looks like a French Mastiff to me." Jean Paul stared at the dog. "They are very loyal pets and very protective of their masters."

They watched the man exchange words with the captain. The man leaned close to the captain and whispered something in his ear. The captain said something back. Then the man answered and handed him a slip of paper. Henri pulled a pouch from his coat pocket. With his free hand, he shook some coins into the captain's hand.

"He did board at the last moment, probably hoping to not attract too much attention or questions," Alexandra commented.

Trying to keep hidden from the roaming revolutionaries who might stop them and cross-examine them, they slid up to the side of the ship close to the gangplank. They tried to blend in with the sailors and passengers.

Jean Paul and Alexandra kept their eyes on Henri as he paced from bow to stern. Finally, he sat down, leaned against the wheelhouse, took out a pen and pad of paper, and began to write.

"I'm sure it's Henri." Alexandra moved closer to the ship. "Henri, Henri," she yelled.

The young man turned toward the sound of her voice. He stared at her and squinted. His faced lit up as if he recognized her. He smiled and waved. He yelled back, but his words were lost in the wind that blew across the water.

"I knew it was him. Well, with a dog like that, I won't worry about Henri. No one will mess with him," Alexandra said.

They stood and watched the sailors get ready to sail. A gust of wind blew the sails and a light rain started. They heard the timbers strain and the ropes slapped and banged against the mast. The French flag snapped with the rising breeze off the water. They waited until the ship pulled away from the dock.

"He'll be fine. Let's get going before the rain gets worse and we get soaking wet. We need to trace your family's genealogy to find out what happened to Henri and the rest of your relatives." Jean Paul squeezed her hand.

"We have to find out how you're related to these people, too. If we can find out about Claudette's children and what happened to them, it might help us find out who really owns Chateau."

Alexandra twisted her ring. She looked around. "We're back. Everyone is dressed in twenty-first century clothes. Come on. Let's get rid of these costumes." She pulled her dress over her head. "Ask the shop keeper where we can find an Internet café." She looked at him and smiled. "Please."

Internet Café - Bordeaux
July 21, 2010

"How do we get into the French ancestry sites? I tried in the States before I left for this trip, but couldn't get in. It was almost impossible to get registered. I thought I would try when I got here, because I would have an address in France." Alexandra sat down next to Jean Paul at a computer in the Internet cafe.

"I'll show you," Jean Paul said.

"I'll get some coffee while you boot up the machine." When she got back, she saw Jean Paul typing on the keyboard.

"The site is hard to access if you don't have a special password. I go in through the French court system's web page that is hooked to the historical society." Jean Paul entered the website, typed in his user name, JP Morneau@att.com and then his password—JPM1974. The web page popped up.

He's three years older than I am, if that's his birth year he's using in his password. She smiled. "Type in the name, Claudette Pache," she said. Alexandra watched the page with the Pache history appear on the screen.

"Here's the page we're looking for." Jean Paul read out loud. "Claudette Marie Pache was born 1759 and died 1793, French citizen. Her mother, Mary Elizabeth Delaney, was born 1731 and died 1779—Irish citizen."

"Well now we know where Claudette's auburn hair came from—her mother." Alexandra smiled.

Jean Paul stared at the screen. "Her father, Jean Gaspard Pache, was born 1729 and died 1769—French citizen.

"My auburn hair come from Claudette." Alexandra asked.

Jean Paul scrolled down the screen. "Claudette married Jacques Louis Pirrot who was born 1757 and died 1787. He was a soldier in King Louis XIV's army. He was loyal to the King. It looks like he did have a brother, Henri Emile, who was born 1758. There's no date of death—no profession listed. He must have been a playboy—gambling and who knows what—living off the family money."

"Henri was Claudette's brother-in-law. She was telling the truth. You know after her husband died, she said he moved into the chateau to take care of her and his niece and nephew. That is until his bad habit of gambling or his loyalty to the King caused him to end up in the Bastille. At least that was his explanation. We have to find out if he did get to the United States and if it was really him we saw board the *Scipion*."

"For that we have to go on a different site," Jean Paul answered.

"Okay, but first let's see if we can trace her children. In the letter we found out that her son's name was Louis."

Jean Paul paged down. "Here he is."

"You found him?"

"Yes, I did. Father Louis Pirrot was born in 1786. He entered the priesthood and became the Bishop of Rouen in NW France and Archbishop of Paris after two years. He died in 1835."

"Well, he was a priest, so we can't trace your ancestors through him. What about his sister, Claudette's daughter?"

"Let's see. Her name was Marie right?" Jean Paul scanned the page. "Here she is. Marie Camille was born in 1787 and died in 1830. She married Doctor Charles Morneau, who immigrated to England, then to Hamburg, returned to Paris, and married Marie. I never knew there was someone in medicine in the family. I don't see anyone else with the title Doctor. There is just a long line of attorneys."

"Look at this." He scrolled through the screen. "There is nothing but boys born in the Morneau family. Here's my father, Louis Paul Morneau, attorney and my mother, Marguerite Girard Morneau, housewife."

"My turn. Oh, can I keep going under your user name?"

"No problem. Go for it. I want to know what happened to Henri."

Alexandra switched chairs with Jean Paul. She entered the Church of the Latter Day Saint's web page. "The Mormons have very accurate records—at least for United States citizens." After she got to the home page, she clicked on family search.org and typed in all the information she had on Henri.

"Remember, if you can't find him that doesn't mean he didn't make it to the United States."

"Well, if he didn't, I'll know I did everything I could to save him…Look! It shows a Henri Pirrot, who lived in Virginia, born 1758 in France, died in 1819 in a flu epidemic. He was a carpenter and married a Catherine Donehey in 1792. She was Irish and a housewife. Maybe that's where I got my red hair. Anyway they had three sons, Charles, Pierre, and Sean. There was no need for the aristocracy so he learned a trade and finally had to work with his hands for a living."

Alexandra laughed as she skipped through the lists of Pirrots and stopped at the top of the page. "Look. Here's a Girard Pirrot, lawyer, who married a Zelda Leche, housewife. They lived in New York City. Those were the names of my grandparents." Alexandra scanned down a few lines and stopped. She sat very still for a moment then ran her finger over the line.

"This is my mother." She pointed to the middle of the screen. "See? Camille Bernard married to André Louis Pirrot. He died in 1976. That was the year I was born. No wonder I never knew him. It says they had one daughter, Alexandra. That's me." She laughed. "I wonder what he did for employment. I asked my mother and grandmother about him, but they always said they would tell me someday. They never mentioned him. I never saw a picture of him. It says that he died in New York City.

I'm going to write to Albany when I get back. There should be some sort of records in the capital. I'll get a death certificate. I don't know why I never thought of that before. I guess I just put it in the back of my mind. There's my mother. She died 1986." She wiped away a tear that ran down her cheek. "I was ten."

"Any more record?" Jean Paul asked.

"No. Now I have to contact Claudette. We have to find out exactly where the chapel is on the chateau property. There are probably records of births, deaths and marriages. There may be land deeds and other important papers hidden there. The churches used to store vital records hundreds of years ago. But the aristocracy usually stored crucial information in their family chapel."

"It's late. Shall we stay here tonight and start back tomorrow?" Jean Paul took hold of her arm and guided her to the door.

"You're right. We won't be able to do anything more tonight." Alexandra looked up at Jean Paul. "Let's start back to the chateau and stop for something to eat on the way. It's not a long drive and I'm anxious to get a good night's sleep and get in touch with Claudette tomorrow so we can get more information."

"That sounds good. I won't be able to go with you to find the chapel. I have to go to the prison in Paris and pay a visit to my client, Monsieur Dumont. You find Claudette and get her to give you directions to the chapel. You can fill me in on everything she tells you and what you find at the chapel when I get back."

Chapter Fifteen

It was late afternoon when Alexandra ran up the stairs of the chateau, threw open the outside door, and stood in the entryway under the chandelier. She took a deep breath, twisted her amethyst ring and waited. Claudette didn't appear. She twisted the ring again—nothing. "Where is she?"

Alexandra wandered through the downstairs rooms of the chateau. She called Claudette's name over and over. She stood in the middle of the library. "This is like looking for the proverbial needle in a haystack. I wish she would show her face. Maybe..." Alexandra ran and didn't stop running until she reached the staircase. Her boots pounded on the marble floor. She took the stairs to the second floor two at a time and stood in front of Claudette's portrait. "Damn...Show yourself. Show yourself Claudette...please."

"That's better—please is better." Claudette floated from the painting and stood in front of Alexandra smiling. "I'm here. What do you want?"

"Finally, you decided to show up," Alexandra shouted.

"No hello," Claudette answered.

"*Bonjour*, Claudette, I need your help and there is no time to waste. I need you to show me how you escaped from the chateau and where I can find the chapel."

"Calm down, Alexandra. Take a deep breath."

"Why does everyone say that to me?"

"Because you are very impatient sometimes. We have lots of time."

"Why are you being difficult? I've helped you, haven't I?"

"I'm just bored. It's fun to see you get mad. You're always calm and collected. You seem to be able to think straight in difficult situations and come up with solutions. You keep a level head. I'm usually the one demanding help."

That's what she thinks. "Why didn't you answer? I've been calling you."

"I didn't know you needed help and to tell you the truth, I didn't feel like answering you. I'm tired. I don't think my brother-in-law will be saved."

"Look. The chapel may contain papers about the chateau and the people who have lived here. Please…I can help you find out some of the answers that you are seeking to your questions—things about your family."

"All right, come on. I was beginning to think that you would never find out anything about my family. Your mother and grandmother never found out anything for me. They were weak. They just enjoyed the dances at Versailles and all the social life. You are strong," Claudette said. "That's why I called you. You are my last chance. If you don't help me, I'll never be able to find peace and cross over. I'll have to wander forever."

"Besides, I was going to tell you something after I examined what is in the chapel."

"What are you hiding? What is the secret?" Claudette stopped.

"Well…I didn't want to get your hopes up, but I found out some things about you children."

Claudette grabbed her arm. "What did you find out?"

"All right, I found out they both escaped from the chateau. Their nanny got them out and hid them in the country with her relatives during the revolution. I don't know who raised them after that, but Louis became a priest, the Bishop of Rouen and Archbishop of Paris. Marie married a doctor and had three children. We can find out more details if we can search the records that are probably hidden in the chapel."

Claudette turned. "I'll be right back."

"Wait! I have something else."

"What is it?" Claudette asked.

"I believe Henri made it to America. He married and had children."

Claudette disappeared into the painting and returned in a few minutes.

"Here's your cape. It will get colder later on. Let's go. Come on, move! I thought you were in a hurry." Claudette pulled Alexandra down the stairs and into a large hall—it was 1793.

Chateau Verny
August 23, 1793

The chairs and tables that had been part of the dining room that Alexandra knew were gone. The room was empty. It looked like a ballroom with a beautiful, polished, wooden floor, with mirrors on three walls—the four sets of French doors were the same—and a large chandelier hung from the middle of the ceiling.

"There's a hidden staircase on the other side of the mirror in the room next to your bedroom. It goes up into one of the towers and then goes down to the kitchen. There's an underground tunnel there that goes to the woods. It comes out on the other side of the woods. We'll start from the kitchen." They turned left and dashed to the huge oak doors. When Claudette pushed them open, Alexandra saw a large, old-fashioned kitchen.

Well, I don't think this room has changed much except for being more modernized. Alexandra passed by a large oak table in the middle of the slate floor. The table stood on thick legs. *I think that table is still in the kitchen.*

Three doors stood in front of them. She watched Claudette pull open the door to her right.

"Nope not this one. I forgot, this is the laundry."

Alexandra peered around Claudette's shoulder. Piles of sheets lay on the floor in front of a large, copper pot encrusted with green. The pot looked as if it held 20 to 40 gallons of water. A large, flat-sided paddle lay on the floor in front of it and next to the paddle was a large bar of soap. She could smell lye. On the shelf above the pot she saw two jars. One was labeled lemon juice, the other sour milk. "What did they use those for?" She pointed to the jars.

"They bleached the clothes with them. The whites were left outside on the grass in the sun for a few days. Lemon juice was rubbed over the stains. After they sat in the sun again, they were washed again in the milk." She pointed to a large kettle next to the wall. "The laundress strained water from boiled potatoes and rice then soaked the clothes that required stiffening in this kettle." Claudette opened the door to her left. "Here it is."

Alexandra laughed to herself as she followed Claudette into the dimly lit pantry. *She knows a lot about the job of the laundress, but I really don't think she has any idea how hard her staff worked. This must have been an interesting life for those living here—aristocracy and household staff—in the late seventeen hundreds. There must have been lots of intrigue and hush-hush information heard in the hidden staircases and tunnels. Who knows what secrets the staff took with them to their graves?*

She looked at the shelves filled with clay jars, cloth bags and wooden boxes. "Some of these look like they have jam in them." She held the jar up close to her eyes.

"It's raspberry jam."

"How do you know?"

"It's my favorite and the only one I knew how to make. My mother-in-law taught me. Come on. We don't have time to dawdle." Claudette moved to the largest of the built-in cabinets and slid her hand along a piece of paneling near its hinges. She pushed. The cabinet scraped along the floor as it slid open, leaving a mark on the flagstone.

"Alexandra we have to go down ten steps." Claudette bent down and grabbed a tin box inside the door. She opened it, pulled out two candles and some matches. She scraped the match along the floor. When it ignited, she lit both candles. "Here. There's a tunnel at the end of the stairs that will lead us under the gardens and woods. When we come out on the other side, we'll be in a field. The chapel is about a fifteen minute walk."

Alexandra noticed, in the dim glow of the candlelight, a flight of stairs to her left. They went up. *Those must be the ones that lead to the room next to mine. When I have time, I'll have to take the branch going to the tower. No telling what I'll find. This chateau is an eerie maze of narrow passageways. I want to explore them all.*

"You'll see our family cemetery. All the original graves are there. Only the public cemeteries reuse some of the graves after a hundred years."

Alexandra followed Claudette down the narrow stone staircase that was steep and shallow. She hugged the wall as she moved off the last step into the old tunnel. She brushed the thick cobwebs out of her face at the end of the staircase. After the last concrete step, her feet hit the dirt. The dust made her sneeze.

She looked up. "Are you sure these beams will hold? Dirt is falling on me. Let's hurry. The beams look as if they will crack any minute. If they do, the dirt will come falling in on top of us and we'll be suffocated. No one will ever find us. Do you know how damp and cold it is in here?" She shivered. Panic bubbled in her throat. She felt a thud. She turned. A piece of wood bracing the ceiling fell in front of her. "Hurry, dirt is falling. Let's get out of here." She gasped, inhaled deep breaths and coughed.

"We're in an underground tunnel; what do you expect?" Claudette answered.

Another small board fell from the wall next to Alexandra. "The tunnel may collapse." Alexandra couldn't believe it. Claudette was becoming more reasonable. She was the one in a panic. Being buried alive was not how she wanted to spend her last day on earth. Then she realized Claudette could be cavalier. She was already dead.

"Don't worry, we're almost there. I told you it would be all right," Claudette said.

Alexandra kept her eyes on the walls and ceiling. Finally, she felt a cool breeze. They were at the end. Alexandra breathed a sigh of relief. She was right behind Claudette when they walked up several steps and moved out into the heavy over-growth of trees that swayed in a gentle breeze.

Alexandra loved this time of day. It was peaceful, quiet, and lovely. They pushed on through long grass and bushes and then stepped onto mowed grass. It was at that moment Alexandra realized something very wrong. Feeling a twinge of unexpected uneasiness, she shivered. The stillness suddenly seemed unnatural. Behind them, Alexandra heard a rustle and the sound of a branch breaking—heavy footsteps pounded toward them. The ground trembled. Now Alexandra had a very bad feeling. She felt a sudden chill and tried to reassure herself that it would be all right. That everything would be fine.

Suddenly all hell broke loose. Claudette held her finger to her lips. "Sssssh. Stand very still," she whispered. Shaking her head, she pulled Alexandra back into the heavy over-growth. Her body stiffened. She waited.

Alexandra stood like a statue as she stared at the group of men wearing red caps in various styles and points of cleanliness, with tricolor cockades, as they ran from behind the trees. Alexandra tried to back up, but they surrounded her and Claudette.

"Hide your ring," Claudette whispered through clenched teeth.

Alexandra froze. It was too late to run. Chills went down her spine. *Stay calm. Don't show panic.* Her chest tightened. *They were lying in wait. I'm in trouble, big trouble.* The face of the gypsy flashed in front of her eyes. The words of the woman who had stood in front of the church rang in Alexandra's ears.

A man covered with dirt writhed like an angry snake grabbed at her. She felt her heart bang violently against the walls of her chest.

"*Fermé la bushe!*" the leader screamed. "Shut up!" He hit Alexandra in the head with the butt of his gun. Then hit her in the stomach knocking the wind from her. Alexandra felt pain, but managed to stay on her feet. Her whole body felt clammy.

Alexandra twisted her ring so that the stones were on her palm side of her hand. Then she stuck her hand in the pocket of her cape—just in time. She felt a gun in her ribs again as she fought to stand. Her heart banged against the walls of her chest. She tripped and fell.

"Get up," the man yelled.

Alexandra, coughing and choking, felt as if she were strangling. She feeling her lungs fill with air as she struggled to stand. She managed to get to her feet, but stumbled when the she felt the man with matted, greasy hair push her with his gun toward a wagon filled with hay. She managed to endure his harsh treatment. He made her skin crawl.

Alexandra glanced at Claudette, who caught her as she swayed, losing her balance.

"Can you stand up? I'll help you walk. How's your head?" Claudette asked.

"I think it's bleeding, but not badly. No blood running down my face. I'll be fine. I'll just have a giant headache tomorrow." Alexandra looked up at the rebel who stood in the wagon. She felt the filthy grime on the man's hands.

He leered at them as he pulled her and Claudette up into the cart. "Sit down and be quiet." He shoved Alexandra against the wood bench behind her. She staggered and landed with a thud on the hard bench of the wagon. She felt her forehead. It still hurt.

"Where are you taking us?" Alexandra screamed.

"Shut up. Sit down," the man shouted.

Alexandra sat and leaned her back against the side of the wagon. She closed her eyes fighting a wave of panic. Her face felt wet. *My forehead is bleeding more than I thought it was. I thought it was just a scratch.* She pressed hard on her wound with her cape. A wolf cried in the hills behind them.

"Well, at least we don't have to walk to wherever we're going." Alexandra looked at the expression on Claudette's face. "Okay, it was a bad joke." Alexandra felt the wagon begin to move down a rocky road. She felt every bump. Chills ran down her spine.

It was dusk. The fields they passed were filled with shadows, but Alexandra could see they were empty of rebels. Candles flickered in the stone houses along the road. The scenery seemed serene to her. She looked intently at the men who captured them. They were anything but calm and peaceful.

A cloud passed over the moon and stars. It was black outside. The woman next to her began to cry. Alexandra moved closer to her. She wrapped her arms around the woman and held her gently.

The first stop was at a church. They pulled a priest from the sanctuary. He sat praying after he was pushed into the cart. The stop after St. Radegonde church was at a small chateau. Alexandra heard screaming. She turned around and saw the rebels drag an elderly couple from their home. The guard with the matted hair kept hitting her legs as he shoved the woman in a dressing gown into the cart.

Poor thing she's having trouble. Alexandra tried to help her.

"I'm in my dressing gown. Did you see what they did? They didn't let us get dressed." She looked back at their house. "They set fire to it. Our house is gone."

Her husband extended his hand to Alexandra. "Charles Delacoix, my wife Babette." The woman began to cry. Alexandra moved closer to her. She wrapped her arms around the woman and held her gently. Then she picked up the woman's head and leaned it on her husband's shoulder.

Next they picked up a family with five children. The mother tried to console the child who sobbed noisily as she moved to Alexandra and sat next to her. "What's going to happen to us?" She rested her head in Alexandra's lap.

"It will be all right." Alexandra stroked the child's back. She listened to the pounding of the horses' hooves. The night fell around them as she leaned back. She wondered what was going to happen.

The wagon stopped several more times. Somehow, on the way, the rebels packed ten more men and women into the small farm cart. Alexandra rode shoulder–to-shoulder with aristocrats who had been dragged from their homes. She looked at their faces—they looked bewildered and petrified. Their hands shook. The expressions on their faces betrayed their anxiety and they seemed to have no understanding of their ultimate fate, just fear about where they were going. She could see that their only crime was being born to wealth. The night fell around them. She searched her brain to remember history so that she might learn what was going to happen to them.

Claudette leaned close to Alexandra. "I have a secret to tell you before we get to our destination. We may get separated so I'll tell you now." She held her hand near her mouth covering her lips. Claudette whispered into Alexandra's ear. "I got revenge on my gardener. He was walking in the upstairs hallway with Monsieur Dumont."

"What did you do?" Alexandra asked. She already knew what had happened. Jean Paul's client was innocent.

"I killed him. I stabbed him in the heart." She grabbed Alexandra's hand. "I told you to hide your ring. Put it in your pocket. Do it right now. The guard isn't looking." Claudette stared at it as Alexandra slid the ring off and pushed it deep into her pocket. "Where did you get it? It looks like my engagement ring."

"My mother left it to me when she died." *Interesting—it probably belonged to her.*

The sound of the horses' hooves pounding on the road and the clanging of their harnesses didn't drown out the crying and moaning of the occupants of the wagon. The noises roared in Alexandra's ears.

Charles Delacoix watched Alexandra. He leaned close to her and tapped her on the shoulder. "Our lives are in terrible danger." He said no more when he saw the guard look up and stare at him. Charles Delaciox moved away and rested his large frame against the side of the wagon. He removed his spectacles, pulled a piece of cloth from his breast pocket, breathed on the lenses and began to wipe them.

The clouds moved slowly in a light breeze clearing the sky. A halo around the full moon cast an eerie glow.

Paris
August 23, 1793

Claudette sat staring straight ahead shaking her head from side to side. No tears dripped down her cheeks. She had the look of resignation. She seemed to be submitting to her fate.

"Claudette, where are we going?" Alexandra whispered in Claudette's ear. She pulled her cape tightly around her. "You know, don't you? Please tell me." Alexandra realized Claudette had been through this horrific time before. She looked out of the wagon and stared at the scenery, not really seeing it. She realized she was re-living a dreadful time in Claudette's life. "What is going to happen Claudette?" she asked.

"We're going to the Conciergerie Prison." Claudette sighed.

The last stop before the guillotine. It was not only the cool air that made Alexandra begin to shake. *Why is Claudette replaying her life and why am I a part of it?* Her head still ached from the blow; she laid it on her knees.

As soon as they passed the walls of Paris, fireworks and moonlight lit up the sky and road. It was very bright. Alexandra could see the faces of the angry crowd. Men and women ran wildly beside them as the wagon slowed down. They threw whatever they could find in the street. Alexandra felt a rock hit her in the back. She ducked down, afraid she might be killed by flying rocks.

The wagon bumped and jerked on the cobblestones of the Paris streets. Alexandra looked out into the city and saw the outline of the La Conciergerie Prison. Fireworks went off close by the prison's gates that stood near the Cathedral of Notre Dame. The famous Catholic Church on an island in the middle of the Seine River.

The screams and cheers got louder the closer they got to the fortress. *What a strange dichotomy—the death machine near a place of God.*

The prison's three huge, gray, stone towers stood high in the sky—they made it looked very formidable against the light of the moon.

It was built in the fourteenth century as a palace and turned into a prison in 1391. Alexandra remembered from her European history book. It was on the Ile de la Cité in the middle of the Seine River.

Alexandra felt the bumps as the wagon's wheels rolled onto a float—oarsmen rowed them to the island. Alexandra stared straight ahead. She didn't make eye contact with anyone in the wagon. Right now she didn't want to see the fear on their faces. There was nothing she could do to help them.

Her palms were sweaty; she wiped them on her jeans. Alexandra sat quietly trying to remember her history. As the float bounced in the water, she recalled that La Conciergerie housed 2780 men and women—held in separate parts of the prison—men in one section and women in another. They were all held in horrible conditions. It was the antechamber to the guillotine. La Conciergerie was the main prison where prisoners were detained before they walked through the Salle de Perus—the room of the doomed—before they were escorted to Concorde Square to be beheaded. She was now afraid. The FBI was never like this. *How am I going to get out of this predicament? I have my ring, but what will I do if I use it and bring some of the rebels with me? And what about Claudette? This is part of the plan I have to see it through.*

Conciergerie Prison
August 24, 1793

It was still dark, but Alexandra guessed it was early in the morning when they reached the inside of the prison. She thought it was probably around four in the morning. The people in the wagon were dragged by their captors into a large room with a tile floor, high ceilings and barred windows. Alexandra glanced around the room. A tribunal, a committee of five men, sat at a long, wooden table. The man in the middle had on an ill-fitting wig and had tiny eyes and a heavy jaw. His drooping, half-closed eyelids and thin, pursed lips made him looked petulant with a look of contempt. He shuffled through some papers in front of him. He handed them to the other judges.

Alexandra's blood ran cold. She looked at men who had looks on their faces that one might see in a nightmare. She noticed none of the prisoners were allowed to speak and how some heaved their chests and sighed as if they seemed resigned to their fate.

Chapter Sixteen

Alexandra hugged her cape close to her body and waited. Her feet began to cramp. The thin soles of her boots were no protection against the hard, cold floor. She shivered. When it was her turn to stand in front of the group, she watched the Revolutionary Tribunal stare at her. They whispered among themselves. As soon as they raised their heads, the man in charge—the one with the bad wig—whispered to a burly, square-chested man with a chiseled face, then banged his gavel. She couldn't believe it when she heard him yell guilty and sentence her to prison without a trial. She had no representation—no lawyer to plead her case. She stood to the side and waited for the rest of the trials. The same scenario repeated itself for each of the people in the wagon—even the children.

Some of the people from the cart sobbed. The woman in the dressing gown fell to her knees and pleaded with the men. She knew immediately that she had to do something to get them both out of the prison. She watched Claudette and saw her tear-stained face. She stood as if made of stone when the judges made their decisions. It was daylight when the trials were over. Two men began to drag Claudette to her cell. She watched Claudette stumble and go limp. Alexandra looked into Claudette's eyes and knew she wept without a sound. Her face was chalk white.

"Wait, let me. I'll help her." Alexandra seized Claudette's arm and gently pulled her to her side and helped her walk from the room. She followed the men as they led them to women's section of the prison and their cells. The sound of the guard's boots pounding on the stone floor sent shivers through her. Alexandra slipped her free hand into her pocket and felt for her amethyst ring. *Thank goodness it's still there. I can't use it now. I have to sit with Claudette and decide how we will escape.*

The squeal of the rusty cell door and the way it scraped on the cement as it opened made her shudder. Then she heard. "Get in there." Alexandra felt herself being shoved by the guard into a cell that was damp and frigid. She felt the cold stone through her boots. Her heart pounded. She heard the scraping of the cell door again as the guard pulled it across the cement floor and then heard a loud crash as it slammed shut.

"Here," the guard yelled. He shoved his hands holding a candle and a match through the bars. "Take it or I'll drop it on the floor, and you never know what's on the floor."

Alexandra heard the march-like thumping of the guard's feet as they moved on with Claudette. She placed her candle into the holder standing on the table and laid the match next to it. She sat down in the hard, wooden chair, scraped the match on the stone floor, and lit the candle. The light from a torch somewhere outside and near the cell shone through the high, barred, narrow window allowed dim light into the cell. Alexandra shook her hair from her eyes and looked around. A pile of straw covered with a thin piece of cloth lay in the corner.

She jumped as she heard little feet scatter across the dirty floor. She looked down. "Oh God, a rat." Then she heard Claudette cry out as she was pushed into the cell just a short way down the hall from hers.

Alexandra listened as the revolutionaries marched down the corridor. She looked up as they passed her cell. They kept their eyes straight ahead. The thudding got quieter and quieter until she couldn't hear their boots pounding on the stone floor. She heard the dull slam of a door shut. *They're far away now. We're safe for a little while.* Her candle sputtered out and left her in the dark except for a sliver of brightness that came through the window and cast shadows on the cell walls. She called out. "Good night, Claudette. Tomorrow morning will be better."

"If only the King hadn't sent money to help the American Revolutionary War—it almost bankrupted our country. Then we had a severe winter and the crops died—there was no food. We shouldn't be in this position. The Rebels hate the aristocracy; they say the problems of France are our fault," Claudette cried out. "They feel as if the royal court at Versailles is indifferent to their plight. They executed the King in January."

"If only." Alexandra put her head down on the table and closed her eyes. She hummed the lullaby her mother sang to her at bedtime when she was a little girl.

Soon daylight from the small, high window bounced off the bars and the walls of the cell. It woke her. She rubbed her shoulders. As she tried to stand, her legs wouldn't hold her. She dropped back into the chair—then stood slowly. Pushing herself up, she used her hands as braces and stood bent over for a few minutes. Her whole body ached.

She pulled her cape tightly around her, trying to keep out the dampness. She walked at a snail's pace—one foot in front of the other—to the door of her cell. It was like she was letting her joints get lubricated so they could move smoothly. She was stiff from the dampness and the position she had been in all night. She needed to get to Claudette's cell. Alexandra looked out through the bars. To her surprise, when she pulled on the handle of the cell, the door opened. *I guess they don't think we'll try to escape so they don't need to watch us closely.* Alexandra walked from her cell, turned left and moved slowly to the cell next to hers.

"I don't believe it." She stopped and stared. Alexandra had expected Claudette to be curled up in a ball crying, but she was sound asleep on her straw-bed with her head lying on folded hands. *Her face looks as if she is in the middle of a wonderful dream. She's, completely relaxed and looks so peaceful.* Alexandra slid into her cell. "Wake up Claudette. The doors of the cells are opened." Alexandra reached down and shook her. "We can leave our rooms."

Claudette jumped and gazed up at her with swollen eyes. Alexandra realized she had been crying before she fell asleep. "If I can get some money, maybe I can get a bed brought in. I'm sure the guards can be bribed."

Don't worry about bribing guards yet. Let's go see where the corridor goes." Alexandra grabbed Claudette's hand and pulled her to her feet. Alexandra began to drag Claudette out of the cell.

Alexandra noticed a book and ink pen on the table. "Are you writing a diary? Where did you get them?"

"I smuggled them in. I had them hide in the pocket of my dress."

"Come on put them away."

"Yes. Wait! I have to hide these. Someday people will see what I went through. The guards can't read, so I'm going to write about my prison experience." Claudette reached for the book and pen on the table. She slid them under the hay where she had been sleeping.

They hurried down the hall. It ended at a door with bars that swung open when Alexandra pushed on it. She walked out of the corridor with Claudette close behind her. They walked down a path that ran along the wall of the prison. When the wall ended, she peeked around the corner of the building.

"A courtyard." Alexandra stopped talking and walked into the yard. She looked up and counted back three windows. She realized that was her cell. "That's where the light came from—torches in the courtyard." She saw torches attached to the wall next to her window. Alexandra looked across the courtyard, she watched several women who gathered around a large fountain like basin that stood in the middle of the small open space. Next to the fountain was an iron fence that separated the two prisons.

Some of the women were washing their clothes in the water that ran from a trough. Other women were talking with the men who stood on the other side of the bars that separated the men's cells from the women's side. One woman held a man's hands through the bars. Everyone's eyes constantly scanned the yard. They spoke in whispered voices to each other as if they didn't know if some of the prisoners might be spies for the guards and listened to what they said.

Alexandra looked around. They all looked depressed. "Come on." She gave Claudette a gentle push toward the fountain. "Splash some water on your face." One of the women stepped back, leaving an opening. "Here, dear, you may have my place."

Alexandra saw Babette Delacroix step back. "How are you Madame Delacroix?"

"I'm all right. What's going to happen to us?"

"It will be fine. Everything is going to be fine."

Claudette called to her. "Alexandra, please come here."

Alexandra moved to the fountain and washed her hands. "What do you want, Claudette?"

"Alexandra, you have to escape. You have to get to the chapel. I need to know everything about my children and husband—also my brother-in-law."

"I told you your brother-in-law did go to the New World. I traced him to the Commonwealth of Virginia in the United States. Then I traced his family through the centuries. Some went to New York City. He was my great grandfather's grandfather. So we're related by marriage, Claudette."

Claudette smiled, but she seemed preoccupied.

"What's wrong, Claudette?"

"They told me my husband died in a battle. I don't believe it."

"Why?"

"Because, he was a friend of Maximilien Robespierre. They were from the same small village and went to school together. They were good friends. Robespierre changed. He wanted a republic where all men were equal. He wanted a world where there was brotherly love. Then he changed. He became a dictator and started to use terror to promote his own power. He turned against the monarchy. The more power he got, the more evil he got. He began to instill fear in the citizens. He started to execute people without a trial. He ordered the King, Louis XVI to death. Anybody who disagreed or challenged him and was part of the aristocracy was sentenced and killed by the guillotine.

"It was probably more than 17,000 people to be exact," Alexandra said. "At least in Paris. Who knows how many more he killed throughout the countryside? He was evil."

"My husband sided with the King. He was loyal to the monarchy. I believe Robespierre was unable to stand the fact that his friend didn't agree with him and had him murdered, or killed Louis himself. This was before the Reign of Terror when the mass executions started."

"I promise I will try to find out how your husband died. If it makes you feel any better, Robespierre died by the guillotine. The people turned against him."

"Thank God. He was very evil."

They heard the clamor of a cart being wheeled down the hallway of the prison. Alexandra and Claudette ran back to their cells.

"Breakfast time. Mangé, eat up." Alexandra reached her cell at the same time the guard did. He came into her cell and dropped a plate on her table and laid a bowl with a small piece of meat in cloudy water next to it. He laughed. "Good thing you got back. No food if you aren't in your cell." She looked at his filthy hands as he pulled a hunk of bread from a large basket. He pulled a ladle from the back pocket of his pants, scooped water from a large bucket and poured it into a cracked, ceramic mug.

Alexandra pulled her chair up to the table and stared at the mug. She pushed it away. It looked like pond scum. Whatever it contained made her nauseous. Alexandra stared at the bowl and pushed it away with her fist. It smelled bad. She was sure if she drank the water or ate the meat she would get sick. She took a bite of the bread. It was stale and hard. She chewed on it slowly, but left most of it on the plate.

A guard marched up and down in front of the cells. He looked at her. "Not hungry?" He laughed.

Alexandra put her head on her table and fell asleep. When she awoke, she dragged her chair into Claudette's cell. "Wake up! We're going to try to escape when it gets dark."

"I'm too weak," Claudette cried out. "I can't." She was lying with her head on the table. She raised her head and rested her chin in her hands. "When did we get here? Where is my bed? Why did all this happen? We were a happy household. I loved everyone who worked for me."

"What's wrong? You were okay a few hours ago. Did you drink the water and eat the meat?" Alexandra looked intently at Claudette, then at the dishes on the table. They were empty. She didn't like the way Claudette looked or acted. Her skin was pale, she shivered and seemed to be confused. Alexandra felt her forehead. *She's burning up.*

"I didn't feel very well when we went to look for the chapel, but I thought I would be all right."

"Why didn't you tell me you were sick before we went into the tunnel? I think it may be the food is making you feel worse—be careful what you eat. Stay covered up and I'll bring Jean Paul back. We'll get you out. The guards don't really watch us very carefully. I remember from history that Marie Antoinette, the queen of France, escaped, but she was caught. It will be dark pretty soon. I'm going to rest for a couple of hours and then leave."

Alexandra lay on her bed of straw staring at the ceiling. All she could do was shut her eyes. Her brain ticked away. A few hours later she pushed open the gate of her cell. She had butterflies in her stomach. She crept to Claudette's cell. This time she saw her sitting on the floor with her back against the wall, hugging her knees to her chest. She was shaking. Alexandra pushed open the cell door and picked up Claudette's cape from the table and tucked it tightly around her. "I'll be back for you. I promise," she whispered. "Stay covered up and only eat the bread and try to sleep."

"Wait!" Claudette fumbled with her cape. She reached into the pocket. "*Voila!* Here, take this." Claudette pressed a key into Alexandra's hand. "This will unlock the chapel." She struggled to push herself up. "The King tried to escape with his family, but they caught him and brought them back to prison. He was executed in January. Don't get caught."

"You don't have to come with me to the gate."

"I just want to make sure you're okay and get away," Claudette said.

Alexandra reached her arm around Claudette's waist. She pulled her up, helping her stand. Claudette walked slowly at Alexandra's side down the dark hallway. "Be careful." When they reached the courtyard, she gave Alexandra a hug and whispered in her ear. "*Au'voir.* You're a good friend." Alexandra watched Claudette's lips move. Alexandra heard her whisper what sounded like a prayer.

Alexandra waited to make sure no one was in the yard. She moved quietly, but rapidly, on tiptoes across the yard. When she reached the gate, she turned, raised her hand and gave a small wave. "*Au'voir,*" she mouthed. Alexandra pushed open the gate just enough to slide through. She wedged her body between the gate and fence. She ran.

Streets of Paris night-time

August 25, 1793

Just passed midnight, Alexandra headed through the gate and disappeared into the hot Parisian night. There were rebels everywhere. They screamed, drank and danced as they celebrated the demise of the aristocracy. Alexandra raced through the tangle of narrow streets. Her lungs burned. She tried to keep to the back alleys of Paris to reduce the chance of getting caught. The night was black. The moon and stars hid behind a thick fog.

When Alexandra heard footsteps and voices, she ducked around the corner of a building, ran in the other direction or crouched in a dark doorway. She tried to make herself as invisible as possible. She waited. When it was quiet, she slowly inched out of her hiding place, looked around and crept down the alley. Hardly breathing, she looked around the corner of the building at the end of the passage.

She wasn't quite sure where she was and had no sense of time. She turned one corner then another. After a little while, she saw the rubble of the Bastille. Some of the shattered stones of the walls were piled on top of one another. They were almost as tall as the original wall. Others had rolled into the yard in front of the doorways making it impossible to enter the prison's towers. *We were lucky we got out when we did.*

She saw the flames of a fire as she crept drew down the alley and drew closer to the source of light. She heard voices and peeked around the corner of the building at the end of the alley. She watched a group of men that sat on the fallen rocks in front of a fire that cracked and spat. They laughed, slapped each other on the back and yelled at each other as they drank out of long, narrow bottles. Alexandra backed down the alley, turned left, and walked down a side street dimly lit with torches. When she was well past the Bastille area, she ran in the direction of the Abbey Cyr. *If I can get there while it's still dark, I can get into the woods and I'll be safe.*

"At last!" Alexandra ran to the gate of the Abbey. She stopped and stared at an old woman who stood at the opening to the courtyard. She looked at her and shuddered at the hideous sores on her face. Alexandra watched as the woman tried to shrink into the wall of the Abbey.

"Hello," Alexandra called out to her.

The woman stared straight ahead—not reacting to Alexandra's voice—but seemed to sense that someone was there. *Maybe she feels the vibrations of another person.* Alexandra leaned closely to the woman's wrinkled face and looked directly into her eyes. They were cloudy as if covered by a film. She waved her hands up and down in front of them. There was still no sign that she saw Alexandra's hand. *She must be blind and deaf. She knows someone is here, but not who it is. Thank God she won't be able to describe me to anyone.*

"Whose there?" the woman asked. She finally decided there was someone near her.

"It's all right." Alexandra patted her shoulder. The woman looked alone and lost to her. Alexandra felt the old woman reach out and grab her. Alexandra gently took her hands and pulled them away from her arms and patted her again. She felt badly, but she had to leave and leave quickly before someone found her.

Alexandra dashed to the dirt road outside the Abbey and slid into the forest across from the gate. She ran, then tripped and fell. She grabbed on to a bush and pulled herself up. Glancing around, she turned to the right and walked several steps. She stopped, spun to the left and stopped again. Desperately she tried to figure out where she was and in what direction she should go. She took a deep breath and went straight. "I'm sure this is the direction I went before."

"The last time I was here the sky was clear. There were stars and a full moon. Tonight is overcast. The sky was filled with clouds. She had no moon or stars to help her this time. She walked onto a path that twisted between the trees. She stumbled again on the roots of a tree and felt a branch of a tree hit her shoulder as she landed on the ground. Alexandra could feel blood running down her leg as she felt hands pull her up. When she looked around, no one was there. "I have to keep moving." Branches hit her face as she ran through the trees.

"I have to get Jean Paul. We have to return to Claudette and get her out of the Conciergerie." She jumped when she heard the crack of thunder. Rain poured through the trees. She saw a road to her left. She ran out of the forest and stood for a moment looking down the road. Alexandra began to walk slowly along the dirt road that began to turn to mud. Her feet sank into the mud. Her heart beat rapidly. She raised her head and let the water run over her face and her parched lips. She heard the rumbling of a wagon. She stared. It was moving toward her.

Alexandra felt the set of hands grab her. They dragged her to the other side of the road and pushed into the ditch behind her. She heard a voice whisper in her ear. "Get down." She looked around again and saw no one.

Alexandra curled into a ball. She took a big gulp of air. She held her breath. She peeked over the edge of the trench and saw a figure—a figure in a long black cape—walk away from the road and vanish into the woods. *It can't be. She's in the Conciergerie prison.* Alexandra hoped that the torrential downpour would hide her. *If they see me, it's back to prison or worse. I could be executed.* She listened to the voices of the people ricocheting off the trees. After the wagon passed by her hiding place, she waited several minutes.

When the rattle of the wagon and the pounding of the horses' hooves became softer, she peeked over the side of the ditch.

When the vociferous yells of the passengers crowded in the wagon sounded far enough away and she was sure that she would not be detected, she sucked in a large breath of air and climbed out of the ditch. Gathering all her strength, she struggled back into the woods.

It's not safe to be on the roads. The mud and rain made it hard to navigate. She trudged with a slow, steady pace through the woods. Soon she saw shafts of sunlight cut through the trees. The early morning light helped her to avoid the hazards of the woods and easier for her to travel faster.

Chapter Seventeen

Mid Afternoon, Giverny
July 23, 2010

Alexandra reached the end of the woods. She twisted her ring and looked out ahead of her. The heavy fog was gone and the rain had stopped. The sun was bright and warmed her. She didn't see the field or the house they had stopped at after they left the Abbey—the night they left Henri there with the nuns. She glanced around and saw nothing but plush fields and vineyards. She was standing in the middle of a road in a small village. She gazed out over the well-manicured lawns of lovely houses. Twenty-first century men and women walked in and out of stores and offices.

Alexandra walked up to the sign at the corner of the street. Looking up, she read, 'Giverny 15 km'. She was so fatigued she could barely put one foot in front of the other. However, she kept moving. She watched a car slow down. The driver leaned out of his window and stared.

What I must look like. She rubbed her throbbing temples as she headed toward a shop that looked as if it might have a telephone. She had left her cell phone on the table in her cell. *Won't they get a surprise when they find a cell phone!* She laughed. *They won't even know what it is.* As she grabbed the handle to open the door, she caught a glimpse of herself in the glass door. Her clothes were wrinkled. Mud caked her cape and boots. Her hair was wet and tangled. Her face was pale with scratches.

She combed her fingers through her hair and rubbed her feet against the mat. The door squeaked as she shoved it open. She marched into the small store. Her muddy, wet boots made a slight squishing noise as she crossed the broad boards of the wooden floor. She approached the man behind the counter. "Can you help me? I need a taxi to Chateau Verny in Giverny."

The man grabbed the phone. He whispered something in French as he looked back and forth from Alexandra to the door. "A taxi will be here in a few minutes." He dropped the phone into its cradle "You can wait, but don't get my shop dirty." He took out a handkerchief from his pants pocket and wiped the perspiration from his face. "It's hot in here."

Is that a hint to get out of his shop? Maybe he thinks I'm scoping out his shop and a bunch of hoodlums will burst in and rob him. Who cares what he thinks. I'll never see him again. "*Merci*, I'll wait outside." Alexandra forced a smile. She wandered out to the front of the store and sat on the curb and waited. "He probably told the driver he had a crazy person standing in his shop who wanted a ride." She laughed. *I hope he didn't call the police and pretended it was a call to a taxi. Relax Alexandra. Everything is going to be all right.*

A few minutes later a taxi slid to a stop in front of Alexandra. The cabbie stared at her as he lowered the passenger side window and yelled out, "The owner called and said someone wanted a taxi. Are you the lady who needs a ride?"

"I'm the one. I need to go to the Chateau Verny."

The driver peered around the street, carefully looking behind her, then out of his back window. She heard the click as the door unlocked.

"What happened to you?"

"I had an accident."

"Get in," he shouted.

I'm not deaf, just in a mess. She threw open the back door, jumped in and plopped down on the seat. Alexandra leaned back and closed her eyes. After a few minutes, she looked out of the taxi at the scenery. *It's so different now. It's beautiful. Not like 1789.* She looked up the mountain to her left and saw the chateau. "Turn here. When we get to the gate, just honk your horn and it will open. After we get to the front door, I'll run in and get you your money."

"No Euros!" He took his foot off the gas pedal and the taxi began to slow down. He glanced over his shoulder and snorted. He slowly turned his head and stared over the steering wheel at the road. He let the cab come to a complete stop.

"Don't stop. Please. Please. Don't worry, the Euros are in my room at the chateau. Hurry! Do I look as if I would cheat you? You'll get paid. I promise."

He laughed and pushed his foot down. He raced up the road at warp speed. The gravel crunched under the taxi's wheels as the driver slid to a stop at the front door. He wiped his brow, turned and leaned over his seat. "That's ten Euros."

Does everyone drive crazily in France? "I'll be right back." Alexandra jumped out of the cab and ran up the steps. She pulled on the handle and tried to open the front door. It didn't budge. *Now they lock it?* Alexandra banged on it with her fist. While she waited, Alexandra looked down. Several men weeding the front garden turned and stared at her. *They must think I escaped from an asylum.*

She raised her hand to knock again. The door opened. Her fist almost hit Jean Paul in the nose. He ducked when he saw it coming toward him. When he stood upright, he stared at her. When Alexandra realized what almost happed, she laughed. After a few seconds, he threw his arms around her and hugged her. "Thank God. You're here. What happened? You look like hell. Have you been rolling in the mud?" he bellowed. Jean Paul softly traced a rough red mark that covered her cheek. "You feel icy cold."

She pulled away. "I need ten Euros for the taxi driver. Then I need your help. No time for conversation."

He dug into his pocket. "I'll pay him. Wait here. Don't you dare move!"

Alexandra waved to the driver and sat down on the top step. She leaned her elbows on her knees and put her chin into her hands as she closed her eyes.

"Where were you?" Jean Paul sat down next to her. "I came back from seeing my client and you were gone. No one knew where you were. You scared me. Stop disappearing on me, please. Do I have to put an ankle bracelet on you?"

"I don't think it would have done any good where I was, I assure you. I'm all right. I came back here and convinced Claudette to take me to the chapel. On our way there we slipped back into the eighteenth century." She took a deep breath. "She led me through a tunnel that went from the kitchen, under the woods and came out in a field. We were still on the property. When we got to the other side of the woods, we were captured and taken by the rebels to La Conciergerie prison."

"Slow down," Jean Paul said.

"No time! I escaped, but Claudette was suddenly too sick to come with me. I don't know what was wrong with her—maybe food poisoning. You should have seen what they expected us to eat. It wasn't like any French food I've ever had." She took a deep breath. "I need your help. I really need your help. We have to go back to the prison and get her out." She grabbed his hands.

"Your hands are ice cold. Take a deep breath."

"Don't worry about me. I'm fine.

"Take a shower and get rid of the mud and change into some dry clothes. I'll get my car and wait for you in front of the chateau." He helped her stand. "Are you all right?"

"Really I'm fine. We have to hurry. We have to get to the area where the prison was during the revolution."

"Okay, change first."

"We'll park your car near the building that used to be the prison in1789. The building now holds the Palais de Justice and offices. They are on the Ile de la Cité—in a busy area of Paris. Of course, you know all that." Alexandra grabbed his arm. "When we get back to 1789, no one will pay attention to us. When I left, the crowds of Paris were in a frenzy. Put on some clothes that don't look too modern—a long coat maybe. I wish we had those costumes we rented in Bordeaux. I'll use my ring and we'll go back to the prison. I hope."

Conciergerie Prison
August 26, 1793

It was late, close to midnight, when they crossed over the bridge to reached the Palace de Justice. Jean Paul slid his Porsche into the public lot. He reached over his shoulder and grabbed hold of his long, dark coat from the backseat. Alexandra held the door handle with a shaking hand and pushed down on it. She threw open her door. She stood and studied the building, then ran up to the side of the building where she thought their cells had been. She stood very still, closed her eyes and said a silent prayer. After Jean Paul reached her side, she grabbed his hand. "Are you ready?" Alexandra didn't wait for him to answer as she twisted her ring.

When she looked up, she and Jean Paul stood outside the front door of the prison. It was 1793. "We're here. I hope we're not too late. We can't be too late," she whispered.

Jean Paul stared up at the prison as he buttoned up his long dark coat. "Are we near the wing where you were imprisoned?"

Alexandra glanced around. Torches lit the outside of the prison and the courtyard. "I'm not sure. Everything looks different at night when you're on the outside. I didn't look behind me when I escaped. I just ran." She grabbed Jean Paul's hand. "We have to find the courtyard where we stood by the fountain. Listen for running water. It's on the women's side. There's a gate in the yard where the women gather. That's where I got out. Our cells were very near to it." She jerked away from Jean Paul and slid her body along the side of the building to the end of its wall. She didn't realize she was holding her breath until she began to feel lightheaded. She staggered, caught herself and leaned against the wall of the building to steady herself. She took several deep breaths and exhaled them to calm herself.

"Are you all right?" Jean Paul pulled her into his arms. "You have to slow down."

"I think this is where the fountain is. Sssssh, I hear voices." She peeked around the corner. "There's a group of guards sitting around a fire in the courtyard. They're next to the fountain. We have to wait until they leave to make their rounds." Alexandra slid down the wall and sat. She pulled up her legs and wrapped her arms around her knees. It helped her to feel warmer and less shaky.

Jean Paul sat next to her and put his arms around her. "You're shaking." He smoothed her hair and tightened his grip.

"I'm fine." She sucked in her breath. She heard her heart hammering in her ears. She felt the warmth of his arm and knew everything would work out. She closed her eyes and waited.

"I don't think I hear voices anymore," she whispered. She stood and peeked around the building again. "It's okay. They've left. Follow me." Alexandra grabbed his hand, pushed on the gate and slid through the opening. She passed the fountain and stopped. She glanced around the courtyard. Once she saw the door leading to the cells, she ran to it. Jean Paul followed her, as she slipped off her boots and walked in her socks down the stone floor of the dimly lit passageway—hardly breathing. There was a dreadful silence. As soon as she reached Claudette's cell, Alexandra came to a dead stop and stood as if frozen. Tears began to run down her cheeks.

"What's wrong?" Jean Paul asked.

"We're too late. She's gone." She ran into the cell and quickly ran her hand under the hay. "I found it."

"What did you find?" Jean Paul asked.

She held up the journal so that Jean Paul could see it. "Claudette wrote in this. Stick this in your pocket."

They heard the pounding of boots on the cobblestones of the prison corridor and the rumbling of wagon wheels and the clanging of horses' harnesses.

"Let's get out of here." Jean Paul grabbed Alexandra's hand and started to run. He pulled her to the gate. "It's starting to get light out. We can't get out the way we came in. The wagon and the guards are behind us. Daylight will make us more vulnerable. It's going to get harder to hide. The wagon sounds as if it is very close," he whispered. "Duck behind the wall after we slide through the gate. Let's go. Quick!"

After the wagon passed, they ran behind it. Jean Paul pulled her down. They hid underneath the wagon when it pulled onto the barge. They crossed the Seine River. The guards didn't notice when the boat landed and Jean Paul and Alexandra broke away and join the crowd walking toward the scaffold. The guards were focused on getting the prisoners to the Place de la Concorde. The crowds didn't notice Jean Paul and Alexandra stop while she pulled on her boots.

When Jean Paul and Alexandra reached the main street, they glanced at the houses crowding either side of the road. "They are decorated as if a festival is being held. I can't believe it. You'd think this was a holiday," Alexandra said.

They followed the crowd, now worked up into a fury, to the square— the Place de la Concorde. Alexandra gazed around. She was surprised how the houses on either side of the square looked. They were not only decorated with banners, but also had the tricolor flag of France hanging from balconies or doors. The red, white and blue moved slowly back and forth in the light breeze.

She stared at the signs hanging from one of the homes. It said 'Unity, liberty, equality, fraternity, or death'. She uttered a quote from somewhere. She couldn't remember where, "Oh liberty, what crimes are committed in your name." She glanced at the woman standing next to her. *She was wearing a necklace of stones. I bet they were pieces of stone pulled from the Bastille.*

Alexandra heard the crowd yelling, "Off with their heads." She looked into their angry faces.

She looked over her shoulder and was gripped with panic. "Oh no!" Alexandra pulled on Jean Paul's sleeve. "Look." She pointed to the cart coming toward them.

The clop, clop hammering of the horses' hooves and the rumbling of the wagon wheels echoed in her head. "It's Claudette." She pointed to the people standing in the open cart. "There, she's standing behind the driver," she screamed.

Claudette stood with two women and six men. The ragged edges of Claudette's shorn auburn hair shone in the morning sun as they peeked out from under her white, linen cap. She wore a plain, white dress. She was pale and drawn. Her cheeks were sunken, her eyes looked dead and her neck was bare.

Alexandra—at the edge of the square—watched the cart pass through the crowd. When the cart passed by her, Alexandra stared up at Claudette and fixed her gaze on Claudette's face. A mist formed over Alexandra's eyes. Then tears streamed down her face. She watched. Claudette stood tall and proud. Her head held high. *She's tearless.* Alexandra dried her cheeks with her sleeve.

As the cart pushed though the mass of revolutionaries, Alexandra heard the crowd cheer, shout obscenities and make sounds that seemed as if they came straight from hell. She stood with soundless tears streaming down her cheeks. Alexandra dried her face with her sleeve again and then clamped her hands over her ears to block out the noise of the crowd and the sound of the horses' hooves.

When the driver brought the wagon to a halt, the mob quieted down. A man dressed in dirty, baggy pants, a shirt with a cockade over his heart, and a red hat that sat cockeyed on his head opened the door to the wagon and let it drop to the ground. The sound of the wood hitting the stone echoed through the square and the crowd went wild again. Jean Paul whispered into Alexandra's ear.

"What?" It was hard to hear over the roar of the crowd.

"You can't change history."

She didn't pay any attention to him. She watched as the priest leaned closely to the condemned and murmur urgently to the group. Alexandra moved closer to the guillotine.

"Prisoner 301," The executioner, Henri Sasone, with drooping eyelids and sagging chin, pulled Claudette from the cart. Drunken men started to yell again. Alexandra stared at her. She saw Claudette bow her head and her lips moved. When her hands were tied behind her back, Alexandra saw them shake, but Claudette remained dignified and calm. Alexandra watched them strap her to a board and then slide her up to the head holder. Alexandra closed her eyes and prayed. She couldn't use her ring. She was too far away from Claudette and she might bring the executioner or anyone else near to her into 2010.

When she looked up, she watched the man, who was short and skinny, prepare Claudette for death. He had a young looking face with deep pockmarks and a sharp, pointed nose. Alexandra was sickened by his look of disdain as he stared at Claudette. Alexandra closed her eyes and listened to the roll of the drums. Then she heard the whistle of the heavy blade as it dropped. She froze and screamed without a sound when she heard the echo of the thud as Claudette's head fell into the basket at the foot of the guillotine. She heard the crowd go wild again and felt sick to her stomach. When she finally opened her eyes, she watched the executioner walked proudly to the bottom edge of the scaffold and hold up Claudette's bleeding head showing it to the crowd. She stared into the street. Blood poured onto the cobblestones in front of the Guillotine. It rushed like a river.

Something made her look to her left. Out of the corner of her eye she saw a man dressed in a double-knotted foulard, brocade waistcoat, and high-heeled shoes. He had a sharp nose, prominent cheekbones, and long, thin lips. His face had a look of cold detachment. He didn't seem to hear the crowd. He stared at her with hard, cold eyes. A shiver went up her spine. She stared into the eyes of treachery and evil and began to shake. His insidious smile made her sick to her stomach. She took a deep breath. "It's Maximilien Robespierre. Maximilien, you'll get yours."

"What did you say?"

Alexandra swallowed deeply. "My God…Why did I let this happen? I should have forced her to escape with me." The words came between sobs.

Jean Paul fixed his eyes on Alexandra. He knew she was going to scream. He covered her mouth with his hand as he whispered in her ear. "You can't change history. It has already happened to her. Remember, you're from 2010. Pretend you're part of the crowd and push through. Don't be polite. Don't worry about whoever gets in your way. Let's get the hell out of here."

Sun Rise, Place de le Concorde

With a burst of adrenaline, Jean Paul pulled Alexandra out of the square. He clamped his hand on her wrist and dragged her through the loud and rowdy crowd. Hordes of people were packed in the square, slowing their escape, and making it almost impossible for Jean Paul to get them out of the area. Jean Paul felt Alexandra shudder.

Alexandra stopped, and stared into the eyes of a small, round man dressed in the clothes of the revolutionaries—the poor. He puffed out his chest. A large cockade—red, white, and blue patch was sewn on his shirt over his heart. He gripped a gun tightly in his hand. His arms flailed. Alexandra thought for a moment that he was play-acting.

"Halt! Down with the aristocracy." He waved the pistol in the air. His eyes, which had a crazed look, shone with determination.

Alexandra didn't move. "He's real…really crazy. That's a serious looking gun," she whispered. "And he's pointing it in our direction."

"Down with the rich. We have no bread—no food. You all must die." He ran toward them and began to shoot.

Jean Paul lunged forward. Before he could grab the gun, the man pointed it at Alexandra's chest. He moved forward, released the safety and pulled back his finger on the trigger. "*Vive la Nation, Vive la République*," he yelled. He shot Alexandra. When the crowd heard the crack of the gun, they scattered, running in all directions.

The last thing Alexandra saw was the man dropping the gun and disappearing into the crowd. Her eyes closed. She tensed. Her stomach tightened. A horrific pain shot through her body. She put her hand on her chest and felt a warm, sticky stream of blood flow through her clothes soaking her fingers. Her legs wobbled. She slid to the ground. The blackness pulled her under.

Jean Paul bent over Alexandra and pulled off his coat and shirt. He bunched up his shirt and pressed it tightly against her chest. Desperately, he pushed on her wound as he tried to stop the bleeding. He broke out in a cold sweat. He wrapped his free arm around her and held her close.

Alexandra felt him holding her tightly in his free arm—her head against his chest. She hung on to Jean Paul as she twisted her ring.

Chapter Eighteen

July 24, 2010

Jean Paul kept his eyes on Alexandra. Her blood was soaking his shirt. He felt as if he was floating. When he looked up, they were on the sidewalk outside the Musée du Louvre.

He had hoped when they got back to 2010 Alexandra would be all right. Unfortunately, she was still bleeding. "Get an ambulance," he yelled. He saw a policeman running toward them as he dug into his pocket for his cellphone. "She's been shot." His throat went dry, his jaw clenched and his eyes blazed with fire.

"An ambulance is on its way," the policeman yelled back. He ran toward them and shouted at the mass of people gathering next to Alexandra to 'keep moving.'

Jean Paul heard the sirens of the ambulance getting closer. "Hang on. Alexandra. The ambulance will be here in a second. You will be on your way to the hospital very soon now."

She felt his lips brush the crown of her head. Then she heard the screech of brakes and voices getting closer to her.

"Get out of the way. Stretcher coming through."

She squinted through a fogged vision and saw the EMTs rolling a stretcher toward her.

"Step back. Let's start an intravenous line as soon as we get her into the ambulance." The voice was next to her ear. "Get a pressure bandage on her chest." One of the EMTs wrapped a blood pressure cuff around her upper arm and attached a portable monitor to her limp body. "Her blood pressure is 90/50, pulse 120. She's fading. She stopped breathing! Get the paddles." His rushed to the ambulance and reached for the machine with the paddles. He rubbed the paddles with gel as his partner started CPR. "Clear!" the EMT yelled. Her body bucked. He looked at the portable monitor. "Okay her heart beat is better."

"Hang an IV drip," yelled his partner.

Jean Paul heard the once erratic bleeps even out. "Will she be all right?" He watched the man start an intravenous drip.

"For now she's okay."

She was aware of the prick of the needle when they stuck it into her arm. The I.V. fluid dripped slowly into her vein. Alexandra felt herself being lifted onto the stretcher. The wheels of the stretcher folded, as she was pulled into the ambulance.

"She's having difficulty breathing. Get the oxygen going." Alexandra heard a voice shout. When the oxygen mask slipped over her nose, she relaxed a little. It was easier for her to breathe.

"I'm going with you." Jean Paul started to jump up into the ambulance to sit beside Alexandra.

"Just a minute! I have to speak with you. I'm Detective Fouché. I'm from the Sûreté."

Jean Paul backed away from the step. "Can't you ask your questions later?" Jean Paul laid his hand on the ambulance door.

"Hang on, lady, we'll get you to the hospital. Coming or going, Sir?" the EMT yelled.

Jean Paul stared at the Detective. "All right, I'll see you at the hospital. Where are you taking her?" He backed away. Raking his fingers through his hair, he left specks of blood.

"To the American Hospital. It's the best one in Paris. It has the finest doctors. Everyone on the staff is bilingual. Meet us in the emergency room." The EMT slammed the door as the ambulance pulled away—its sirens blaring.

Jean Paul turned to the policeman. His brows pulled closely together. His clenched teeth caused a sharp pain to shoot through his jaw. "What is it, Detective?" He sighed.

"Did you see the person who shot her?"

"No." He couldn't tell him what had transpired. It would bring up more questions than he needed right now, or ever. Besides, he knew the detective wouldn't believe him.

"We found a gun a few feet away from where the victim fell. It's a flint locked muzzle loading gun. It's mounted on a fifteen inch dagger with a wood and brass handle. I've only seen a gun like that in a museum. It's from the eighteenth century. Do you know anything about it?"

"Nothing." He moved away from the detective and began to pace. "I have to get to the hospital. Ask your questions later? Meet me at the hospital. I'll answer as much as I can."

"What about the assailant? What did he look like?"

"He looked like an escapee from a mental institution." *I may be right about that. I really don't think the shooter looked like a revolutionary.* "I just told you. I have to go. I'll answer your questions later."

"Are you sure you can't remember anything unusual about him. What was he wearing?"

"Detective, I told you, I don't remember anything."

"All right. What are your names and where are you and the victim staying?"

"I'm Jean Paul Morneau, attorney, and the victim is Alexandra Pirrot, U.S. FBI agent. We're staying at the chateau in Giverny. We were in Paris for the day to do some sightseeing."

"I will keep in touch with the hospital. When they say Mademoiselle Pirrot is able to answer questions, I'll stop by her room. Meanwhile, don't go anywhere. Don't leave Paris."

"Don't worry. I'm not going anywhere." Jean Paul clenched his jaw and ground his back teeth together. He grimaced. *I wish this guy would get lost.*

Hospital
July 24, 2010

As soon as Jean Paul's body passed by the sensors at the entrance of the emergency room, the doors opened automatically and he sprinted through. He dashed to the desk on the left wall of the large, tiled room. "Alexandra Pirrot. She was brought in a short while ago." Jean Paul stood in front of the desk that had a sign that said *Admitting.* "Where is she?" He looked around at the cubicles separated by white curtains.

"Sorry, sir…"

"What? No!" He stopped and looked intently at the woman. He knew his face must have turned ashen. He felt ice cold.

"No…No, sir. She's alive. They took her right up to surgery. Go to the fourth floor—four east—and give them your name. The nurse or doctor will let you know when they finish." She pointed toward the elevators.

Jean Paul ran to the elevators. He bumped into a nurse pushing an intravenous pole, knocking it out of her hand. She reached out for it, but he caught it just before it landed on the floor and pushed it toward her.

"Sorry."

He reached the elevator and repeatedly pushed on the button with his index finger. "At last." He heard a ding and a swishing noise as the door slid open. He banged on the 'close door' button. "Come on, get moving," he yelled as the door slammed shut. *Get a grip.* He hammered on the 'four' with his fist. "Finally!" Jean Paul shouted as the doors closed and he felt the upward motion of the elevator.

When the elevator stopped with a jolt, he leaped out and followed the arrow to the 'four east' waiting room. He needed to calm down. He knew Alexandra was being taken care of and there was nothing he could do but wait. He stepped into a room with worn, but comfortable-looking, furniture; molded plastic chairs were pushed under the two square tables. An upholstered couch with faded material sat across from him. A large ficus tree stood in the far corner. Some of its leaves had fallen on the floor. A man paced up and down and then sat down on one of the molded chairs. A woman punched her cell phone several times before she realized there was no reception in the hospital. She sighed loudly.

The nurse sitting at the nurses' station looked up and smiled. "May I help you?"

Jean Paul cleared his throat. "I'm Jean Paul Morneau, Alexandra Pirrot's husband."

He lied to the nurse at the desk when he told her he was Alexandra's husband, but she had no living relatives in France. "They told me to come up here and said I would be able to find out her condition."

"Oh good, I need you to sign some forms." She moved from behind the desk. Her lab coat was white and starched. Her white clogs made a soft thudding sound as her rubber soles hit the floor. "She woke up just long enough to sign the permission for surgery. Here's the rest. Just sign where I've put the x."

He didn't even look at what he was signing. He handed them back to her nurse and watched her stuff them into a manila file folder. "I'll be right back," she said as she disappeared behind a swinging door with the sign that said 'Operating Room'.

The white walls, tile floor, and antiseptic smell of the waiting room didn't soothe his nerves. He paced while he waited for her to return. Jean Paul walked over to the door that she had disappeared through and stared through the window. He looked down a long hallway. Within a few minutes he saw her come out of a room at the end of the hall. She walked back to the door where he stood. Jean Paul stepped back and moved out of the way as she pushed the door open. "Is she all right?" His eyebrows were drawn together showing deep lines in his forehead.

"Things are going well. No problems yet."

No problems yet. That's a big help. He paced back and forth.

Finally the nurse came over to him. "She'll be all right. Dr. Bernard Papion is operating on her. If anyone can save her, he can. He's the best thoracic and heart surgeon in France. He's famous for his robotic technology."

"So what does that mean—robotic technology?" Jean Paul shook his head.

"When patients are operated on with the robotic technique, the physicians guide the robots. The procedures can be done with finer motions. The patients have smaller scars and less pain. There is a reduced risk of infection, because there are fewer people in the operating room. There is less blood loss. She had lost so much blood before she got to the hospital, it was imperative that her loss of blood, during surgery, be kept at a minimum. She'll be fine."

"Thank you." Jean Paul sat down and flipped through the magazines on the scarred table next to his chair. The pages flew by. He didn't even see what was on them. The conversation of the people in the waiting room ebbed and flowed. He heard a word here and there. None of the patients seemed to be as sick as Alexandra or at least that's what he thought he heard from their relatives' who waited near him.

After what seemed like hours, Jean Paul watched the doors of the surgical unit swung open. A tall man in a green scrub suit and cap with a mask hanging around his neck walked through the doors. Jean Paul thought he looked about his age. The doctor opened the folder when he reached Jean Paul's chair.

"Mr. Morneau?" He smiled.

"Yes?" The back of Jean Paul's neck tensed, his jaw beneath a darkening beard tightened and his eyes were serious.

"I'm Dr. Bernard Papion." He extended his hand to Jean Paul. "The surgery went well. We were able to remove the bullet. It was lodged very close to her heart. The next twenty-four hours will be the most dangerous for her, but she is doing very well for the injury she sustained. She is in very good health—that helps. She is being moved to a critical care room. She will be in 406. Wait five or ten minutes while we get her settled, then you can see her. You can stay all day and all night. If you need to ask me anything, the hospital can always reach me. They have a number that contacts me day and night."

"Thank you, Doctor." Jean Paul breathed a long sigh of relief. He realized he was still gripping the doctor's hand. "Sorry." He smiled. "Thank you again." He dropped the doctor's hand. *My God. He looks just like Henri. I guess in this lifetime he's a doctor and it's his turn to save Alexandra. Last lifetime, Alexandra saved Henri, the brother-in-law.*

"Do you have any questions?"

Jean Paul couldn't think of anything. "Not right now." He ran his hand through his hair as he walked with the doctor toward room 406.

"I want to check her before you see her," Dr. Papion said.

Jean Paul waited outside the room for the staff to leave. Once Alexandra was alone, with all her tubes and leads attached, he pulled a chair up to her bed and flopped into it. *Why her?* He pounded his fist on the arm of the chair. His eyebrows were drawn together. His jaw was set. His eyes were dark blue like the sea during a storm. He didn't hear the nurse come into the room.

"Her pulse is good. She should wake up soon. I'm sure she will be fine. I know it must be alarming to see all the tubes, but they will be taken out soon." The motherly woman in a white lab coat patted Jean Paul on the shoulder. Her crepe-soled shoes squeaked as she left the room.

Jean Paul sat by Alexandra's bed. His eyes were fixed unwaveringly upon Alexandra. He wished she would wake up and talk to him. He didn't move when the night nurse covered him with a blanket. He woke up in the middle of the night and stood over Alexandra. He smoothed her limp and ragged hair from her face. His insides lurched as he watched her.

He thought about the first time he met her in the dining room at the chateau. She was poised and self-assured. Now she looked like a ghost— her face was pale and gaunt. It was as white as the sheets on her bed. Jean Paul dug his fingers through his hair. He watched for any little sign that meant she was waking up—there was none. Her even breathing gave him a hopeful feeling. She was a strong woman. She would be all right. She had to be, he thought.

Jean Paul touched her cheek with a trembling hand. "I love you," he whispered—not believing his own voice. He stared at her. He had given up cigarettes years ago, but now he seriously thought about bumming a couple. However, that would mean he would have to go outside to smoke and he didn't want to leave her bedside. He knew that he felt more than friendship for Alexandra. *I can't lose her now.*

Hospital
July 27, 2010

Alexandra lay very still. She knew people moved around her and that they spoke in hushed voices. It was hard for her to hear what they said over the steady beep, beep of the machine—just out of her view—whose wires were attached to her chest.

She wanted to respond to the voices, but couldn't seem to open her eyes. Her mouth felt dry. She couldn't seem to make her lips move. She was positive one of the voices she heard was Jean Paul. He seemed to be having a conversation with someone—a nurse, a doctor—she wasn't sure. The voices came from a long way off. Finally, she was able to force her eyelids open—just a little.

Through blurred vision she saw a woman in a white lab coat with a stethoscope draped around her neck. As her vision became a little clearer, she saw the nurse change the clear, plastic bag attached to a pole at the side of her bed and adjust the drip of the fluid going into the plastic tubing that eventually went to the needle taped to the top of her hand.

Alexandra turned her head to the side. She saw Jean Paul. He had sunk low in his chair. His feet were propped on the metal bar at the end of her bed. A blanket was pulled over one of his shoulders. His eyes were closed. She looked at his rumpled clothes and tousled hair. His strong jawline was shadowed with a several-days-old beard. *How long has he been here? He looks very male, big and brooding, even in his sleep. The unshaven look makes him seem sexy and tough. Good God! Alexandra. You're lying in a hospital bed, barely able to move.*

She reached out the hand that wasn't attached to the intravenous drip and touched his arm that lay at her side. A shooting pain drummed in her head. Her chest hurt. She slipped back into sleep.

Later in the afternoon, Alexandra awoke when she heard two male voices. One was Jean Paul—she recognized him—the other, a man with a gruff voice. She had heard it before—before she was brought to the hospital. She couldn't identify it. She knew they were arguing. Then the room was quiet. After a few minutes, she made an effort to open her eyes. She wiggled her fingers and toes to make sure they still worked. She eventually looked up at the array of plastic tubing attached to her and decided not to move.

Alexandra kept her eyes open and looked around the room. Jean Paul was still slumped down in a chair next to the bed. A man in a business suit was standing at the foot of her bed. He was staring at her. The man was big—tall and heavy with broad shoulders. He looked like a linebacker for a winning Super Bowl team.

"Looks like she's awake, Mr. Morneau," Detective Fouché said.

Startled, Jean Paul jumped. He sat straight up in his chair. His feet that had been propped up at the end of the bed landed on the floor with a thud.

Alexandra felt his warm fingers tighten over hers.

He looked into her face that was still as white as her pillowcase. As he stood up, he leaned over her bed. He kissed her tenderly. "Alexandra, thank God you're awake." He stared at her opened eyes. A deep scowl carved horizontal lines on his forehead. His heart skipped a beat. She looked so small and lost to him. "I didn't know if you would ever wake up."

Alexandra looked up at him and stared into his eyes that had turned deep blue like the sea before a storm. She smiled. "I'm okay," she mouthed.

"Now that the hellos are over, can I get answers to some of my questions? Detective Fouché—from the Sûreté, Ms. Pirrot," he said as he moved closer to her and extended his hand. "Ms. Pirrot, just a few questions."

She tried to speak, but her lips wouldn't move—they were dry and stiff. "I'm so thirsty," she finally managed to whisper.

"Detective, don't you see her condition?" Jean Paul picked up a glass of water and held the straw to Alexandra's mouth. "She can barely speak."

"I can wait." He stepped back few steps.

"Be careful, dear. Take small sips." Jean Paul smiled. He couldn't believe she was finally awake.

After a few sips, Alexandra nodded to the detective. "May I help you, Detective Fouché?" she whispered.

"Did you know your assailant? Did he say anything to you?"

"No, I never saw him before. The only thing I heard him say was 'Halt.' He mumbled something about rich people. I'm not sure what it was." Alexandra was sure he would act like a bulldog that grabbed a huge bone and wouldn't let go until he found out who shot her. She felt she had to tell him something that would pacify him for a while. "Detective, he had a French accent and looked deranged." Her voice was low and hoarse.

"Can you tell me a little more?"

"He was a little taller than me—five foot six or five foot seven." Alexandra stopped. She took a deep breath and slowly exhaled it. "And very heavy. I really don't remember anything more…Wait, he was dressed in baggy clothes."

"The bullet they took out of you was from the antique gun we found at the scene of your shooting."

Alexandra shrugged her shoulders. She glanced at him and then motioned for Jean Paul to give her more water.

"Okay, we'll keep looking, but we probably won't find him. We haven't been able to trace the gun. The fingerprints we found on it are not in the system. I'll be back if I need anything else." He nodded. "If you remember anything more about what happened, call me." He pulled a card from the inside pocket of his jacket and laid it on her bedside table. "You too, Monsieur Morneau."

He didn't think they were telling him everything they knew, but he couldn't prove it. A lawyer and a FBI agent would be hard to take on if they didn't want to cooperate. They would know how to hide facts, but why would they want to hide something that would help get the shooter?

"Thank you very much, Detective Fouche," Alexandra said. "I appreciate you trying to find my assailant. I'm sorry I can't be of more help. If I think of anything more, I'll get in touch with you."

She stared at Jean Paul's haggard face and the dark circles under his eyes. "Have you been here the whole time?"

"Yup."

"How long have I been out?"

"Three and half days. Do you remember anything?" he asked when the detective left.

"Just running from the square after Claudette was guillotined."

"Sssssh." He stroked her face and held her to him. He smoothed her auburn hair that cascaded around her face. He didn't know she was crying, until he felt the wetness of his shirt. "I should have protected you better."

Alexandra felt the steady rhythm of his heartbeat. "I left her to die."

"No. Don't think that way, Alexandra. You can't change history. You went back in time to help her get some answers—not to save her. She needs to rest in peace and you are helping her to do that. You aren't supposed to stop her death—that already happened. You're here to give her answers."

"We still have to get some of those answers." Alexandra closed her eyes. "There's one answer that I got. It will help your case. When we were in the wagon going to La Conciergerie, Claudette confessed to the murder of Mr. Dumont's business partner."

"What! Why did she do it?"

"She thought...apparently he looked exactly like the gardener who turned her in to the revolutionaries. In her mind, when she saw the business partner, she thought it was the gardener and now she could to get her revenge—revenge for taking her away from her family. She wasn't able to see her children grow up because she was killed by the rebels. She was guillotined. Claudette had no idea why the gardener reported her. She was good to the people who worked for her at the chateau. She said she always treated them well."

Chapter Nineteen

Jean Paul strolled into Alexandra's hospital room.

"Wait!" Alexandra shouted when she saw him. She was standing in her lacy underwear. She grabbed her blouse and jeans and held them in front of her half-naked body trying to hide as much of herself as possible. She felt warmth creep from her chest to her forehead.

It was too late. Jean Paul stood mesmerized. "Where did you get the clothes?" Jean Paul finally asked?

"I had a nurse buy me some things. I gave her my size or the size I used to be. I'm afraid I've lost a lot of weight. Turn your back." She pulled on her jeans and buttoned her apricot blouse. She looked down. "I'm afraid they're hanging on me. But at least I can go back to the chateau in street clothes and not in a hospital gown and robe." She gathered up the waist of her jeans and tightened her belt. She pulled on her socks and sneakers, and slipped the make-up she had applied before he had arrived into a plastic bag. She ran a brush through her hair.

"Are you sure you're all right? Are you well enough to leave the hospital?"

"Yes, the doctor discharged me with a couple of meds—an antibiotic and something for pain. My pain is minimal. I feel great. I'm very tired of being in bed. I need to get in to the fresh air. Dr. Papion wouldn't have discharged me if he wasn't sure I'd be okay. The only thing he insisted on is that I visit his office before I go back to the States."

He pulled her close and found her mouth. Their lips never parted as he drew her closer. His hands ran down her back and spine. He kissed her throat.

"Excuse me." Alexandra looked up and saw a nurse standing next to them. "I brought a wheelchair." She smiled. "You're all signed out."

"She'll be fine," she said to Jean Paul. The nurse walked with them to the door. She waited while Jean Paul walked to the parking lot to get his Porsche.

Jean Paul drove up and slid into a parking place at the curb. "Better than Cinderella's carriage." The nurse winked at Jean Paul.

"Thank you very much for all your good care." Alexandra smiled.

"Take good care of her. Don't let us see her again," the nurse said, nodding to Jean Paul.

Jean Paul laughed. "Don't worry. I'm not letting her out of my sight." He covered her lips with his. He was aware of her heart beating as she snuggled into his arms and returned his kiss.

Alexandra looked over her shoulder and waved to the nurse as they pulled away.

"We have to make one stop before we go back to the chateau," Jean Paul said.

"Where are we stopping?"

"At Saint-Pierre prison, outside the city of Versailles. Monsieur Dumont has been incarcerated there since he was arrested. He's not going to be prosecuted. I just have to sign some papers and he can go home. I'm meeting his wife there. She'll bring him home."

"You got him out! How did you do it? I know you didn't tell them about Claudette ghost jumping out of her portrait, did you?"

Jean Paul laughed. "No, they eventually admitted there wasn't enough evidence—no weapon, no confession. With no proof, they didn't have much of a case. He also had an alibi that they finally decided to believe."

"Who's they?" Alexandra asked.

"A judge, the investigating officer, and the public prosecutor. The poor man suffered horrific conditions, but thank God he was strong and was able to survive. The prison was built in 1760. Many prisoners commit suicide. Some people are never heard from again after they are incarcerated. Nobody in charge at the prison will admit what happens to them. Dumont was in a cell that once was a dungeon. It had a solid, metal door and a small peephole. There was no window. The prison had rats, lice, and unsanitary conditions. They don't have torture machines anymore; just being there is agony enough. I wasn't allowed to see him for almost a day after he was incarcerated. The prison officials let me into his cell exactly twenty hours after he was jailed. I'm amazed he is still sane."

"I'd like to talk with him about what he saw that day in the hallway. After he gets settled at home, of course," Alexandra said.

Historical Society-Vincennes
August 14, 2010

Alexandra ran down the stairs of the chateau. She took a deep breath and reached the driveway just as Jean Paul's car pulled up. She watched the convertible top of his Porsche slide down into the back of the car. "After we search the records at the historical society we'll have some lunch. Vincennes is only four miles outside the Paris city limits."

It was a beautiful day. Alexandra had seen the scenery along the road to Paris in all kinds of conditions. Today, it was probably the most picturesque. It was warm and sunny. The yellow machines had started to prepare for harvesting the grapes, the little town squares were filled with people shopping and children were playing games in the streets. Alexandra watched the field and houses fly by as they drove.

Jean Paul pulled up to the gate of the historical building. He handed his credentials to the guard, who scanned them into a machine and then pointed to the parking area. "Park to the right of the building. It will be a short walk to the door—just a few minutes," the guard said.

"*Merci.*" Jean Paul nodded to the guard.

"All the navy and army records are stored here. Apparently the records go back to the seventeenth century. The records are very thorough. You can find physical descriptions of the veterans, birth, manner of death and date, education, rank, where the veteran served, where they are buried. They also list information about their family members," Jean Paul said. "Besides the family chapel at the chateau, this is probably the only place we'll be able to find any information about Claudette's husband and his family."

This may be the only place we'll be able to find information on how her husband died and where he served can be found," Alexandra said.

"What did you show him?"

"An ID that gets me into all the important places. An ID for the Justice Department." Jean Paul parked the car as close as he could to the building. He grabbed Alexandra's hand as they walked to the main entrance. "I didn't want you to have to walk too far."

"You don't have to treat me like an invalid. I'm fine. But thank you." She squeezed his hand.

They walked up the stairs to the front door and stopped at the desk just inside the building. A man in a black suit, white shirt, and navy blue tie sat on a chair in front of a metal desk. He was staring at a computer.

"*Bonjour*," Jean Paul said. "We're looking for any records you have on Jacques Louis Pirrot, eighteenth century." He showed his I.D. card. "This is Alexandra Pirrot.

Alexandra echoed his greeting.

"Pierre Carpier, Sergeant," the guard answered as he scanned Jean Paul's I.D. "We've put almost all the records in the computer. Let's see if he's been entered." The man scrolled to the eighteenth century. "What did you say his name was?"

"Jacques Louis Pirrot." They watched him type in the name.

"You're in luck. His history is sketchy, but he's listed. Here, look." He turned the screen so they could see the information.

"You're right, it's sketchy, but there is some information," Jean Paul said as he scanned the computer page.

"My French is pretty good but I can't translate that fast. Could you please tell me in English?" Alexandra asked.

"*Oui*." The guard pushed a button that automatically translated the information to English. "All done." He brought up a split screen—French on one side, English on the other." Alexandra followed along as he began to read. "Jacques Louis Pirrot, born 1759 and died in June of 1787. He served with distinction. Pirrot was a lieutenant in the King's regiment. That would be King Louis XVI. The one beheaded during the French Revolution. Pirrot's wife's name was Claudette. Married in the 1780s, no exact date mentioned. He had two children. No physical description. Seems like the family had a private cemetery. He was buried there. A lot of French families of the aristocracy had private chapels in their family cemeteries where they stored their important papers. Records like marriage licenses, death notices, last will and testament and so on would probably be there."

"How did he die? Does it say?" Alexandra asked.

"Let's see." He read down a few lines. "He didn't die in battle. Seems like a friend shot him by mistake."

"What was the friend's name?" Alexandra moved closer to the screen.

The guard studied the screen for a few minutes moving his index finger down the screen. "Ah, here it is. Here's another notation made sometime after his death. The name is Robespierre."

"Not in battle?" Jean Paul nodded to Alexandra.

Sergeant Carpier looked back at the screen. "No, it says the family was told he died in battle, by the order of Robespierre. Later it was discovered by the military that Robespierre shot him by mistake. Seems like he wrote a letter to a friend just before he was guillotined. How you say—a death bed confession," he said as he chuckled.

"I'm sure a tyrant like Robespierre wouldn't want Claudette's husband for a friend, since he was loyal to the King. Who investigated the death?" Alexandra asked.

"There's nothing in the records about that. Sorry I couldn't be more help."

"Thank you very much. Sergeant Carpier. You have been a big help. You answered a lot of our questions." Alexandra smiled. "Mistake my foot," she whispered to Jean Paul on the way to the car. "Claudette was right. She suspected it was Robespierre who murdered her husband."

Montmartre

"Come on, let's go into Paris." Jean Paul took hold of Alexandra's arm. "I'm hungry. Where do you want to go?"

"You pick the place." Alexandra smiled. "It's your city."

"Let's go to Montmartre—La Rive Gauche. I know a great café." Jean Paul drove quickly through Paris traffic and parked his car at the bottom of the hill. "The carnival spirit is in full gear all year round there. You'll enjoy it."

"This is wonderful." They passed private mansions that hid behind locked gates. She stopped and peeked behind the iron fences at their beautiful gardens. As they walked up the steep hill on the narrow streets toward the top, Alexandra rested and watched a street artist. As she started to leave he yelled, "Mademoiselle, come back, *s'il vous plait*." He waved to Alexandra to sit on the stool. "I want to draw you." She turned and sat down on the stool in front of him. Jean Paul stood beside the artist and watched him sketch. The artist quickly drew her. When he finished, he ripped off the sheet of paper, rolled it up and handed it to her.

Alexandra dug into her purse. "Combien?"

"As you Americans say, it's on the house," he said with a distinctive New York accent.

"Thanks. You sound as if you're from the United States."

"I am. Been here ten years. Never lost the accent of the City. I try to sound French but it's hard. " He laughed. "But I'm beginning to feel as if I'm a native."

"I'm beginning to feel that way also."

She waved as they continued up the hill. *"Merci beaucoup."*

"Let me see it again." Jean Paul leaned over and took a good look at the drawing as Alexandra unrolled it. "Looks just like you. He's good."

"*Merci*, Monsieur," the artist called to them as they continued up the hill.

"Where are we going?"

"I want to show you Paris from the best view in the city. It's at the top of the street and uphill. Are you up for it?"

"Yes."

They passed fish and butcher shops and bakeries and small cafés as they walked up to the Sacré-Cœur Basilica at the head of the street. When they passed a fruit market, Jean Paul stopped and bought two apples.

"Are you doing all right?" Jean Paul handed her one.

"I'm doing fine. Just a little slower than usual, but it forces me to enjoy the scenery. Thanks for the apple. I'm getting hungry." Alexandra looked up at the dome of Sacré-Cœur that stood at the head of the street.

"Okay, then let's go." He led her into the Basilica. She walked through the sanctuary studying the statues and altar.

They walked the extra two hundred and ninety-five feet to the dome. Alexandra leaned on the ledge and looked out over Paris.

"How can the Basilica stay so white with all the weather and pollution?" Alexandra asked.

"It's made of travertine stone quarried in Chateau Landon. It constantly exudes calcite. That's what ensures that it remains white. The people of Paris wanted a spiritual revival. The construction was started in 1875. They commissioned the architect, Paul Abode. He was the one who designed it."

When they reached the walkway at the top, Alexandra looked down on Paris. "I see Notre Dame. That's the Ile de la Cité?" She tried to identify more landmarks. "There's the Eiffel Tower." She felt someone pushing to get to the rail and moved back.

"I love Paris. It's a wonderful city."

"Ready for lunch? It's easier going down."

"I'm starved."

Outside the Basilica they watched the street mimes, stilt walkers, and clowns entertain the crowds of people. They walked downhill. The café was halfway down the block. Jean Paul stopped outside a small restaurant. "It's small, but the food is excellent." He motioned to the man standing in the doorway. "*Bonjour*, Anton." Jean Paul waved to the waiter.

"*Bonjour*, Monsieur Morneau. And who is the beautiful, young woman?"

"My American friend, Alexandra Pirrot." He grabbed her hand. They followed the waiter inside and to a table overlooking the street. "*Merci*," Jean Paul said.

"We'll have the catch of the day and a salad. Okay?" he asked as they sat down at a small table.

"Fine. And some wine."

They sat and talked about the information they found at the historical society.

"We have to find the chapel on the chateau grounds. I think it may be near the cemetery and pond that I can see from my window. There's something that looks like a building. It covered with vines so it's hard to tell what it is."

It was dark when they left for the chateau. Alexandra was mesmerized by the view. "It is truly the City of Lights."

Monsieur Dumont greeted them as they opened the front door.

"How are you feeling? Are you getting rid of the stench of the prison and the horrific conditions?" Alexandra smiled. "I knew you were innocent. I met your ghost and the murderer of your business partner. Hopefully, I'll be able get her to cross over before she creates any more mayhem. I have to get some information for her and then, with a bit of luck, she'll be gone."

"Oh, thank you. I don't want any harm to come to my wife and me. I feel better that I am not the only one that has seen the ghost." He gave her a hug. *"Merci."*

"She really isn't a bad person. She was getting revenge because she thought your business partner was the gardener who turned her in to the revolutionaries. I guess he could have been a twin of her betrayer." She smiled.

"I feel better and I'm putting prison behind me," he said. "Goodnight, I will see you at breakfast."

Jean Paul pulled her close to him. "You knew just how to make him feel better. I'm positive we'll find the chapel and all the information that will help Claudette pass over."

Paris and Ile de la Cite
August 17, 2010

"We have an invitation to my parents' home for dinner. They live on the Ile de la Cité. My father called and said he found some documents from the 1700s in the attic and that he had a surprise for me. He said he had no idea how they got there or how long they had been there."

"Did he give you any idea or a hint at what they were?" Alexandra asked.

"No. Apparently he and my mother were storing his old records from cases he litigated years ago and came across some papers stuffed in an old book. He's not how sure how old the papers are, but said they looked well over one hundred and fifty years old. He said a couple had dates on them. The years on them were 1785, 1795, and 1801. The rest of them he said he couldn't read."

"I would love to go. Can we leave early and walk around Paris?"

"Sure. We'll leave about noon and have lunch somewhere nice."

"I'd love to visit the Museé D'Orsay," Alexandra said. "I'm fascinated by the Impressionists. It's my favorite period of art."

"All right, we'll leave about eleven."

"I'm going to park my car on the Ile de la Cité, near Notre Dame. That's next to where my parents live. We can take the underground to the Arc de Triomphe and walk down the Champs-Elysées. Wear comfortable shoes. It's about a mile and a half mile walk. After lunch we can go to the Musée D'Orsay. It's very close to my parent's home."

When they arrived at the Arc de Triomphe station, Alexandra and Jean Paul walked through a tunnel and came up to the street. Alexandra waited for a break in the traffic and rushed across the street. She hurried to the Arc and walked under it. She looked at the eternal flame—the memorial to an unknown French soldier killed in battle during World War I.

Then, hand-in-hand, Jean Paul and Alexandra battled the traffic to get to the sidewalk. They started their walk on the Champs-Elysées. Alexandra peeked into boutiques, auto showrooms, small markets, shops, and other retail shops. At the fifth cafe, Alexandra said, "Let's stop for a cup of coffee—my treat."

They sat outside at the café and people-watched for a while and then began to walk again.

"Ready to go. Do you want to buy anything?"

"No, not now. I just want to look," Alexandra answered.

When they reached the winged statue—Spirit of Liberty—at the Place de la Concorde, Alexandra looked around. "I remember this place," she said. "Only too well."

Jean Paul looked at her and pulled her to him. "Don't think about it—all that is over. There was nothing you could do. I keep telling you history can't be altered." He gave her a hug "Cheer up. Are you hungry?"

"*Oui, trés* hungry. I skipped breakfast."

Jean Paul raised his hand and hailed a cab. The taxi slid to a stop at the side of the curb. After they got settled in the back seat, Jean Paul leaned forward. "Maxim's, *s'il vous plait.*"

The ride to Three Rue Royale didn't take too long. When she jumped out of the cab, Alexandra stared at the deep red awning with gold letters spelling out the name of the restaurant. The facade of wood and huge glass doors with brass handles hadn't changed in years. She remembered seeing a picture of Maxim's in the 1930s. "How did you know this was on my list of restaurants to eat in?"

"I didn't, but it has great food."

The restaurant was crowd. Alexandra instantly smelled the aroma of herbs and spices.

The maître d' showed them to a table that looked out into the avenue.

"Perfect," Jean Paul said. When they sat down, he looked at Alexandra. "How do you like the art nouveau interior décor?"

"I love it. I feel as if I'm in 1890. The combination of nature—stems and flowers—and people are wonderful. The pastel colors, curvilinear lines, the flower-like halos behind beautiful, young women in graceful, flowing robes are unique. I do believe the painting behind you was done by Mucha. He used writhing plants and flowing lines. His women were painted with a combination of flowing hair and nature."

"Maxim's was opened in 1893, just after the dawn of Art Nouveau, by a waiter Maxim Grillard. It's now owned by Pierre Cardin, the French clothes designer who has branched out into the gourmet food business," Jean Paul said.

They ate and talked. It was easy for both of them to engage in conversation. They seemed to realize how much they had in common. After lunch, Jean Paul hailed another cab and they were off to the museum on the Ile de la Cité.

"Have you ever been to the D' Orsay?" she asked.

"I've never had time. I've seen a lot of the art before they took it from the Louvre and hung it here after they built this museum. It was built in an old train station, you know."

"Yes, it's an interesting building. Let's start on the second floor." She headed for the marble staircase and pulled Jean Paul along with her. "I love this art. It's less formal, more casual, with brilliant colors. The way they were able to show light and its changing quality is unbelievable to me." She wandered through the paintings of Vincent Von Gogh, Monet, Cezanne, Gauguin, and Renoir. She stood in front of Renoir's 'Bathers' and sighed. "I wish I had talent like that. When I took a History of Art course in college, the impressionist artists were my favorite.

She glanced at her watch. "Should we be heading for your parents' house?"

Chapter Twenty

"Yes, I think we can walk from here. How are you doing?"

"I'm absolutely fine. I want to get your mother some flowers."

"There's a flower market on the way—so no problem."

They strolled through streets with secondhand bookstores, gardens, and magnificent houses behind fences and gates. When they reached the flower market, she wandered through the stalls. She picked some white roses and lilies and a mixture of other white flowers. "Do you think I can get these wrapped, *s'il vous plaît?*" Alexandra said to the sales woman in front of her. She was directed to a table near the entrance.

"I'm so glad not to be thinking about Claudette for a while. I need a break and meeting your parents is a wonderful way to a take a breather and relax. I'm so happy I'm getting to meet them." She smiled at Jean Paul.

A few blocks from the flower market Jean Paul came to a stop at an elegant townhome. He punched numbers in a keypad and pushed open the gate. They walked up a circular driveway to the oak door of the home.

Jean Paul opened the door of his parents' home and yelled, "Hello."

Alexandra was surprised when a handsome woman with white hair, clad in a light blue silk suit that matched her ice blue eyes, entered the hallway. Her smile was welcoming. She gave Jean Paul a hug. "This must be Alexandra!" She extended her hand. "Please come in." She made Alexandra feel comfortable immediately.

Alexandra recognized the same regal nose and slender fingers that reminded her of Claudette.

"It's chilly out there tonight. We've heard so much about you," Jean

Paul's mother said.

Alexandra felt her face warm. She handed her the flowers. "Thank you for inviting me to your home."

"How sweet of you," Jean Paul's mother said. "Thank you." She rang a small bell sitting on the antique entrance hall table.

A young woman in a black and white uniform immediately appeared in the hallway.

"Please put these in water, Marie. They are beautiful, Alexandra. Come with me." Jean Paul's mother led them to a living room. Alexandra peeked at the antiques and Oriental rugs as she followed. Their home reminded Alexandra of her home in New York City. When they entered the living room, Alexandra saw a man sitting in a winged-back chair. He was an older version of Jean Paul. He stood. "Good evening, my dear." He grasped her hand with both of his when she extended it. He moved to the hearth where logs cracked in the burning fire and stood next to her with his back to the fire.

"Good evening, Mr. Morneau. Thank you both for having me." She turned to Jean Paul's mother.

"Please dear, this is Louis." She extended her hand toward her husband and smiled lovingly. "And I am Marguerite. Jean Paul, please get your friend an aperitif."

"What would you like?"

"A dry sherry, please," Alexandra requested.

"Here, sit next to me." Marguerite sat down in front of the fire and patted the loveseat next to where she sat. "We have fires in the evenings, even in the summer. These old, stone houses hold in the cold and dampness. We've had lots of rain lately."

Alexandra took the sherry Jean Paul handed her.

"We are so glad Jean Paul brought you to dinner, especially since he told us you just recently got out of the hospital. "How do you feel?"

"I'm all healed and feel great."

Jean Paul hardly ever brings anyone around to meet us. You must be very special."

Alexandra put her hand to her face. She knew it must be pink—if not bright red. Her cheek felt hot. She looked at the floor for a second and then looked up and smiled.

"Don't pay attention to my mother." Jean Paul turned to his mother. "Would you like something to drink?"

"Yes, dear. I'll have a sherry also."

"Mother, I'm busy with work. You know that. I don't even get here very often."

Alexandra looked at Jean Paul and noticed how much he did resemble his father, even though he had some of the same facial expressions as his mother.

"Yes, yes, I know, but a mother likes to see her son once in a while."

"There's my brother—how often do you see him?"

"Well, your brother lives in England. But actually, he gets here more than you do. Jean Paul's brother is in computers, Alexandra, so he has more time off. If he brings his computer, he can do his work wherever he is. His sister, Camille, is very busy, too. She was supposed to be here tonight, but she got tied up in Paris. She will be very sorry that she missed you both."

"My mother's name was Camille. It seems as if many names have been used over and over through the generations in our families," Alexandra said.

"Yes. Jean Paul said you are related to the family who owned the chateau during the Revolution…as are we.

Alexandra smiled. "There are so many similarities between our families…" She heard soft footsteps. She glanced toward the doorway.

Marie stood, her hands folded in front of her. "Dinner is served, Madame."

"Thank you, Marie. Please." She extended her hand and gestured toward the dining room. She wrapped her arm through Alexandra's. "Come, Gentlemen. Follow us."

"The table looks beautiful." Alexandra gazed at the crystal and silver place settings. When she sat down, she studied the cream china with its gold band on the edge. *It looks like Limoges.* "Your china looks a lot like the service I inherited from my grandmother." Alexandra looked at her flowers. They were arranged in a low, crystal vase and sat in the middle of the table. She began to feel right at home.

"Your flowers tie everything together. They are the finishing touch," Marguerite said. "Louis, please pour the wine. I hope everyone is in the mood for fish?"

"I love it. After all that horrible hospital food, it will be wonderful to have a home-cooked meal."

"What happened to you?" Marguerite asked. "Jean Paul said that you were shot."

Alexandra glanced at Jean Paul. He looked noncommittal. *I guess I'm on my own.* "Yes, we were in a crowd and someone rushed up to us and shot me. I never saw him before."

"No one is safe anymore. There are all kinds of lunatics on the streets." She glanced at Jean Paul. "I know my son will make sure you are protected from now on." She reached over and patted Jean Paul on the arm.

Jean Paul smiled. He reached for Alexandra's hand and squeezed it.

During dinner, Marguerite talked about their family and Paris. Alexandra talked about her vacation—the places she had visited and some of the research she had done on her family history. She told them about Henri and his life and family. She left out the parts about the ghosts and the part about returning to 1789. Alexandra just talked about what they found at the Internet café. She was pleased when Marguerite suggested that they have their coffee in front of the fire. The living room reminded her of her home—in fact, Jean Paul's home was much like hers. She looked around. The living room was so comfortable.

When Louis finished his coffee, he rose. "Ladies, will you please excuse us? I need to talk a little business with my son." Jean Paul followed his father. "It won't take us too long," he said from the doorway.

"More coffee?" Jean Paul's mother asked Alexandra as she reached for the coffee pot. Alexandra held up her cup. "You take it black—correct?" Marguerite tipped the silver-covered pot over Alexandra's cup.

"Black, thank you. A habit I got into when I joined the FBI. I drank so much coffee. I dropped the cream and sugar. They made it seem as if I was drinking an ice cream soda and didn't give me as much of a jolt. I needed the coffee high to keep me awake sometimes when I worked long hours."

"Louis and I lived in New York City when we were first married. He was with the Diplomatic Service. I miss it sometimes. It was very exciting. We traveled all over the world. However, I was finally ready to settle down and start a family and I decided to stay put in one place. When he left the service, we came back to France. Louis opened a law practice." Marguerite smiled. "Now that he is retired the only place we go is to our home in the South of France. We don't visit there very often. I spend my time attending garden clubs and book clubs and visiting with my friends. It's nice to be able to do whatever you want to do."

"That's what I'm doing on my vacation and enjoying every minute," Alexandra said.

"I sometimes miss the old days, but life is much more normal now."

Marguerite asked many questions about New York City—Broadway plays, the new maestro of the symphony, and shopping.

"Tell me about your work with the FBI? You must travel a lot. Do you enjoy it?"

"I get to see a lot of places and meet a lot of good and bad people. I was a lawyer and joined the agency after college. Maybe I'll practice when I retire."

Jean Paul and his father reappeared, and Alexandra decided that Jean Paul looked very pleased with what his father had shared with him. Louis offered everyone a liqueur and then sat down. He asked Alexandra a lot of questions about the FBI. He seemed to know a lot of people in the Bureau, including Alexandra's boss. The conversation went on smoothly. It was almost as if they had all known each other for years. Alexandra felt Jean Paul watching her as she talked with his parents.

"Well, it's time that I get back to the chateau. I have a busy day tomorrow," Alexandra said. "Thank you so much. I've had a lovely evening."

"When will you bring her back, Jean Paul?" his mother asked.

He looked at Alexandra and smiled. "How about next weekend? Okay with you?"

"I would love that. I've had a wonderful evening. It was so nice to meet both of you."

Marguerite stared at Alexandra for a minute and then glanced at her son. "Just a moment." She left the room. When she returned, she held a long narrow box in her hands. "This is for you. We found it in the attic in the box where we found the papers—the papers from the chateau."

Alexandra untied the purple ribbon around the box. Her eyes opened wide. She saw a thin, silver, open heart with a briolette-shaped amethyst surrounded by diamonds hanging in the middle of the heart. It hung on a delicate S link silver chain. "Oh, Marguerite, this is beautiful. I can't accept this. It's too much."

"Yes, you can, my dear. I believe it belongs to the Pirrot side of the family. It's yours now."

"I don't know what to say…Thank you so very much." Her eyes filled with tears as she hugged Jean Paul's mother. "This is so sweet of you."

Marguerite smiled. "We will see you next weekend. I hope."

"I'm looking forward to it," Alexandra said.

She sat with her hand in Jean Paul's as they drove to the chateau. She was quiet.

He took her hand and squeezed it. "You're not saying anything."

"I don't know what to say. The evening was wonderful…the gift…I felt right at home."

"They liked you. I didn't know about the necklace, but my mother was right. You should have the necklace. It's part of your family."

"I like your parents very much and I felt very comfortable with them. Your house is very much like my home in New York City. I loved sitting in front of the fireplace. My mother, grandmother, and I used to do that after dinner very often."

"Don't you want to know what my father found?"

"Oh, yes. I was so over whelmed by the necklace that I forgot."

"My father gave me a copy of the deed that proved my family owned the chateau in 1789. He found it tucked in a book in the attic that was in the box with some jewelry and other papers. They felt the deed was the only important document. The others were death certificates, birth certificates, architectural drawings, and letters from people he never heard of. He said maybe his grandfather had stored the box there. My grandfather seemed to know more about family history than anyone else. I guess the piece my mother gave you was with them. We should put his papers and what we find in the chapel together. It will help us get a good look at the family."

"Tomorrow we'll find the chapel and then we can put all the pieces together." Alexandra leaned back and closed her eyes. "I hope."

Chateau Verny-early morning
August 18, 2010

Alexandra waited for Jean Paul in the entrance hall. She smiled when she saw him running down the stairs. He was in good shape. His breathing wasn't even labored.

"I brought Claudette's letter to her children and her diary. If we find anything important at the chapel we can put everything together."

"Good idea. Then we can go back and study all of them when we have time," Jean Paul said. "What was written in her diary?"

"Not much. She described her first days in prison and how it was being persecuted by the Revolutionaries." Alexandra moved toward the back of the chateau.

"I'm not going back into the tunnel. It's not a long walk, but when I was in there with Claudette, it looked as if it was going to collapse. The beams that were supposed to support the ceiling were cracked. Dirt fell on our heads as we walked. The rocks embedded in the dirt to make the walls were crumbling. It was dusty and cold. I thought there would be a cave-in. It's unsafe. It should be filled in. I was right—there are branches of the tunnel that go all over the chateau. Let's explore them when we have time."

"What room were you in when entered the tunnel? What part of the chateau?"

"We went in through the kitchen, behind the pantry."

"All right, let's start outside to the back of the chateau. We'll walk from the kitchen and go straight through the woods from there."

"Claudette said it would be about a fifteen minute walk after we left the woods."

"Come on, let's go." Jean Paul grabbed her hand and pulled her to the back of the chateau.

"All right, there's the kitchen," Alexandra said.

They walked through the gardens and wedged them themselves between the branches of the hedges so they could get to the woods.

Jean Paul glanced around. He found a narrow path leading to the edge of the woods. They trudged through the trees and bushes. Jean Paul held back the tree branches as he led the way.

"Thank you. I won't get all scratched up this time." Alexandra smiled up at Jean Paul. *I'm getting a real tour of the woods of France.*

"Here we are." He pulled her into the over-grown grass at the edge of the woodland.

"This is where we were captured the night we were taken to the prison. We're just a few feet from the mowed area. I think if we walk straight ahead we'll find the chapel. I can see a large group of chestnut trees from my window and a small pond next to a cemetery. It looks like a bucolic area. The chapel is probably in that area."

They walked hand-in-hand. Jean Paul let go of her hand and stopped. He bent down. Paying no attention to him, Alexandra looked ahead of them—she stood on her toes to see if she could see the chapel.

When he stood up he brought a bouquet of daises from behind his back. "These are for you. I couldn't resist."

"Thank you. You're so nice. Wait, I see it. I see the chapel."

The chapel had settled into over-grown grass and bushes. She began to run and stopped at the pond.

"Look! There it is—the chapel is next to the cemetery. It looks as if the gardeners take care of this area. The grass around the chapel is a little long, but the headstones are all standing straight, although the slates are in various degrees of disrepair. The weather has caused a lot of the carved names and information to wear away and some of them are so chipped and cracked they're impossible to read. The grass seems to have been mowed—no weeds. The gray blocks at the end of the graves are barely above ground on some of the graves."

Alexandra walked over to them. "Look." She pointed to the stone next to her. "I can't read that one, but this one says Jacques Louis Pirrot—it's impossible to read anymore. This one says Claudette Pache Pirrot. The date she died was August, 1793. She's in a beautiful spot under a huge chestnut tree and next to the water." Alexandra bent down and placed the daisies near the headstone. "Do you mind?"

"Of course not, I think it's very caring of you."

"The pond must be spring fed. There are carps swimming in it."

"It's almost hard to see the chapel until you're right on top of it. All the trees and bushes around it hide it from view, from the road and my room." With tears in her eyes, she turned around and looked at the chapel. It was stone with a slate roof and long narrow windows without glass. The tears began to run down her cheeks. She felt Jean Paul wrap his arm around her and heard him say. "It's all right."

"Let's go to the chapel."

She looked down. "Here are the children's graves. I don't recognize any of the other names."

"Here." He offered her a handkerchief. "Let's go inside." Jean Paul jiggled the padlock on the door. "It's locked up tight."

Alexandra reached into her pocket and smiled. "Claudette gave me the key the night I escaped from La Conciergerie." It took her three tries to insert the key in the lock. Her hands were shaking. Finally she heard it snap. She pulled the padlock off and threw open the door. "How beautiful." Alexandra stared down the middle aisle at a marble altar with a solitary cross—no statues of saints guarding it. Small cherubs sat near the floor at each corner.

"I wondered if Claudette and her household worshiped here?" she asked.

Jean Paul pulled out a twenty-first century lighter and walked around the small room. He lit the candles in the sconces lining the walls. "Someone must have been here since the time Claudette lived at the chateau. The candles are not modern, but they are not as old as the eighteenth century. They look hand-dipped—not store bought."

Alexandra moved down the center aisle. Two benches that looked as if they would each seat four people sat on either side of her. "It's so dusty in here." She brushed off the bench nearest her and wiped her hands on her jeans before she sat down. She looked around, trying to see if there was anything that looked like it held papers. She leisurely walked around the room, running her hands along the walls. "There's nothing here. The papers must be hidden in the altar."

She moved to front of the altar and brushed off the thick dust on the top. "There must be a button to open a panel or drawer." She ran her fingers along the sides and front of the altar. "I found it. The button is behind the Cherub at the left-hand corner." She stuck her finger in the dent and pushed on the button. A panel near the bottom popped open. She peered into the space large enough to hold a box about a foot long and a bundle of papers.

"Be careful," Jean Paul said. He leaned down and looked into the space. "It seems all right."

Alexandra reached into the opening and pulled out a metal box. She struggled to pull off the top.

"Here, let me help," Jean Paul said. He easily pulled it off.

"I could have done that. My hands were shaking, I was so excited."

Jean Paul laughed. "Sure."

Alexandra grabbed the box from him. She began to riffle through the papers. "Here's the original deed. Only it has your family name listed as the owners. There are lots of other documents." She began to flip through the papers again. "Most of them are certificates of marriages, births, deaths." She looked into the empty space and took out more papers.

"Oh no, here's a dagger. It was tucked between the box and letters. She pulled it from the pile and examined it. "Looks as if there is dried blood on the blade. Do you think that's what Claudette used to murder Mr. Dumont's business partner?"

"Maybe, or perhaps there are other murders we haven't discovered. It really doesn't matter now. The murder of Mr. Dumont's business partner will just go down as an unsolved crime. Let's look at the letters." Jean Paul leaned over Alexandra and looked at the letters tied together with a red, satin ribbon.

Alexandra pulled off the ribbon. She ran her fingers through them. The letters scattered on the floor. She picked up the letter nearest her. She withdrew a folded sheet from the envelope and opened it carefully. "A lot of this is too damaged, probably by dampness, for me to read. But essentially it talks about Claudette's children." She strained her eyes to read. "*Louis born in 1786, educated at the College de Navarre, ordained in 1807 as a priest. His last post was Archbishop of Paris. He died on the last day of the last month of the year—the 31st. The year was 1835. Marie Camille 1787-1825 married a doctor and had three sons.* Looks like she did well for herself." Alexandra glanced at the second page. "It's part of a letter from Monique. Here's what she said."

Dear Madame Pirrot,

Here's the mail I collected when the rebels left the chateau. They left after they ruined a lot of the furniture and some of the rooms. They left your letters scattered around the chateau. I gathered them up and put them here in our hiding place, where I hope you will find them. Your children are fine. I have hidden them with my family in England.

Your faithful friend, Monique

"Monique was the nanny mentioned in Claudette's letter." She looked down. "Here's one from Henri."

My Dear Sister-in-Law,

I am on my way to the New World. I saw the woman who was with you when I escaped the Bastille. She was at the ship this morning and waved to me. Our trip will take six to eight weeks.

My first morning started with reasonable calm. I sat outside and watched the coast of France melt away and read to kill a few hours. Within five minutes a single drop of rain fell on my hair. Then suddenly the sky darkened and thick dark clouds rolled in. The waves began to churn. The sailors ran as the lightening shattered through the clouds like a crackling explosion. The sky turned a charcoal gray. The wind picked up. It was a gust that almost picked me up and threw me over board. It did rip the book from my hand. The sea became knife gray. A starboard lifeboat swung loose, snapped from its chains and broke the rail as it dropped into the sea. A sailor was almost swept through the opening of the rail and into the sea.

The captain yelled for us to get to our rooms. I struggled to stand and then made my way gripping the life rope to my room. It took all my energy to get there and to close my door against the gusting gale. But I did it and felt safer when I latched it closed.

Before I could get there the rain came down in a deluge. The wind got worse. I got soaking wet before I reached my room. I got chills from my wet clothes that sagged against my wet skin. I put on my only other clothes and left my wet ones to dry. They will most likely be stiff and uncomfortable. But it is nothing like the misery I suffered at the Bastille. I tried to sleep as the boat pitched back and forth. We were restricted to our rooms.

Many passengers in first class and below are ill, but are feeling better on this third day now that the sea has not calmed down. I am lucky the nuns paid my passage in first class. I am more comfortable than the people below. I don't feel the roll of the ship as they do. I feel sorry for the sailors who are feeling ill and have to work.

It is now the second week that I am at sea. The weather has become warm and I can see the islands in the distance. Once we off-load the cargo and load up new supplies, we will leave for Virginia in the New World. I shall try to make a new life and learn a trade as a carpenter—since there is no need for an aristocrat. As soon as I am settled, I will make arrangements for you to get passage and join me. I was not able to sell your engagement ring. I didn't have the heart to do it. I will give it to my wife and then to one of my children if I am lucky enough to sire some so that they can pass it through the generations. I will leave this letter with the captain so that when he returns to France he can see that it is delivered to you. I hope you and your children are well.

Your loving Brother-in-Law, Henri

"There! There it is. More proof we're related. It matches the information we found at the Internet café."

Jean Paul nodded. "You're right you're related to the Pirrot side of the family. I don't see anything about the Dumonts. They must have been related to one of the Revolutionaries and the chateau was passed down without papers."

"I guess if we don't find anything in the official records of Giverny that the chateau belongs to the Dumonts, my father's paper and the deed we found will give the chateau back to us—my family."

She pulled Claudette's letter and diary out of her pocket and placed it with the others. "I know it will be yours soon, Jean Paul." She raised her finger to her closed lips. "Sssssh. I'm sure there is someone in the chapel with us," Alexandra whispered. "I heard a noise coming from the entrance."

They looked up. Claudette stood near the entrance. Alexandra could see the scar around her neck as she walked toward her. Before Alexandra reached the doorway, Claudette disappeared. Alexandra dropped the papers, grabbed Jean Paul's hand and ran from the chapel. They stood at the outside of the entrance of the chapel and watched Claudette float to her headstone beneath the chestnut tree in the corner of the cemetery.

Claudette looked back at them and smiled as she gave a small wave, then turned away. The sun shone brightly as she stood over her headstone. She pulled her cloak tightly around herself and evaporated into her grave.

Alexandra stared. "She's gone. She has crossed over."

"We're done here. Let's put everything back and return to the chateau," Jean Paul said.

Alexandra looked over her shoulder. It was quiet except for the whispering of the grass as it blew in a light breeze.

Epilogue

Chateau Verny
September14, 2010

She had wandered through the French Revolution and stayed in one piece. Now she sat on the patio with Jean Paul, enjoying a cup of coffee. Together they looked out over the gardens.

"No matter how much I twist my amethyst ring. I can't get Claudette to reappear. Secrets from the past will always bind me to Claudette. However, I don't think we'll have any more visits from her." Alexandra stared into the woods. "She came to me because she needed my help. When she found out the information she wanted, she found peace. She left us the day we saw her in the chapel's cemetery. She was able to cross over. The ring is now just a beautiful piece of antique jewelry."

Jean Paul stood and pulled her to her feet. His grip was firm and his hands felt warm. "You are the bravest, strongest and most beautiful woman I have ever known. I fell in love with you the first day I met you." Slight crinkles formed at the corners of his eyes. He put his hand under her chin. He turned her face to his and cradled it in his hands with gentleness.

She never felt so loved or cherished. Alexandra hugged him tightly. "When was the last time I said that I love you?" Alexandra asked.

A smile played at the corner of his mouth.

"What? What's wrong?"

He shook his head and laughed at her question.

She felt a warmth creep up her face. "Well..." Alexandra stared at him. "What's wrong?"

"Actually, you never have told me you love me," Jean Paul said.

She leaned close to his ear and laughed. "I love you," she whispered, putting her arms around his neck and pulled him to her. She finally had given up holding back the words. She realized someone capable of true love puts others above themselves—that was Jean Paul. He wasn't like James. She pressed her lips to his.

Alexandra stood at the entrance of the chateau with Jean Paul. "It's been wonderful. My vacation is over. The FBI needs me, but I'll be back very soon," Alexandra said.

Madame Dumont stood in front of them. "Thank you for letting us stay on," Madame Dumont said. She wiped the tears that began to run down her cheeks with her apron. She grabbed Jean Paul's hand.

"We need you both here. We need people who know how to run an inn," Jean Paul said.

Alexandra walked with Jean Paul to the front door. She gave Madame Dumont a hug. As Jean Paul left to get his car, Alexandra stood with Jacques next to her with her suitcase. When Jean Paul's pulled his Porsche up to the door, he pushed the button on his key ring. The trunk popped open.

Jacques heaved the suitcase up and stowed it in the trunk of the Porsche, then opened the car door for Alexandra. He looked as if he wanted to say something to her as she jumped into the car. She looked at him. "Yes, Jacques what is it?"

"Thank you, Miss, for helping our ghost."

Alexandra smiled and waved to the Dumonts and Jacques. "*Au'voir*, I'll be back before you know it."

As they drove to the airport, Alexandra watched the scenery fly by. It was so beautiful now. It was hard for her to realize that it had been torn apart by the Revolution. She couldn't believe the lives of people from hundreds of years ago had intertwined with those living today. She thought about how they seemed to be the same people going through centuries as different individuals. *Alexandra, don't think about it anymore. It was a wonderful adventure. One I will never forget. Nobody would believe what happened unless they had been there.*

"I had a wonderful time visiting the beaches at Normandy. I will never forget watching the breathtaking sunrise with you the first morning we were there. World War II was another war that caused destruction and the loss of hundreds of lives in France. I wonder if we have a connection to someone who lived then and might need our help." She laughed.

"That's not funny. No more ghosts. Promise me you'll only

investigate cases with people who live in our universe," he said as he pulled into a parking space at the airport.

"I won't. Believe me, you can't compare what I've experienced to anything I've been involved with in the FBI. It was so much worse. I'll stay with the FBI cases, I promise."

He wrapped his arms around her as they walked through the airport. "I will miss you," he said. His voice was deep and husky.

"You are the most magnificent man. I am so happy you've come into my life."

Jean Paul stood at the gate of her Air France flight in Terminal E. "I'll see you in two weeks. You are going to be a big help to me. Together we'll solve the murder of the French diplomat my client rented his condo to." He held her close. "I don't want you to go."

"We'll be together soon," Alexandra said.

Jean Paul gathered her into his arms. He put his hand under her chin. Turning her face to his, he kissed her softly.

"I'll arrive at Kennedy Airport at seven forty p.m. Then I'll have to go through customs. The cab ride shouldn't take very long—depending on traffic. I'll be home before ten."

"Last call for Air France flight 010," came over the loud speaker.

"Call me when you get home." He hugged her again.

"I love you." Alexandra kissed him.

As she walked to the plane doors, Alexandra heard her mother singing the lullaby she used to sing to her before she went to sleep.

"The past and the present have been brought together, Mother." Alexandra had tears of joy in her eyes.

THE END

Did you enjoy *Beyond The Mist?* If so, please help us spread the word about Joyce Humphrey Cares.

•Recommend the book to your family and friends

•Post a review on retailer sites and Goodreads

•Tweet and Facebook about it

ABOUT THE AUTHOR

Joyce Humphrey Cares lives in Central Florida. A voracious reader since childhood, she finally decided to take a stab at writing. She combines her love of history and the places she has traveled when she weaves her stories.

When she is not writing, Joyce is a Guardian ad litem volunteer, builds and decorates dollhouses, plays golf, and plans her next trip to a place where she can return home and write a romantic suspense or time travel story.

She is a member of Romance Writers of America, Sunshine Romance Authors, and the Florida chapter of Mystery Writers of America.

She may be contacted at joycecares01@gmail.com or at her webpage www.joycehumphreycares.com.

Other Books
It Started With Forbidden
Degrees of Wickedness
It Happened Yesterday